WE

Yevgeny Zamyatin

WE

A new translation, with an Introduction, by
Natasha Randall

Foreword by Bruce Sterling

THE MODERN LIBRARY

NEW YORK

2006 Modern Library Paperback Edition

Translation and introduction copyright © 2006 by Natasha S. Randall
Foreword copyright © 2006 by Bruce Sterling

Published in the United States by Modern Library, an imprint of The
Random House Publishing Group, a division of Random House, Inc., New York.

MODERN LIBRARY and the TORCHBEARER Design are registered
trademarks of Random House, Inc.

LIBRARY OF CONGRESS CATALOGING-IN-PUBLICATION DATA
Zamiatin, Evgenii Ivanovich, 1884–1937
[My. English]
We/Yevgeny Zamyatin; a new translation by Natasha Randall;
with an introduction by Bruce Sterling.—Modern Library paperback ed.
p. cm.
ISBN 0-8129-7462-X (pbk.)
I. Randall, Natasha. II. Title.
PG3476.Z34M913 2006
891.73'42—dc21 2006042032

Printed in the United States of America

www.modernlibrary.com

4 6 8 9 7 5 3

FOREWORD

MADMEN, HERMITS, HERETICS,
DREAMERS, REBELS, AND SKEPTICS

Bruce Sterling

Yevgeny Zamyatin has a sound claim to the invention of the science fiction dystopia. This book, Zamyatin's only novel, barely saw publication during his tragically shortened lifetime. The Russian text spread by hand-typed samizdat manuscripts in the St. Petersburg literary circles and through tattered, covert copies of a single émigré publication in Prague.

An English translation existed well before any full Russian version saw print. George Orwell, author of *1984*, managed to find and read it. Orwell thought that Aldous Huxley, author of *Brave New World*, had probably read it. Written with radical invention, deliberate verbal obscurity and cunning political intent, *We* is a rather hard book to read or to translate. Traditionally, it's a hard book even to find.

Zamyatin's many friends and disciples considered him a mannered overseas sophisticate with advanced and dangerous ideas. He'd been exiled in Finland. He had built ships in distant Britain. In person he came across as a dapper, tweedy naval engineer. Russians nicknamed him "the Englishman." He managed the translations from English for a Russian publishing house, where he carefully studied the socialist H. G. Wells.

Nevertheless, *We* is a book that could only have come from Russia, or, rather, from the unique time and space that was revolutionary Petrograd. It's a science fiction novel set centuries in the future, but this story will spring to life if you can imagine it dressed in full, period regalia, with violently agitated Russian Constructivist costumes and a spacey, ethereal Theremin soundtrack.

Zamyatin was a revolutionary writer by nature, so this scrambling, visionary text isn't much of a novel. *We* takes the form of a diary by a future engineer-turned-writer (a Zamyatin stand-in, basically). Our hero, in an unwise attempt to please the authorities, writes a personal confession. He is the chief designer of a mighty spaceship. His literary boasting is meant to aid his regime's schemes to invade other planets and brainwash their inhabitants.

Nobody living in this regime seems to believe in its surreal and brutal totalitarian tenets. So, our hero's confident self-psychoanalysis soon goes awry. He's a government drone with serious woman-troubles (much like Winston Smith, the hero of *1984*). Once he is able to confide the overheated contents of his heart and soul to paper, our narrator, D-503, goes straight off the rails. D-503 turns out to be quite a dedicated diarist. His burning urge to literary expression is enough to wreck his career, alienate his best friend, and drive his steady girlfriend to madness.

As Zamyatin had put it in an earlier theoretical essay, "I Am Afraid": "True literature can exist only where it is created, not by diligent and trustworthy functionaries, but by madmen, hermits, heretics, dreamers, rebels, and skeptics." So this book is a kind of negative bildungsroman: it's about a diligent and trustworthy functionary who shirks his work, fools the cops, dumps a woman who loves him and wants his baby, has a wild affair with a decadent revolutionary, and even helps to hijack a spaceship, all for the sake of belles lettres.

After completing *We* in late 1920 or early 1921, Zamyatin showed the manuscript to a few friends but was denied publishing permission. When it did appear in print, thanks to the mischievous Czechs, and well out of reach of the Soviet secret police, a predictable hell broke loose. How predictable? For Zamyatin, trouble was very predictable.

Zamyatin was first arrested in 1905, at the age of twenty-one, as a Bolshevik student activist. He was beaten up by Tsarist cops, kept in solitary for months, and exiled to the provinces. This exemplary punishment merely fertilized his eccentricities. Zamyatin was able to sneak back from Finland into St. Petersburg in disguise, where he obtained an engineering degree while squatting in the city illegally. In 1911, the cops rediscovered Zamyatin. This time he was sent into Russian internal exile, where he whiled away the time composing satires. In 1914 one of these satires, "In the Backwoods," was published. This time, not just Zamyatin but also his publisher faced arrest. The entire print run of the magazine was also rounded up, and Zamyatin's book was put before a judge, but he somehow avoided jail.

Zamyatin then was sent to England to supervise the construction of Russian icebreakers, where, as a brief change of pace, he satirized the British. However, life without Mother Russia never seemed to agree with him. He quickly returned to Russia between the revolutions of 1917, where, as a noted former troublemaker, he was given a literary job by Maxim Gorky. This period was the high point of Zamyatin's life and career, though Soviet Revolutionary Petrograd was no Miami Beach. There, in 1922, he published a Poe-like horror tale called "The Cave," about miserable post-revolutionary Russians simply trying to stay fed and unfrozen in their wintry, unlit apartments.

Zamyatin was arrested by the new Soviet authorities in both 1919 and 1922. When not writing fantastic fiction, hiding it, and/or trying to publish it, Zamyatin spent much time and energy writing about writing. As a participant in early Soviet "NeoRealism" and the guru of the "Serapion Brothers" clique, he was eager to create a tough-minded, sparse, revolutionary futurist-fantasy literature, one that wasn't mushy, hazy, bourgeois, and Symbolist, but "written with 90-proof ink." Zamyatin believed that the future could be out-guessed by out-guessing the next revolution. How? The seeds of revolutions were already visible as the rantings of today's heretics.

They could also be found in arcane areas of intellectual exploration that had not yet been popularized and acculturated.

Thus the genuinely weird sensibility of D-503, the hero and narrator of *We. We* is one of the first attempts to write about the future through the consciousness of someone born there and living there. Our hero's unique, personal Newspeak is a colorful tossed salad of the wildest avant-gardism of the 1920s: Einstein, curved space and the fourth dimension, Marxist dialectic, Freud, free love, math, engineering, aviation, and rocketry. It's a syncretic, wildly imaginative text that combs the world's library of innovation, science, and dissent, in order to address the one topic it can never directly confront: the cruel descent of the Bolshevik rebellion into frozen dogma and totalitarian stasis.

A passionately literary work, *We* is (almost) entirely devoid of literary referents. Our hero's metaphors are scientific and mathematical, to the extent that even women's faces are described as geometric vectors or mathematical symbols. In this rigid world of supposed efficiency and utopian perfection, our hero's maddened thoughts are splintered, multi-planar, almost Dadaist. Often, when right on the brink of some revelatory higher sense, his sentences simply . . .

These Zamyatin word-games, this attempt to be futuristic and think futuristically rather than merely describing futurity from the perspective of the present day, was Zamyatin's literary breakthrough. This book reads like nothing else on earth before or since. He was entirely grounded in the time and space of Petrograd, yet he managed to take flight.

Yevgeny Zamyatin is orbiting in a literary space all his own with this one. It is a work without real ancestry, and its descendants have rarely matched its visionary daring.

The term "science fiction" was not yet invented when Zamyatin composed this prescient text. It is nevertheless extremely science-fictional. It has whole sets of sci-fi themes and conceits that were entirely fresh when Zamyatin created them: hermetically sealed cities, synthetic food, unisex suits, *Metropolis*-like crowds of drones marching through cyclopean apartment blocks, whizzing, roaring trips in giant spaceships, mind control through brain surgery. . . .

They're clichés now, of course: but they were only reduced to clichés through decades of effort by lesser artists.

The book was fiercely attacked by Stalinist party-line critics. Zamyatin's works were removed from Soviet libraries and he was forbidden to publish. In 1931, Zamyatin and his wife were allowed by Stalin to emigrate to Paris. He continued to consider himself a Soviet writer, always hoping to return whenever the Regime would allow him to write. Some Russian literary émigrés were able to thrive in Paris, but Zamyatin wasn't one of them. Unable to finish a historical novel, he wasted away in silence and poverty, and he died on March 10, 1937.

There's little doubt that he had foreseen and expected this fate. Like his hero, he even seemed to somehow relish his own immolation: "The flame will cool tomorrow, or the day after tomorrow.... But someone must see this already today, and speak heretically today about tomorrow. Heretics are the only (bitter) remedy against the entropy of human thought."

—

BRUCE STERLING, author, journalist, editor, and critic, was born in Texas in 1954. Best known for his science fiction novels, he also writes design criticism, travel journalism, and a weblog. He is currently living in Belgrade.

INTRODUCTION

THEM

Natasha Randall

We is a novel of revolution. It is the sum of the utopian enthusiasms, which gestated in the nineteenth century and were delivered in the early twentieth. But change was afoot in 1920, the year the novel was written: these Russian enthusiasms were entering a sort of singular Bolshevik utopian rigor mortis. By 1923, Yevgeny Zamyatin wrote:

> It is an error to divide people into the living and the dead: there are people who are dead-alive, and people who are alive-alive. The dead-alive also write, walk, speak, act. But they make no mistakes; only machines make no mistakes, and they produce only dead things. The alive-alive are constantly in error, in search, in questions, in torment.[1]

The "greens" (peasants), the "blacks" (anarchists), and the Whites were being reduced to ashes while the only remaining ideology was forging the idea that man could be made mechanical. Zamyatin, an engineer, quantified this moment in his anti-utopia, fast-forwarding the cogs and wheels of early Soviet society *ad absurdum*. There is not one detail of life in the One State that doesn't illustrate a given theory or discovery of his day.

The Bolshevik Revolution was buoyed by an enormous "utopian propensity" in the Russian population. The country had been poised for apocalypse at the turn of the century, and though their anticipations went unrealized, they were eager for a new world nonetheless. Some sought the creation of a universal language for all mankind. Others promoted the idea of geanthropism, the emancipation of women. Yet others upheld pedism, the liberation of children. And the Anarcho-Biocosmists made plans for a social revolution in outer space. There were versions of machinism, primitive reticence, antiverbalism, nudism, social militarism, revolutionary sublimation, and suicidalism.[2] All these ideas were being incarnadined by 1920.

That year, Trotsky was disciplining Russian society into a militarized labor force. Pastoral Russia had risen to its newfound *volya* (free will) but was now struggling against this new yoke. The Bolsheviks were building the new Soviet Man, who would outpace his human peers. The peasantry would bond into the strongest proletariat amalgam. The stuff of daily life was churned through the time and motion studies of the American engineer Frederick Winslow Taylor. Russia was electrified—literally—and the darkest corners of the old life were irradiated with industrial ideas. The year 1920 was perched at the dawn of film, radio, and the automobile. It was also the year that the word *robot* came into being (originating in the Russian and Czech word *rabotat',* which means "to work"). The Bolsheviks with their militaristic, urban-centric, industrial aggression were conquering all of Russia.

Meanwhile, Petrograd of 1920 was being reconstructed from the remnants of St. Petersburg after a ruinously long involvement in World War I and further shortages were caused by the civil war efforts. The privileged classes, known as "former people" (*byvshie lyudi*), had piled their suitcases and furniture onto carts and abandoned their comfortable apartments to the proletariat. Mansions were divided into cramped communal apartments and palaces had been expropriated for government purposes. The city was rife with starvation. Garbage flowed down the Moika and Fontanka canals.

Winters were cruel—people wore coats and hats indoors, and firewood was so scarce that Petrograders burned furniture, pianos, and books to get through. According to historian Richard Stites, the population of Petrograd fell from 1,217,000 to 722,000 during the years of War Communism between 1918 and 1921.[3]

But, in all this, the arts were thriving, feeding on the stuff of ideas. Amongst the loudest avant-garde voices of the time were the Futurists with their provocative antics. The Proletarian Culture movement, Proletkult, was also in full swing after being established in 1917 with plans to engender a new proletarian cultural universal. By 1919, it became an enormous movement with half a million participants.[4] Their ideas included god-building, tectology, and human mechanization. And it was these ideas that form the core of Zamyatin's *We*.

The proletarian poet Alexei Gastev, described by Nikolai Aseev as the "Ovid of engineers, miners and metalworkers," was the most active advocate of Frederick Winslow Taylor's ideas about men and machines. Gastev was the head of the Central Institute of Labor, founded in 1920.[5] Any reader of *We* will recognize Gastev's experiments with Soviet workers as the basic material for the One State. Besides, Zamyatin's title is borrowed from the Proletkult, whose writers had composed poems and plays with the title "We" before Zamyatin's own work emerged.[6] In his cultural history of Russia, *Natasha's Dance,* Orlando Figes describes Gastev's research excellently:

> Hundreds of identically dressed trainees would be marched in columns to their benches, and orders would be given out by buzzes from machines. The workers were trained to hammer correctly, for instance by holding a hammer attached to and moved by a special machine, so that they internalized its mechanical rhythm. The same process was repeated for chiseling, filing and other basic skills. Gastev's aim, by his own admission, was to turn the worker into a sort of 'human robot'... Gastev envisaged a utopia where 'people' would be replaced by 'proletarian units' identified by ciphers such as 'A,B,C, or 325, 075, 0, and

so on.' These automatons would be like machines, 'incapable of individual thought', and would simply obey their controller. A 'mechanized collectivism' would 'take the place of the individual personality in the psychology of the proletariat'. There would no longer be a need for emotions, and the human soul would no longer be measured 'by a shout or a smile but by a pressure gauge or a speedometer'.[7]

Zamyatin, at the time, was living in the Dom Isskustv, the House of Arts, established by Maxim Gorky, where the provision of work and lodging was meant to protect writers, artists, and musicians from the harsh conditions of the time.

For three years after that we were all locked up together in a steel projectile and, cooped up in darkness, whistled through space, no one knew where. In those last seconds-years before death, we had to do something, to settle down to some sort of a life in the hurtling missile. . . . And all the writers, all those who had survived, were constantly bumping into each other in the cramped space—Gorky and Merezhkovsky, Blok and Kuprin, Muyzhel and Gumilyov, Chukovsky and Volynsky. . . . In the frozen, hungry, typhus-ridden Petersburg, there raged an epidemic of cultural and educational activities. Since literature is not education, all poets and writers became lecturers. And in place of money there was a strange new unit of exchange—the ration, obtained by abandoning poems and novels for lectures.[8]

Between 1917 and 1921, the latter part of which Zamyatin was living at Dom Isskustv, he wrote a novel, a play, two tales, fifteen stories, fourteen fables, four vignettes, and a dozen articles.[9] He was an active participant in the House of Arts and House of Writers (Dom Literatorov) and was also instrumental in the founding of the All-Russian Union of Writers (VSP). As an editor of the World Literature series, Zamyatin oversaw translations of H. G. Wells, George Bernard Shaw, Romain Rolland, and Jack London. He also delivered lectures on literature and taught a very important workshop for young creative-writing talent. In 1921, Zamyatin's pupils would form a literary group called the Serapion Brothers, which included the likes of Mikhail Zoshchenko, Lev Lunts, Vsevolod Ivanov, Veniamin Kaverin, Konstantin Fedin, Nikolay Tikhonov, Mikhail Slonimsky, and Viktor Shklovsky. And it was during this time of editing, teaching, and administrative duties that Zamyatin wrote *We*, most likely from 1920 to late 1921.[10]

As a writer, however, Zamyatin had been suspected of antipathy toward the Revolution and the Bolsheviks since his return to Russia in 1917. According to Alex M. Shane, he was considered a bourgeois writer and an internal émigré.[11] As such, his new novel had a rocky reception. After he had put his finishing touches to *We*, its publication was announced several times but the manuscript never made it into print in the Soviet Union during his lifetime. It was considered too dangerously satirical, and even Gorky, Zamyatin's sponsor for much of the 1920s, would later say: "Zamyatin is too intelligent for an artist and should not allow his reason to direct his talent to satire. [*We*] is hopelessly bad, a completely sterile thing. Its anger is cold and dry; it is the anger of an old maid."[12] It wasn't until 1988 that the manuscript was published in the Soviet Union.

The earliest, most reliable Russian text of *We* is that published by *Izdatel'stvo Imeni Chekhova* (Chekhov House Publishers) in 1952. In a strange twist of Zamyatinesque fantasy, I discovered that Chekhov House was supported by the Eastern European Fund of the Ford Foundation, established by Henry Ford in 1936. Just prior to that, Henry Ford had instigated operations that used the principles of Frederick Winslow Taylor to promote efficiency in his automobile factories—as did Lenin to advance his super-population in 1920. As extraordinary as it might sound, the name Henry Ford became well known throughout Russian villages in the 1920s—better known, in fact, than the names of many party leaders. Lenin had imported Ford Motor Company tractors in large numbers after the revolution. Peasants affectionately called these tractors "Fordzonishkas" (they also were said to have named their children after Ford in the early years of the Soviet era!), and the terms *fordizatsiya* and *teilorizatsiya* (Fordization, Taylorization) were used in Soviet universities in the 1920s.[13] And it was exactly this effect, the mechanizing of Russia, thanks to American industrial thought, that Zamyatin so fiercely satirized in his novel. Indeed, in 1922, Max Eastman, defender of the revolution in Russia, said, "I feel sometimes as though the whole modern world of capitalism and Communism and all were rushing toward some enormous efficient machine-made doom of the true values of life."[14]

As a writer, Zamyatin was very much of his time. He crafted *We* with the precision and efficiency of a Taylorist worker, using every atom of the novel for his own aims to convey the "hypertrophy of the power of the machine and the power of the state—any state."[15] The book is rife with symbols and its language as tight and suggestive as a coiled spring. In his essay "On Literature, Revolution, Entropy, and Other Matters," he describes writing and his conception of the fast "language of thought":

> The old, slow, creaking descriptions are a thing of the past; today the rule is brevity—but every word must be supercharged, high-voltage. We must compress into a single second what was held before in a sixty-second minute. And hence, syntax becomes elliptic, volatile; the complex pyramids of periods are dismantled stone by stone into independent sentences. When you are moving fast, the canonized, the customary eludes the eye: hence, the unusual, often startling, symbolism and vocabulary. The image is sharp, synthetic, with a single salient feature—the one feature you will glimpse from a speeding car.

As an engineer, Zamyatin was able to translate science and mathematics into his fiction. After all, his hero, D-503, is a mathematician, and it is through his syllogisms that we traverse his chronicles. Any mathematician will tell you, at first glance, that the computational elements of *We* are naïve—that the One State barely looks beyond the four rules of arithmetic. But the mathematical fabric of the novel is seamless, where mathematics travels through *We* almost as an allegorical supertext. There are books that explore the nuts and bolts of *We*'s mathematics,[16] but fortunately language comes to our rescue in instances such as when D-503 explains that he is afraid of the square root of minus one ($\sqrt{-1}$) because it is an "irrational number" (it is also, in fact, an imaginary number, but Zamyatin chose the word *irrational* with distinct purpose). In his *Universe of the Mind*, Yuri Lotman said: "Modern science from nuclear physics to linguistics sees the scientist as inside the world being described and as a part of that world. But the object and the observer are as a rule described in different languages, and consequently the problem of translation is a universal scientific task."[17] This was Zamyatin's feat—he rendered emotions in equations, relationships in geometry, and philosophy in calculus while delivering a page-turning story.

Aside from the mathematics, *We* is perhaps the most explicitly codified novel ever written. Given the sheer volume of symbols and allusions in the text, it is hardly surprising that *We* is said to be "the second most studied Russian novel of the twentieth century among Western scholars."[18] A sampling of the scholarship available will tell you that "Auditorium 112" in the story refers to the prison cell (no. 112) where Zamyatin was incarcerated on two occasions. The name of the duplicitous secret agent S-4711 may refer to the launch date of the *Saint Alexander Nevsky* icebreaker that Zamyatin worked on in 1917. Biblical undertones of the Myth of the Fall in the One State (Eden) are woven through the narrative.[19] Pavlov's experiments appear when a young cipher is corrected with an electrical whip and yelps "like a puppy." The color yellow represents freedom, life, and the old irrational world.[20] Every material that Zamyatin conjures has something else to say beyond its simple semantics. Onomasticians and toponymists have a field day with this book.

Of particular interest to language fiends, and to this translator, is Zamyatin's relationship to the sounds of words. He told the artist Yuri Annenkov of the qualities he ascribes to certain sounds and letters. L is pale, cold, light blue, liquid, light. R is loud, bright, red, hot, fast. N is tender, snow, sky, night. D or T is stifling, grave, foggy, obscuring, stagnant. M is kind, soft, motherly, sea-like. A is wide, distant, ocean, misty mirage, breadth of scope. O is high, deep, sea-like, bosom. I is close, low, pressing.[21]

In pursuing this new translation, I was intensely aware of Zamyatin's sounds. I chose lingual and labial permutations that matched Zamyatin's where I could. I distinctly recall the moment of deciding to render *sverkayushchii* (a very important word in the novel) as "sparkling" rather than "gleaming." Added to the patterning of consonants and vowels in *We*, Zamyatin's rhythm is carefully wrought. But this occurs at the level of the sentence. Zamyatin's sentences are rife with rhythmic markers of syntax—particularly the dash, the colon, and the ellipsis.

> To me, it is entirely clear that the relation between the rhythmics of verse and prose is the same as that between arithmetic and integral calculus. In arithmetic we sum up individual items; in integral calculus we deal with sums, series. The prose foot is measured, not by the distance between stressed *syllables*, but by the distance between (logically) stressed *words*. And in prose, just as in integral calculus, we deal not with constant quantities (as in verse and arithmetic) but with variable ones. In prose, the foot is always a variable quantity, it is always being either slowed or accelerated. This, of course, is not fortuitous: it is determined by the emotional and semantic accelerations and retardations in the text.[22]

These rhythmics in Zamyatin's narrative are what I hope to have captured with this new translation. I strived to preserve his tempi through a translation of punctuations between idioms. There are unexpected shifts of tense. He omits verbs and other grammatical elements. He avoids the words *like* and *such as*, preferring direct metaphor. I kept his sentence fragments. There are neologisms like *javenishly*, which describes the way a doctor laughs at D-503. Zamyatin insists on the leitmotif as a device to achieve artistic economy, so these signifiers are necessarily translated consistently throughout the book. Overall, Zamyatin approaches the design of his meticulous text with extreme logic. His character D-503, the voice of his novel, speaks in equations. In my rendering here, D-503's sentences pivot cause and consequence around colons, like they would around an equal sign (=).

The syntactical pacing and pulsing in both the Russian and this translation may seem strange at first, until you surrender to Zamyatin's "language of thought." In his essay "On Language" (1919–20), Zamyatin explained: "[I]f you try to follow the language of thought in your own mind, you will not find even the simplest sentences—only shreds, fragments of simple sentences. Only the most essential elements of a sentence are used: sometimes only a verb or only an epithet, an object . . . At first glance this assertion may seem paradoxical: why should fragments of sentences, scattered as after an explosion, have greater effect on the reader than the same thoughts and images arranged in regular, steady, marching ranks? . . . [because] you meet the reader's natural instinctive need. You do not compel him to skim . . ."

My gratitude goes to Christian Hawkey for his terrific counsel, to Barbara Diamond, to my mathematician father, to Alexander Simonovsky, to Josée Waring, and to my grandmother. Thanks also to the Bakhmeteff Archive for their help.

NOTES

1. From Zamyatin's essay "On Literature, Revolution, Entropy, and Other Matters" (1923), as translated by Mirra Ginsburg in *A Soviet Heretic: Essays by Yevgeny Zamyatin* (University of Chicago Press, 1970), p. 110.

2. Stites, Richard, *Revolutionary Dreams: Utopian Vision and Experimental Life in the Russian Revolution* (New York, Oxford: Oxford University Press, 1989), pp. 55 and 69.

3. Ibid., p. 53.

4. Ibid., p. 71.

5. Figes, Orlando, *Natasha's Dance: A Cultural History of Russia* (New York: Metropolitan Books, Henry Holt and Company, 2002) p. 463.

6. Aleksei Gan wrote a play in 1919–20 that conceived of a population of nameless people, known only by graphic symbols (see Heller, Leonid,

"Zamiatin: Prophète ou témoin? *Nous Autres* et les réalités de son époque," *Cahiers du monde russe et soviétique*, vol. 22, no. 2/3 [April–September 1981], pp. 138–40). Vladimir Kirillov also wrote a poem called "We" (see "My," in *Stikhotvoreniia: Kniga Pervaia 1913–1923 G.* by Vladimir Kirillov [Moscow: Izd-vo "MOSPOLIGRAF," 1924]), p. 58.

7. Figes, p. 464. Here, Figes is drawing his research from Stites and Ernst Toller in *Which World? Which Way? Travel Pictures from Russia and America* (London: S. Low, Marston & Co., Ltd., 1931).

8. From Zamyatin's essay "Alexander Blok" (1924), as translated by Mirra Ginsburg in *A Soviet Heretic*, p. 205.

9. Shane, Alex M., *The Life and Works of Evgenij Zamjatin* (University of California Press, 1968), p. 37.

10. These details of Zamyatin's involvement in literary life in Petrograd were researched with gratitude to Alex M. Shane's *The Life and Works of Evgenij Zamjatin*, pp. 34–37.

11. Ibid., p. 40.

12. As translated by Alex M. Shane in a footnote on p. 27 of his book, Maxim Gorky wrote this in a letter to I. A. Gruzdev, *Sobranie Sochinenii v Tridtsati Tomakh* (Moskva: Gos. Izd-vo Khudozh lit-ry, 1955), p. 126.

13. Stites, p. 148.

14. As quoted by Irving Howe in "The Fiction of Anti-Utopia," in *The New Republic*, April 25, 1962.

15. Zamyatin says this in an interview in 1932, published in *Les Nouvelles Litteraire*, Paris.

16. There is a very lively book called *O Sintetizme, Matematike i Prochem* . . . (1994), written by Edna Andrews, Thomas Lahusen, and Elena Maksimova, which delivers mathematical explorations of *We*.

17. Lotman, Yuri, *Universe of the Mind: A Semiotic Theory of Culture* (London, New York: Tauris, 1990), translated by Ann Shukman, p. 269.

18. Cooke, Brett, *Human Nature in Utopia: Zamyatin's* We (Evanston, Illinois: Northwestern University Press, 2002), p. 18.

19. Beauchamp, Gorman, "Zamiatin's *We*" in *No Place Else: Explorations in Utopian and Dystopian Fiction* (Carbondale and Edwardsville: Southern Illinois University Press, c. 1983), eds. Rabkin, Eric S., Greenberg, Martin H., Olander, Joseph D., pp. 56–57.

20. Proffer, Carl R., "Notes on the Imagery in Zamyatin's *We*," in *Zamyatin's We: A Collection of Critical Essays* (Ann Arbor, Michigan: Ardis Publishers, 1988), ed. Kern, Gary.

21. My thanks to Professor Edna Andrews for drawing my attention to this in her essay "Text and Culture: Continuous Discontinuation in Lotman and

Zamjatin" in *Russian Literature XLIX* (2001), pp. 347–69. The material comes from Annenkov's memoirs, *Dnevnikh Moikh Vstrech; Tsikl Tragedii* (New York: Mezhdunarodnoe literaturnoe sodruzhestvo, 1966).

22. From Zamyatin's essay "Backstage" (1930), as translated by Mirra Ginsburg in *A Soviet Heretic,* p. 197.

KEYWORDS:

A Declaration. The Wisest of Lines. An Epic.

I am merely copying, word for word, what was printed in the *State Gazette* today:

IN 120 DAYS, THE CONSTRUCTION OF THE INTEGRAL WILL BE COM-PLETE. THE GREAT, HISTORIC HOUR WHEN THE FIRST INTEGRAL WILL SOAR THROUGH OUTER SPACE IS NIGH. SOME THOUSAND YEARS AGO, YOUR HEROIC ANCESTORS SUBJUGATED THE ENTIRE EARTHLY SPHERE TO THE POWER OF THE ONE STATE. TODAY, YOU ARE CONFRONTING AN EVEN GREATER CONQUEST: THE INTEGRATION OF THE INFINITE EQUATION OF THE UNIVERSE WITH THE ELECTRIFIED AND FIRE-BREATHING GLASS INTEGRAL. YOU ARE CONFRONTING UNKNOWN CREATURES ON ALIEN PLANETS, WHO MAY STILL BE LIVING IN THE SAVAGE STATE OF FREEDOM, AND SUBJUGATING THEM TO THE BENE-FICIAL YOKE OF REASON. IF THEY WON'T UNDERSTAND THAT WE BRING THEM MATHEMATICALLY INFALLIBLE HAPPINESS, IT WILL BE OUR DUTY TO FORCE THEM TO BE HAPPY. BUT BEFORE RESORTING TO ARMS, WE WILL EMPLOY THE WORD.

IN THE NAME OF THE BENEFACTOR, LET IT BE KNOWN TO ALL CI-PHERS OF THE ONE STATE:

ALL THOSE WHO ARE ABLE ARE REQUIRED TO CREATE TREATISES,

EPICS, MANIFESTOS, ODES, OR ANY OTHER COMPOSITION ADDRESSING THE BEAUTY AND MAJESTY OF THE ONE STATE.

THESE WORKS WILL BE THE FIRST CARGO OF THE INTEGRAL.

ALL HAIL THE ONE STATE, ALL HAIL CIPHERS, ALL HAIL THE BENEFACTOR!

As I write this, I feel something: my cheeks are burning. Integrating the grand equation of the universe: yes. Taming a wild zigzag along a tangent, toward the asymptote, into a straight line: yes. You see, the line of the One State—it is a straight line. A great, divine, precise, wise, straight line—the wisest of lines.

I am D-503. I am the Builder of the Integral. I am only one of the mathematicians of the One State. My pen, more accustomed to mathematical figures, is not up to the task of creating the music of unison and rhyme. I will just attempt to record what I see, what I think—or, more exactly, what we think. (Yes, that's right: we. And let that also be the title of these records: We.) So these records will be manufactured from the stuff of our life, from the mathematically perfect life of the One State, and, as such, might they become, inadvertently, regardless of my intentions, an epic poem? Yes— I believe so and I know so.

As I write this: I feel my cheeks burn. I suppose this resembles what a woman experiences when she first hears a new pulse within her—the pulse of a tiny, unseeing, mini-being. This text is me; and simultaneously not me. And it will feed for many months on my sap, my blood, and then, in anguish, it will be ripped from my self and placed at the foot of the One State.

But I am ready and willing, just as every one—or almost every one of us. I am ready.

KEYWORDS:

Ballet. Quadratic Harmony. X.

Spring. From beyond the Green Wall, from the wild, invisible plains, the wind brings the yellow honey-dust from a flower of some kind. This sweet dust parches the lips—you skim your tongue across them every minute—and you presume that there are sweet lips on every woman you encounter (and man, of course). This somewhat interferes with logical reasoning.

But then, the sky! Blue, untainted by a single cloud (the Ancients had such barbarous tastes given that their poets could have been inspired by such stupid, sloppy, silly-lingering clumps of vapor). I love—and I'm certain that I'm not mistaken if I say *we* love—skies like this, sterile and flawless! On days like these, the whole world is blown from the same shatterproof, everlasting glass as the glass of the Green Wall and of all our structures. On days like these, you can see to the very blue depths of things, to their unknown surfaces, those marvelous expressions of mathematical equality—which exist in even the most usual and everyday objects.

For instance, this morning I was at the hangar, where the Integral is being built, and suddenly: I noticed the machines. Eyes shut, oblivious, the spheres of the regulators were spinning; the cranks were twinkling, dipping to the right and to the left; the shoulders of the balance wheel were rocking proudly; and the cutting head of the perforating machine curtsied, keeping time with some inaudible music. Instantly I saw the greater beauty of this grand mechanized ballet, suffused with nimble pale-blue sunbeams.

And then I thought to myself: why? Is this beautiful? Why is this dance beautiful? The answer: because it is non-free movement, because the whole profound point of this dance lies precisely in its absolute, aesthetic subordination, its perfect non-freedom. If indeed our ancestors were prone to dancing at the most inspired moments of their lives (religious mysteries, military parades), then all this can only mean one thing: the instinct for non-freedom, from the earliest of times, is inherently characteristic of humankind, and we, in our very contemporary life, are simply more conscious . . .

To be continued: the intercom is clicking. I lift my eyes: it reads "O-90," of course. And, in half a minute, she herself will be here to collect me: we are scheduled for a walk.

Sweet O! It has always seemed to me that she looks like her name: she is about ten centimeters below the Maternal Norm, which makes her lines all rounded, and a pink O—her mouth—is open to receive my every word. Also: there are round, chubby creases around her wrists—such as you see on the wrists of children.

When she entered, I was still buzzing inside out with the flywheel of logic and, through inertia, I started to utter some words about this formula I had only just resolved (which justified all of us, the machines and the dance): "Stunning, isn't it?" I asked.

"Yes, the spring, it is stunning . . ." O-90 smiled pinkly.

Wouldn't you know it: spring . . . I say "stunning" and she thinks of spring. Women . . . I fell silent.

Downstairs. The avenue is crowded: we normally use the Personal Hour after lunch for extra walking when the weather is like this. As usual, the Music Factory was singing the March of the One State with all its pipes. All ciphers walked in measured rows, by fours, rapturously keeping step. Hundreds and thousands of ciphers, in pale bluish unifs,* with gold badges on their chests, indi-cating the state-given digits of each male and female. And I—we, our foursome—was one of the countless waves of this mighty tor-rent. On my left was O-90 (a thousand years ago, our hairy fore-bears most probably would have written that funny word "my" when referring to her just now); on my right were two rather unfamiliar ciphers, a female and a male.

The blessed-blue sky, the tiny baby suns in each badge, faces un-clouded by the folly of thought . . . All these were rays, you see—all made of some sort of unified, radiant, smiling matter. And a brass beat: Tra-ta-ta-tam, Tra-ta-ta-tam—like sun-sparkling brass stairs—and with each step up, you climb higher and higher into the head-spinning blueness . . .

And here, like this morning in the hangar, I saw it all as though for the very first time: the immutably straight streets, the ray-spraying glass of the sidewalks, the divine parallelepipeds of the transparent buildings, and the quadratic harmony of the gray-blue ranks. And then: it was as if I—not whole generations past—had personally, myself, conquered the old God and the old life. As if I personally had created all this. And I was like a tower, not daring to move even an elbow, for fear of scattering walls, cupolas, ma-chines . . .

And then, in an instant: a hop across centuries from + to −. I was reminded—obviously, it was association by contrast—I was sud-denly reminded of a picture in the museum depicting *their* olden day, twentieth-century avenue in deafening multicolor: a jumbled crush of people, wheels, animals, posters, trees, paint, birds . . . And do you know, they say that it was actually like that—that it's actually possible. I found that so improbable, so ludicrous, that I couldn't contain myself and laughed out loud.

And then there was an echo—a laugh—coming from the right. I spun around: the white—unusually white—and sharp teeth of an unfamiliar female face were before my eyes.

*It is unlikely this comes from the ancient word *Uniforme*.

"Forgive me," she said, "but you were observing your surroundings with such an inspired look—like some mythical god on the seventh day of creation. It looked as though you actually believed that you, yourself, had created everything—even me! I'm very flattered . . ."

All this was said without smiling, and I'd even go as far as to say that there was a certain reverence (maybe she was aware that I am the Builder of the Integral). And I don't know—perhaps it was somewhere in her eyes or eyebrows—there was a kind of strange and irritating X to her, and I couldn't pin it down, couldn't give it any numerical expression.

For some reason, I became embarrassed and, fumbling, began to justify my laughter to her with logic. It was perfectly clear, I was saying, that the contrast, the impassable chasm, that lies between today and yesterday . . .

"But why on earth impassable?" What white teeth! "Across the chasm—throw up a bridge! Just imagine it for yourself: the drums, the battalions, the ranks—these were all things that existed back then too. And consequently . . ."

"Well, yes, it's clear!" I cried (it was an astonishing intersection of thoughts: she was using almost exactly my words—the ones I had been writing just before this walk). "You see, even in our thoughts. No one is ever 'one,' but always 'one of.' We are so identical . . ."

Her words: "Are you sure?"

I saw those jerked-up eyebrows forming sharp angles toward her temples—like the sharp horns of an X—and again, somehow, got confused. I glanced right, then left and . . .

She was on my right: thin, sharp, stubbornly supple, like a whip (I can now see her digits are I-330). On my left was O-90, totally different, made of circumferences, with that childlike little crease on her arm; and at the far right of our foursome was an unfamiliar male cipher, sort of twice-bent, a bit like the letter "S." We were all different . . .

This I-330 woman, on my right, had apparently intercepted my confused glance and with an exhale: "Yes . . . Alas!"

In essence, her "alas" was absolutely fitting. But again, there was something about her face, or her voice . . .

I—with uncharacteristic abruptness—said: "Nothing alas about it. Science progresses, and it's clear that given another fifty, a hundred years . . ."

"Even everyone's noses will be . . ."

"Yes, noses," I was now almost screaming. "If, after all, there is any good reason for enviousness . . . like the fact that I might have a nose like a button and some other cipher might have . . ."

"Well, actually, your nose, if you don't mind me saying, is quite 'classical,' as they would say in the olden days. And look, your hands . . . show, come on, show me your hands!"

I cannot stand it when people look at my hands, all hairy and shaggy—such stupid atavistic appendages. I extended my arms and with as steady a voice as I could, I said: "Monkey hands."

She looked at my hands and then at my face: "Yes, they strike a very curious chord." She sized me up with eyes like a set of scales, the horns at the corners of her eyebrows glinting again.

"He is registered to me today," O-90 rosily-joyfully opened her mouth.

It would have been better to have stayed quiet—this was absolutely irrelevant. Altogether, this sweet O person . . . how can I express this . . . She has an incorrectly calculated speed of tongue. The microspeed of the tongue ought to be always slightly less than the microspeed of the thoughts and certainly not ever the reverse.

At the end of the avenue, the bell at the top of the Accumulator Tower resoundingly struck 17:00. The Personal Hour was over. I-330 was stepping away with that S-like male cipher. He commanded a certain respect and, now I see, he had a possibly familiar face. I must have met him somewhere—but right now I can't think where.

As I-330 departed, I-330 smiled with that same X-ishness. "Come by Auditorium 112 the day after tomorrow."

I shrugged my shoulders: "If I am given instructions to go to the particular auditorium you mention, then . . ."

With inexplicable conviction, she said: "You will."

The effect of that woman on me was as unpleasant as a displaced irrational number that has accidentally crept into an equation. And I was glad that, even if only for a short while, I was alone again with sweet O.

Arm in arm, we walked across four avenue blocks. On the corner, she would go to the right and I to the left.

"I would so like to come to you today and lower the blinds. Today, right now . . ." O shyly lifted her blue-crystal eyes to me.

You funny thing. Well, what could I say to her? She came over only yesterday and knows as well as I do that our next Sex Day is the day after tomorrow. This was simply that same "pre-ignition of thought" as happens (sometimes harmfully) when a spark is issued prematurely in an engine.

Before parting, I twice . . . no, I'll be exact: I kissed her marvelous, blue, untainted-by-a-single-cloud eyes three times.

KEYWORDS:

A Jacket. The Wall. The Table of Hours.

I looked through all that I wrote yesterday and I see: I was not writing clearly enough. I mean, all this is of course completely clear to any one of us. But how do I know: it may be that you, unknown reader, to whom the Integral will be carrying these records, have only read the great Book of Civilization up to the page that describes the life of our ancestors nine hundred years ago? It may be that you don't know terms like the Table of Hours, the Personal Hour, the Maternal Norm, the Green Wall, the Benefactor. It is amusing to me—and at the same time very laborious to explain all this. It is exactly as if a writer of, let's say, the twentieth century, were made to explain in his novel the meaning of the words "jacket," "apartment," or "wife." But then again, if his novel is to be translated for barbarians, would it make any sense to carry on without notes about the likes of "jackets"?

I am certain that the barbarian, looking at a "jacket" would think: "What's this for? Just more to carry on my back." I have a feeling that you will think exactly the same thing when I tell you that none of us, since the Two-Hundred-Year War, has been beyond the Green Wall.

But, my dear friends, you must try to think a little now—it will help matters. It is clear that the whole of human history, as far as we know, is the story of transition from a nomadic mode of life toward an increasingly settled one. Surely it follows then that the most settled mode of life (ours) is also the most perfected life (ours)? It was in previous eras that people rushed about the Earth from end to end, when there were nations, wars, trade, the discoveries of different Americas. But why—and for whom—is this necessary anymore?

I will allow: becoming accustomed to this kind of settledness was not effortless or immediate. During the Two-Hundred-Year War, all roads were destroyed and grasses grew over everything and, initially, it must have been very uncomfortable to live in cities, which were cut off from one another by green thickets. But what of it? I imagine that after man's tail fell off, he, likewise, didn't immediately know how to fend off flies without the help of his tail. He, at the beginning, undoubtedly mourned his tail. But can you imagine yourself now with a tail? Or can you imagine yourself on the street, naked, without a "jacket"(perhaps you still walk around wearing "jackets")? Well, that is how it is here: I cannot picture a city without the dressing of the Green Wall, I cannot picture a life not expressed in the numerical overlay of the Table.

The Table . . . Right now, from the wall of my room, from the panel of gold underlay, the burgundy numbers are looking me in the eye, sternly but tenderly. I am involuntarily reminded of that which the Ancients called "icons," and I feel like making up poems or prayers (the same thing). Ah, if only I were a poet, I would rightly exalt you, O Table, O heart and pulse of the One State.

All of us (perhaps you, too), as children, read at school that greatest of all ancient literary legacies: *The Railroad Schedule.* But even if you put that next to the Table, you will see it is graphite next to diamond: in each is the same C, carbon, but how eternal, how transparent, how dazzling is the diamond. Who is not made breathless when racing and rumbling through the pages of the *Schedule*? But the Table of Hours—it transforms each of us into the real-life, six-wheeled, steel heroes of a great epic. Each morning, with six-wheeled precision, at the exact same hour, at the exact same minute, we, the millions, rise as one. At the exact same hour, we uni-millionly start work and uni-millionly stop work. And, merged into a single, million-handed body, at the exact same Table-appointed second, we bring spoons to our lips, we go out for our walk and go to the auditorium, to the Taylor Exercise Hall, go off to sleep . . .

I will be totally frank: the absolutely exact solution to the mystery of happiness has not yet fully materialized even here. Twice a day—from 16:00 to 17:00 and from 21:00 to 22:00—the united powerful organism scatters to its separate cages. These are written into the Table of Hours: the Personal Hours. In these hours you will see chastely lowered blinds in the rooms of some; others are walking along avenues, deliberately, to the brass beat of the March; and others still, like me now, are at their desks. But I firmly believe—call me an idealist or fantasist—I believe that sooner or later, one day, we'll find a place in the general formula for these hours too, one day all of these 86,400 seconds will be accounted for in the Table of Hours.

I've come to read and hear many unlikely things about the times when people lived in freedom, i.e., the unorganized savage state. But the most unlikely thing, it seems to me, is this: how could the olden day governmental power—primitive though it was—have allowed people to live without anything like our Table, without the scheduled walks, without the precise regulation of mealtimes, getting up and going to bed whenever it occurred to them? Various historians even say that, apparently, in those times, lights burned in the streets all night long, and all night long, people rode and walked the streets.

This I just cannot comprehend in any way. Their faculties of reason may not have been developed, but they must have understood more broadly that living like that amounted to mass murder—literally—only it was committed slowly, day after day. The State (humaneness) forbade killing to death any one person but didn't forbid the half-killing of millions. To kill a man, that is, to decrease the sum of a human life span by fifty years—this was criminal. But decreasing the sum of many humans' lives by fifty million years—this was not criminal. Isn't that funny? This mathematical-moral mystery could be solved in half a minute by any ten-year-old cipher here among us; but they couldn't do it—not with all their Kants put together (because not one of their Kants ever figured out how to build a system of scientific ethics based on subtraction, addition, division, and multiplication).

And then, isn't it absurd that the government (it dared call itself a government!) could fail to impose any control on sexual lives? It was whoever, whenever, and however much you wanted . . . Absolutely unscientifically, like wild animals. And, like wild animals, obliviously giving birth to children. Isn't it funny to know crop breeding, poultry breeding, fish breeding (we have specific information that they knew how to do these things), and not to be able to get to the top rung of that logical ladder: child breeding? Not to pursue those ideas all the way to our Maternal and Paternal Norms?

It is so funny, and so unbelievable, and yet I'm nervous of what I've just written: perhaps, you, unknown reader, think I'm a malicious joker? Suddenly you're thinking that I simply want to make a little fun of you and in mock seriousness I am telling you the most absolute junk.

Well, first, I am not capable of joking—every joke, by function of its omissions, contains a lie; and, second, One-State Science confirms that the life of the Ancients was exactly so, and One-State Science cannot be mistaken. Yes, after all, how could there have been any logic to their government if all their people lived in that state of freedom, i.e., like wild animals, monkeys, herds? What could you possibly expect of them, when even today, on rare occasions, from some distant undersurface, from the shaggy depths of things, you can hear the wild echoes of monkeys?

Fortunately, it rarely happens. Fortunately, these are only minor incidentals: they are easily repaired, without having to stop the perpetual, great progress of the whole machine. And to expel the offending cog, we have the skillful, severe hand of the Benefactor and we have the experienced eye of the Guardians . . .

Yes, by the way, I have just remembered: that twice-bent, S-shaped man—it seems I once had the occasion to see him emerging from the Bureau of Guardians. Now I understand why I instinctively felt a certain respect for him and a sort of awkwardness, when in his presence that strange I-330 was . . . I should confess that that I-330 . . .

The sleep bell is ringing: 22:30. Until tomorrow.

KEYWORDS:

The Barbarian and the Barometer. Epilepsy. If Only . . .

Until now, everything in life had been clear (it is not in vain that I have, it seems, a certain predilection for this particular word "clear"). But today . . . I don't understand it.

First: I actually received instructions to be at Auditorium 112, like she said I would. Even though the probability of that was

$$\frac{1,500}{10,000,000} = \frac{3}{20,000}$$

(where 1,500 is the number of auditoriums and 10,000,000 is the number of ciphers). And secondly . . . but then again, I'd better tell you everything in the right order.

The auditorium. An enormous, sun-saturated hemisphere of glass expanses. Circular rows of noble, spherical, smoothly sheared heads. My heart sank slightly as I looked around. I suppose I was searching for something: would that pink half-moon glimmer on the pale blue waves of unifs—where were those sweet lips of O? I spotted someone's unusually white and sharp teeth, just like . . . no, no, I'm mistaken, it isn't . . . This evening, O is coming over—at 21:00—so my desire to see her here was completely natural.

There's the bell. We stood and sang the Hymn of the One State, and on the stage, the phonolector sparkled with its golden loudspeaker and keen wit: "Esteemed ciphers! Not long ago, archaeologists uncovered a book from the twentieth century. In it, an ironical author tells the story of a barbarian and a barometer. The barbarian noticed: every time the barometer pointed to 'rain,' it actually rained. And then, one day, when the barbarian wanted it to rain, he tapped out just enough mercury so that the level would indicate 'rain' " (on the screen, a barbarian in feathers, tapping out the mercury; the sound of laughter). "You laugh: but does it not seem to you more appropriate to laugh at the Europeans of that epoch? Like the barbarian, the European wanted 'rain'—rain with a capital R, algebraic rain. But he stood before the barometer like a big wet chicken. At least the barbarian had more gumption and verve and—though barbarous—logic: he was able to establish that there is a connection between effect and cause. Having tapped out the mercury, he achieved that first step along the great path, toward . . ."

At this point (I repeat: I am writing all this, without hiding a thing)—at this point, I temporarily became sort of waterproof to the invigorating torrent pouring from the loudspeakers. It suddenly occurred to me that I had come here in vain (why "in vain"? And how could I have not come, seeing as I had instructions to do so?); it seemed to me that everything was empty, just a shell. And, straining, I returned my attention to the phonolector when it started to address its main subject: our music, our mathematical composition (the mathematician is the cause, the music is the effect), and the description of the recently invented musicometer.

". . . By simply turning this handle, any of you could produce up to three sonatas an hour. What a struggle this was for our ancestors. They could create only if they drove themselves to fits of 'inspiration,' a strange form of epilepsy. And here is an amusing illustration of their results: the music of Scriabin, twentieth century. This black box" (at this point the curtains moved apart on the stage and there stood their ancient instrument) "they called this box 'grand' or 'forte,' which again proves how much all of their music . . ."

And so it went on—again, I hardly recall any of it, very possibly because . . . well, yes, I'll tell you straight: because it was I-330 who went up to the "grand" instrument. It is likely that I was astonished by her unexpected appearance on the stage.

She was in the fantastical attire of an ancient epoch: a tightly fitting black dress, the sharply emphasized white of her bare shoulders and neck, and a warm, heaving, breathing shadow between her . . . and those blinding, almost evil teeth . . .

A smile—a sting, aimed here—down below. She sat and played. It was wild, convulsive, colorful—like everything back then: lacking even a shadow of rational mechanics. And, of course, all those around me were right: they were all laughing. Except a few . . . including me—but why wasn't I?

Yes, epilepsy is a psychic sickness—a pain . . . a slow, sweet pain—a sting—and you wish it would go deeper, hurt more . . . Then, slowly—sunshine emerges. Not our kind of sunshine, the pale-bluish-crystalline kind, which disperses evenly through our glass bricks—no: it was a wild, rushing, burning sun, expelling itself, shedding itself in little tufts.

The person sitting next to me glanced to the left—at me—and giggled. For some reason, I distinctly recall seeing on his lips: a microscopic spit bubble jump out and burst. This bubble brought me to my senses. I was myself again.

Just like everyone else, I was just hearing a silly, fussy clatter of strings. I laughed. Things became easy and simple. The talented phonolector had portrayed this wild epoch too realistically—that was all.

With particular pleasure, I then listened to our contemporary music. (It was demonstrated at the end for the sake of contrast.) Crystal chromatic degrees converging and diverging in infinite sequences and the summarizing chords of Taylor and Maclaurin formulae with a gait like Pythagorean pant-legs, so whole-toned and quadrilateral-heavy; the melancholy melodies of diminishing oscillations; pauses producing bright rhythms according to Frauenhofer lines, the spectral analysis of planets . . . What magnificence! What unwavering predictability! And how pitiful that whimsical music of the Ancients, delimited by nothing except wild fantasy . . .

As usual, in orderly rows, by fours, we all walked out through the wide doors of the auditorium. Nearby a familiar twice-bent figure flashed past; I bowed respectfully.

Sweet O was supposed to be coming over in an hour. I felt pleasantly and usefully excited. Once home, I hurried to the building office, handed my pink ticket to the monitor, and received permission for blind-lowering. This permission is only given to us on Sex Days. Otherwise, we live in full view, perpetually awash with light, in among our transparent walls, woven from the sparkling air. We have nothing to hide from one another. This also eases the arduous and distinguished task of the Guardians. Otherwise, who knows what could happen? It's possible that it was exactly those strange nontransparent habitations of the Ancients that gave rise to that sorry cellular mentality of theirs. "My (*sic!*) house is my castle"— they really should have thought that through!

At 22:00, I lowered the blinds and at that same minute O walked in, a little out of breath. She offered me her pink little mouth and her pink ticket. I tore the pink ticket but couldn't tear myself away from the pink mouth until the very last moment at 22:15.

Afterward, I showed her my records and spoke—very well, I think—about the beauty of the square, the cube, the straight line. She listened so charming-pinkly, and suddenly from those blue eyes: a tear, another, and a third, right onto the open page (page 7). The ink ran. So now I'll have to copy it out again.

"Dear D, if only you—if only . . ."

"If only"? "If only" what? Again with her old refrain: a baby. Or maybe this is a new thing, to do with . . . to do with that other woman? Could it be that . . . No, that would be too stupid.

KEYWORDS:

A Quadrilateral. The Masters of the World.
A Pleasantly Useful Function.

Again, something's not right here. Again, I've been talking to you, my unknown reader, as though ... well, let's say, as though you were my old comrade R-13, the poet with African lips, a person everyone knows. Meanwhile, you—on the moon, on Venus, on Mars, on Mercury—who knows you? Where and who are you?

Here's the thing: imagine a quadrilateral—a living, beautiful square. And this quadrilateral is asked to describe itself, its existence. But you see, the last thing that would occur to the quadrilateral mind would be to mention its four equal angles: it just doesn't see them—they're just a given, every day. Well, that's me, permanently in that same sort of quadrilateral predicament. Whether it's the business of the pink ticket or something similar: to me, it's all the equivalent of four angles, but for you, it may be more vividly evident than Newton's binomial theorem.

So here goes. Some ancient sage once said something clever (accidentally, of course): "Love and hunger are the masters of the world." Ergo, to take control of the world, man must take control of the masters of the world. Our ancestors finally conquered Hunger with a heavy cost: I am talking about the Two-Hundred-Year War, the war between the city and the countryside. It is likely that savage

Christians stubbornly clung to their "bread"* out of religious prejudice. But in the thirty-fifth year before the founding of the One
State, our modern petroleum-based food was invented. True, only
0.2 percent of the population of the earthly sphere survived. But in
exchange for all that—the cleansing of thousand-year-old filth—
how glistening the face of the earth has become! In exchange for all
that, this zero-point-two percent has tasted bliss in the ramparts of
the One State.

Isn't it clear that bliss and envy—they are the numerator and the
denominator of the fraction known as happiness. And what would
be the point of those countless sacrifices in the Two-Hundred-Year
War if, in our life, there still remained good reason for enviousness?
But it did remain, because noses were still "button" noses and "classical" noses (our prior conversation on the walk), and because some
achieved the love of many but many achieved the love of none.

So it's natural that having subjugated Hunger (algebraically = to
the sum of material goods), the One State began an offensive
against the other master of the world—against Love. Finally, even
this natural force was also conquered, i.e., organized and mathe-
maticized, and around three hundred years ago, our historical *Lex
Sexualis* was proclaimed: "Each cipher has the right to any other cipher as sexual product."

And the rest are technicalities. You are thoroughly examined in
the laboratories of the Bureau of Sex, the exact sexual hormone
content of your blood is determined, and then they generate a corresponding Table of Sex Days for you. Then you make a statement
that on your given day you would like to make use of this (or that)
cipher, and you receive the appropriate ticket book (pink). And
that's it.

It's clear: if there is no good reason for enviousness, the denominator of the fraction of happiness is brought to zero and the fraction is transformed into a glorious infinity. And that very thing,
which was to the Ancients the source of innumerable silly tragedies,

---

*This word has been preserved only in the form of a poetic metaphor. The chemical
composition of this material is not known.

has been converted to a harmonic, pleasantly useful function of the organism, exactly like sleep, physical labor, ingestion, defecation, and the rest. From this you will see how the great strength of logic purifies everything, no matter what it touches. Oh, if only you, unknown people, could also know this divine strength, if only you could learn to follow it through.

. . . Strange: I was writing today about the highest of heights in human history and all the while breathing the cleanest mountain air of thought, but, meanwhile, there were clouds and cobwebs and a cross, some kind of four-pawed X, inside me. Maybe it was my own paws, since they were in front of me on the table all this time—my shaggy paws. I don't like talking about them and I don't like them: they are evidence of the savage epoch. Could there actually be, within me—

I wanted to cross out that last part because it goes beyond the bounds of my preselected keywords for this record. But then I decided: I won't cross anything out. Let my records—like the most sensitive seismograph—produce the crooked line of even the most insignificant brain oscillations. Sometimes it is exactly these oscillations that serve as forewarning of . . .

Okay, this is really absurd, this really actually should be crossed out: we have channeled all the forces of nature—there cannot be any future catastrophes.

And now everything is clear to me: that strange feeling inside is all due to that very quadratic predicament of mine, about which I spoke at the beginning of this record. And there is no X in me (it's not possible). It is simply that I am afraid that some kind of X exists in you, unknown readers of mine. But I believe you won't judge me too harshly. I believe you will understand that it is more difficult for me to write than for any author in the course of all human history: some wrote for their contemporaries, others for their descendants, but no one ever wrote for their ancestors or beings who resemble their own distant, savage ancestors . . .

KEYWORDS:

An Incident. That Damned "Clear."
Twenty-Four Hours.

I repeat: I have charged myself to write this without hiding a thing. Therefore, however sad it is, I ought to record here that, obviously, even today, the process of hardening, the crystallization of life has not yet been completed, it hasn't reached the ideal—there are still a few stages to go. The ideal (clearly) is a state where nothing actually happens anymore, but meanwhile, there are still things that . . . Well, take something like this, if you like: I read today in the *State Gazette* that a Celebration of Justice will take place on Cube Plaza in two days' time. So, you see, once again some cipher has disrupted the progress of the great State machine. Once again, something unforeseen, something that couldn't be calculated in advance, has occurred.

And, besides that, something happened to me. True, it was during the Personal Hour, i.e., the hour specially reserved for unforeseeable circumstances, but all the same . . .

At around 16:00 (more exactly, ten minutes to 16:00), I was at home. Suddenly, the telephone:

"D-503?" (A female voice).

"Yes."

"You free?"

"Yes."

"It's me, I-330. I'm flying by for you now and we'll set our course for the Ancient House. Agreed?"

I-330 . . . That I-330 annoys me, repels me—almost spooks me. And that's exactly why I said: "Yes."

Five minutes later and we were already in the aero. A May sky of blue majolica and the light sun in its own golden aero, buzzing along behind us, not rushing ahead, not falling behind. But there, up ahead, was a cloud whitening our view like a cataract, stupid and puffy, like the cheeks of the ancient "Cupid"—and it was somewhat irking me. The wind dries your lips when the front window is open—you lick your lips incessantly without meaning to and incessantly think about your lips.

Dull green dots were already visible, though still far off—there, behind the Wall. Then a slight, involuntary sinking of the heart—down, down, down, like descending a steep hill—and we were at the Ancient House.

The whole, strange, fragile, blind structure is wrapped in a glass shell: otherwise, of course, it would have collapsed long ago. At the glass door was an old lady, wrinkled all over, especially her mouth: all pleats and gathers, the lips already tucked inside. Her mouth was overgrown somehow—it was totally unbelievable that she could speak at all. But then she did speak: "Well, now, my dears, you've come to look at this little house of mine?" And the wrinkles beamed (that is, it is likely that they formed an optical image that created the impression that they were "beaming").

"Yes, grandma, I felt like seeing it again," I-330 told her.

The wrinkles beamed: "What a sun, eh? . . . Well, what's up, what? Ooh, mischief-maker, ooh, mischief-maker! I kno-o-ow, I know! Oh, all right: go in alone; I think I'm better off here, in the sunshine . . ."

Hmm . . . It would seem that my companion is a frequent visitor here. I want to shake something from myself, something is bothering me: it's still that same untethered visual image, that cloud on the smooth blue majolica.

As we climbed up the wide, dark staircase, I-330 said: "... Love her—that old woman."

"What for?"

"Don't know. Maybe—for her mouth. Or maybe for no reason at all. Just because."

I shrugged my shoulders. She continued, smiling a little bit, or maybe even not smiling at all: "I feel very guilty about it. It's clear that one should not 'love for the sake of it' but 'love for something's sake.' All natural forces should be ..."

"It's clear ..." I began. I caught myself immediately on that word and secretly glanced over at I-330: had she noticed?

She was looking down somewhere: her eyes lowered, like blinds.

It reminded me of walking along the avenues in the evening, at around 22:00, and among the brightly lighted, transparent cages there are darkened ones with lowered blinds, and behind those blinds—what is happening, what is behind her blinds? Why did she call me today and what is all this?

I opened the heavy, creaky, opaque door and we were in a dark, disorderly space (they called this an "apartment"). There stood that strange, "grand" musical instrument, amid the wild, disorganized, crazy multicolor of tones and shapes—like that ancient music. White smoothness overhead; dark-blue walls; the red, green, orange bindings of ancient books; the yellow bronze of a candelabra and a statue of Buddha; and the lines created by the furniture all mangled by that epilepsy, not adhering to any sort of equation.

I bore this chaos with great strain. But my companion had, seemingly, a stronger constitution.

"This is my most favorite ..." Suddenly she caught herself and that sting-smile of white, sharp teeth appeared. "To be more precise: this is the most ridiculous of all of their 'apartments.' "

"Or, even more precisely: of their nation-states," I corrected her. "Thousands of microscopic, perpetually quarreling nation-states, relentless, like ..."

"Well, yes, that's clear," said I-330, apparently very serious.

We crossed the room where two little children's beds stood (in that epoch, children were private possessions). And more rooms, the glimmering of mirrors, gloomy closets, intolerably multi-colored sofas, a vast "fireplace," and a mahogany bed. The only evidence of our contemporary, excellent, transparent, and eternal glass was in their pathetic, fragile, mini-quadrilateral windows.

"And to think: these people 'loved for the sake of it,' burning, suffering..." Again her eyelids lowered like blinds. "What a ridiculous, spendthrift waste of human energy—don't you think?"

She spoke somehow from within me, she spoke my thoughts. But there was still that annoying X in her smile. There, behind those blinds, inside her, something was going on—I don't know what—and it exasperated me. I wanted to quarrel with her, to scream at her (to be exact), but I had to agree anyway—not agreeing is not allowed.

Then we stopped in front of a mirror. At that moment, I only saw her eyes. An idea came to me: aren't human beings constructed as haphazardly as these ridiculous "apartments"? Human heads aren't transparent, and their only tiny windows: the eyes. It was as if she had guessed what I was thinking and she turned. "Well—here are my eyes. So?" (This, of course, was said without words.)

Before me were two terrifyingly dark windows, and within them a very unknown, strange life. I could only see fire—some kind of inner wood-fire was blazing there—and there were figures, who looked just like . . .

It was only natural, of course: I had seen a reflection of myself. But, in fact, it was so unnatural and unlike me (obviously, the depressing effects of the circumstances) that I distinctly felt frightened, felt caught, a captive in this wild cage, I felt myself gripped by the wild whirlwind of ancient life.

"You know what," I-330 said, "go out into the next room for a minute." I heard her voice come from in there, from within, from the dark windows of her eyes, where that wood-fire burned.

I went out and sat down. From a little shelf on the wall, the snub-nosed, asymmetrical physiognomy of some ancient poet (Pushkin, perhaps) was faintly smiling at me. Why on earth am I sitting here and compliantly suffering this smile? And what is the point of all this: what am I here for, what is this ridiculous situation? This irritating, repulsive woman, this strange game ...

Back in there, the door to the closet banged, silk rustled, and I could barely restrain myself from going in—and, though I don't exactly remember, I probably felt like saying many very harsh things.

But she had already come out. She was in a short, old-fashioned, bright-yellow dress, a black hat, black stockings. The dress was made of light silk and I could clearly see: her stockings went very high up, a good deal higher than the knee, and the open neck, the shadow between ...

"Listen, you, clearly, want to try to be original, but don't tell me that you ..."

"Clearly," I-330 interrupted, "to be original means to somehow stand out from others. Consequently, being original is to violate equality ... And that which in the idiot language of the Ancients was called 'being banal,' for us just means doing your duty. Because ..."

"Yes, yes, yes! Exactly," I burst out, "and one has no business, no business in ..."

She walked up to the statue of the snub-nosed poet and hanging the blinds of her eyes over those wood-fires—there, within, behind her windows—she said, in what seemed to be total seriousness this time (perhaps to mollify me), a very reasonable thing: "Don't you find it surprising that once upon a time people put up with the likes of him? And didn't just put up with him but adored him. What slavish spirit! Don't you think?"

"Clearly ... that is to say, I meant ..." (That damned "clearly" again!)

"Well, yes, I understand. But it's likely, in essence, this was a case of the masters becoming more powerful than their rulers. Why didn't they isolate them and destroy them? In our world ..."

"Yes, in our world ..." I began. And suddenly she burst out laughing. I could see this laughter with my eyes: the ringing, severe, stubbornly supple (like a whip), crooked line of this laughter.

I remember I was shaking all over. Now I wanted to grab her—I don't remember anymore what I wanted to do . . . but I had to do something—it didn't matter what. I mechanically opened my golden badge, glancing at the time. It was ten minutes to 17:00.

"Don't you think it's time?" I said with as much politeness as I could muster.

"And what if I asked you—to stay here with me?"

"Listen, you . . . are you aware of what you are saying? In ten minutes I am obliged to be in the auditorium . . ."

". . . And all ciphers are obliged to go through the prescribed course of art and sciences . . ." I-330 said, mimicking my voice. Then she raised the blinds. She lifted her eyes: the wood-fire burned through the dark windows. "I know a doctor in the Bureau of Medicine. I am registered to him. And if I ask him—he'll give you a certificate that says you were sick. Well?"

I understood. I finally understood where this game was going.

"What are you saying! Do you know, as an honest cipher, I am obliged, in theory, to report you immediately to the Bureau of Guardians and . . ."

"And what about not 'in theory'?" A sharp smile-sting. "I am deadly curious: will you go to the Bureau or not?"

"Are you staying?" I grasped the door handle. The handle was bronze and I heard: that same bronze in my voice.

"Just a minute . . . may I?"

She walked up to the telephone. She dialed some kind of number—I was in such shock that I didn't make a mental note of it—and she yelled: "I will wait for you at the Ancient House. Yes, yes, alone . . ."

I turned the bronze cold handle: "Would you mind if I took the aero?"

"Oh, yes, of course . . ."

There, at the entrance, the old woman dozed in the sun like a plant. Again, I was amazed that she opened her overgrown mouth and that she began to speak: "And she . . . your—what, she stayed in there alone?"

"Alone."

The old woman's mouth tucked inside again. She shook her head. From the look of it, even her weakly brains understood the utter absurdity and risky nature of that woman's behavior.

At exactly 17:00, I was in the lecture. And there, for some reason, it came to me that I had told the old woman an untruth: I-330 was there, but she was not alone now. Maybe it was this—that I had involuntarily lied to the old woman—that so tortured me and interfered with my listening. Yes, she was not alone: that was the thing.

At 21:30, I had a Personal Hour. I could have gone to the Bureau of Guardians and issued a statement today. But after that silly incident, I was tired. Also, the lawful period within which you can issue statements is forty-eight hours. I'll make it there tomorrow: a whole twenty-four hours remain.

KEYWORDS:

An Eyelash. Taylor. Henbane and Lily of the Valley.

Nighttime. Green, orange, blue; a red "grand" instrument; a dress, yellow as a lemon. Then the bronze Buddha; it suddenly raised its bronze eyelids and then sap started to flow from it—from the Buddha. And from the yellow dress, more sap. And sap dripped down the mirror, and oozed from the big bed, and from the children's beds, and now from me myself—and with it oozed an indistinct, morbidly sweet horror.

I awoke: a moderate bluish light. The glass of the walls was sparkling, the glass chair and table, too. All this was calming; my heart ceased to pound. Sap, the Buddha . . . what is this absurdity? It is clear: I am sick. I have never had dreams before. They say that for the Ancients, it was absolutely usual and normal to have dreams. Yes, of course, it seems their whole existence was just such a horrific carousel: green, orange, Buddha, sap. But we, here and now, know that dreams are a serious psychic disease. I also know: until now my brain was chronometrically regulated and gleaming, a mechanism without a single speck, but now . . . Yes, particularly now: I feel some kind of foreign body in there, in my brain, like a fine eyelash in the eye—the rest of you doesn't feel it, but the eye with the eyelash in it can't forget about it for a second . . .

The small, bright, crystal bell in the bed's headboard rings: 07:00. It's time to get up. On the right, on the left, through the glass walls, it's as if I am seeing myself, my room, my nightshirt, my motions, repeating themselves a thousand times. This cheers me up: one sees oneself as part of an enormous, powerful unit. And such precise beauty: not one extraneous gesture, twist, or turn.

Yes, that Taylor was, without doubt, the most brilliant of the Ancients. True, he didn't think everything through, didn't extend his method throughout life, to each step, around the clock. He wasn't able to integrate his system from an hour to all twenty-four. But all the same: how they could have written whole libraries about the likes of Kant—and not take notice of Taylor, a prophet, with the ability to see ten centuries ahead?

Breakfast was over. The Hymn of the One State had been sung harmoniously. In fours, we went to the elevators, harmoniously. The rustling of the motors was almost audible—and rapidly down, down, down—with a slight sinking of the heart . . .

And, just then, for no reason, that ridiculous dream surfaced again—or some sort of implicit function of the dream. Ah, of course, only yesterday I had that same sinking feeling in the aero— on our descent. But all that is over with: period. And it's a very good thing, too, that I was so decisive and harsh with her.

I rushed along in a wagon of the subterranean rail to the location of the Integral, where its elegant body stood on stocks, still immobile, not yet animated by fire, glistening under the sun. Closing my eyes, I fantasized in formulas: in my head I calculated again the escape velocity that would be needed to launch the Integral from the Earth. With each fraction of a second, the mass of the Integral would change (consuming combustion fuel). This equation turned out to be very complicated, with transcendental quantities.

Penetrating my fantasy: here in the solid, numerical world, someone sat down next to me, someone gently bumped me and said, "Pardon me."

I slightly opened my eyes and at first I saw something fly swiftly into outer space (it was an association with the Integral). It was a head and it was able to fly because there were protruding pink wing-ears on each of its sides. And then the crooked line of an overhanging back of the head and a stooping spine—twice-bent—the letter "S" ...

And there was an eyelash inside the glass walls of my algebraic world again—there is something unpleasant that I am supposed to do today.

"It's okay, don't worry." I smiled at my neighbor and exchanged bows with him. His badge flashed digits: S-4711 (of course, I had associated him with the letter "S" from the very first moment—it was a visual impression, unregistered by my consciousness). And his eyes flashed: two sharp gimlets, quickly revolving, boring deeper and deeper and now screwing into my deepest depths, where they will see what I myself won't even ...

All of a sudden, the eyelash became completely clear to me: he was one of them, the Guardians, and basically, there was no more postponing it, I had to tell him everything right now.

"I, if you will, was at the Ancient House yesterday ..." my voice was strange, flattened, planar. I tried to cough it clear.

"Well, that's excellent. It does provide material for very edifying conclusions."

"But, you see, I wasn't alone. I accompanied cipher I-330, and, you see ..."

"I-330? Good for you. A very interesting, talented woman. She has many admirers."

... Perhaps he, too—back then on the walk—maybe, he was registered to her, too? No, bringing this up with him is just not possible, it's inconceivable: that is clear.

"Yes, yes! And how, and how! Very." I smiled—broadly and stupidly—and I felt: this smile makes me look naked, silly ...

The gimlets reached my deepest depths, and then, rapidly revolving, screwed themselves back into eyes; S double-smiled, nodded at me, and slid along to the exit.

I hid behind my newspaper (it seemed to me that everyone was looking at me) and soon forgot about the eyelash, about the gimlets, about everything: I was very alarmed by what I was reading. It was one short line: "According to reliable witnesses, new evidence has been found of an organization, which continues to elude us to this day, whose aim is the liberation of the State from its beneficial yoke."

"Liberation?" Astounding: the extent to which this criminal instinct is deep-rooted in humankind. And I consciously say: "criminal." Freedom and crime are so indissolubly connected to each other, like ... well, like the movement of the aero and its velocity. When the velocity of the aero = 0, it doesn't move; when the freedom of a person = 0, he doesn't commit crime. This is clear. The sole means of ridding man of crime is to rid him of freedom. And we have only just gotten rid of that ("only just" means centuries within a cosmic time-scale, of course) and now suddenly some pitiful half-wits have gone and ...

I don't get it: why didn't I, yesterday, go to the Bureau of Guardians immediately? Today, after 16:00, I will go, without fail ...

I left at 16:10 and at that exact moment I saw O on the corner—in total pink rapture over our encounter. Now, she has a simple, round intellect, I thought. How opportune: she will see what's going on and give me the support I need to ... But then, no: I am not in need of support. I was firmly decided.

The pipes of the Music Factory rang out the March harmoniously—the everyday March. What indescribable charm—this everydayness, repetitiveness, this reflectivity!

O grasped my hand. "A stroll?" Those round blue eyes opened widely to me—blue windows to the interior—and I penetrated inside without getting caught up on anything: there is nothing inside, that is, nothing extraneous, unnecessary.

"No, no stroll. I need to ..." I told her where I was going. And, to my amazement, I saw: that pink circle of a mouth forge into a pink half-moon, with its horns facing downward, as if from something sour. This enraged me.

"You female ciphers, it seems, are incurably corroded by prejudice. You are completely incapable of thinking in the abstract. Pardon me—but this is pure dimness."

"You are going to the spies . . . hmph! And to think I went to the Botanical Museum and got you a sprig of lily of the valley . . ."

"Why 'and to think'? What is this 'and to think . . .'? How utterly female." I grabbed her lily of the valley angrily (I admit). "So, here it is, your lily of the valley, well? Sniff it: pleasant, yes? So at least you have that much logic. Lily of the valley smells good: that's right. But apparently you can't say that about odor itself, about the concept of 'odor'—that it is 'good' or 'bad'? You can't, can you? There is the odor of the lily of the valley and there is the loathsome odor of henbane: both are odors. There were spies in the ancient state and there are spies among us here . . . yes, spies. I am not afraid of words. But it is absolutely clear: in those days, a spy was henbane and now, a spy is lily of the valley. Yes, lily of the valley!"

The pink half-moon trembled. Now I understand why—but at the time it appeared as though . . . I was convinced that she was about to start laughing. So I yelled even louder: "Yes, lily of the valley! And there is nothing funny about it, nothing funny about it!"

Round, smooth spheres of heads were floating by and turning to look. O tenderly took me by the hand.

"You're something today . . . Are you perhaps sick?"

The dream—yellow—the Buddha . . . Then everything became clear to me: I had to go to the Bureau of Medicine.

"Yes, it's true. I am sick," I said very joyfully (this was a completely inexplicable contradiction: there was no reason to be joyful).

"Then you must go to the doctor right now. You do understand: you are obliged to be healthy—funny that I have to point it out to you."

"Oh, sweet O, well, of course, you are totally right. Absolutely right!"

I did not go to the Bureau of Guardians: I couldn't, I needed to go to the Bureau of Medicine. They kept me there until 17:00.

In the evening—it didn't matter by then, since the Bureau of Guardians was closed anyway. O came over that evening. The blinds were not lowered. We were solving a puzzle from the age-old book of problems: this is very calming and cleanses the thoughts. O-90 was over the notebook, her head bent toward her left shoulder and her left cheek propped up by her tongue in concentration. How childlike, how charming. And inside me, once again, everything was good, precise, simple . . .

She left. I was alone. I took two deep breaths (this is very beneficial before sleeping). And all of a sudden, an unexpected odor—reminiscent of something very unpleasant . . . I soon found it: a sprig of lily of the valley was hidden in my bed. Immediately, everything whirled about, rising up from the depths. Well, this was simply tactless on her part—leaving me these lilies of the valley. Yes: I never went to the Guardians, no. But it's not my fault that I'm sick.

KEYWORDS:

The Irrational Root. R-13. A Triangle.

It was long ago, in my school years, when $\sqrt{-1}$ happened to me. My memory of it is clearly carved: a bright spherical hall, hundreds of round, little-boy heads, and Pliapa, our mathematics teacher. We called him Pliapa—he was rather vintage and disheveled, and when the monitor inserted his plug from behind, the loudspeaker started up "Plya-plya-plya-tshhhhh," and then the lesson began. One day, Pliapa explained "irrational numbers" and I remember I wept, I beat my fists upon the table and wailed: "I don't want $\sqrt{-1}$! Take $\sqrt{-1}$ out of me!" This irrational root had sunk into me, like something foreign, alien, frightening, it devoured me—it couldn't be comprehended or defused because it was beyond *ratio*.

Now, once again it's that $\sqrt{-1}$. I looked over these records once more and it was clear to me: I have been outwitting myself, lying to myself, all in order not to see $\sqrt{-1}$. It was all junk—that I was sick and all that—I could have made it there. A week ago I know I would have gone without a moment's thought. Why is it that now I . . . Why?

Even today. At 16:10 exactly, I stood before the glittering glass wall. Above me, the golden, sunny, clean radiance of the letters on the signboard of the Bureau. Inside, through the glass, a long line of pale bluish unifs. Faces flickering like icon-lamps in ancient churches: they had come to perform a heroic deed; they had come to surrender their loved ones, friends, or their selves to the altar of the One State. And I—I strained toward them, to be with them. But I couldn't: my legs were deeply soldered to the glass flagstones. I was standing there, stupidly watching, lacking the strength to move from that spot . . .

"Hey, mathematician, daydreaming?"

I winced. Pointed at me: black, laughter-lacquered eyes and thick African lips. It was the poet R-13, an old friend—and with him was pink O.

I turned angrily (I think, if only they hadn't bothered me just then, I would have, once and for all, torn that $\sqrt{-1}$ out of myself, with the flesh still stuck to it, and I would have walked into the Bureau).

"Not daydreaming—but admiring, if you don't mind," I said rather sharply.

"Indeed, indeed! You ought to be a poet, my friend, not a mathematician but a poet! Ha, ha, come over to our side, to the poets, eh? Well, what do you think—I can set you up in a second—hmm?"

R-13 speaks gutturally; words gush out of him, out of his thick lips, they spray—every "p" is a fountain. "Poets"—a fountain.

"I serve and will continue to serve knowledge." I clouded over: I don't like or understand jokes, but R-13 has an idiotic habit of joking.

"Oh come on—knowledge! This knowledge of yours is utter cowardice. Yes, that's it—really. You just want to build a little wall around infinity—and you're afraid to look behind it! Yes. Peek over it and you'll have to squeeze your eyes shut—ha!"

"Walls are the foundation of anything and everything human . . ." I began.

R sprayed a fountain, O laughed pinkly, roundly. I waved them away: go ahead, laugh, it doesn't matter. I wasn't up to this. I needed something to eat, to stifle this damned $\sqrt{-1}$.

"You know what," I suggested, "why don't you come over and spend some time at my place, we can solve problems." (I recalled that quiet hour yesterday—perhaps it could be the same again today.)

O cast a glance at R, then cast a clear, round glance at me, cheeks tinting a little with the soft, exciting color of our tickets.

"Well, today I . . . today I have—a ticket to go to him," she nodded toward R. "And in the evening he is busy . . . so . . ."

The wet, lacquered lips smacked good-naturedly: "Well, okay. We only need half an hour together—right, O? And as to your math puzzles—I'm not a great puzzle enthusiast, but basically—well, let's go to my place and sit for a while."

I was terrified of being left with myself—with this new stranger, I mean, who, by some strange coincidence, has my digits: D-503. And so I went with them to R-13's. True, he is not precise or rhythmic and he has a kind of twisted, laughable logic, but we are friends all the same. It was not just an accident that he and I both chose sweet, pink O three years ago. This binds us together somehow even more strongly than our years together at school.

Next, we were in R's room. It was as if—well, everything was exactly like mine: the Table, the glass of the chairs, table, closet, and bed. But as soon as R walked in, he moved one of the chairs, then the other—and all perspectives became displaced, everything departed from the regulation dimensions, became non-Euclidean. R is still the same, hasn't changed. When it comes to Taylor and mathematics—he always lagged behind.

We reminisced about old Pliapa: how we, as little boys, would sometimes glue little thank-you notes all over his glass legs (we really loved Pliapa). We reminisced about the Scripture-instructor.* The Scripture-instructor was exceptionally loud-spoken—wind would even blow from his loudspeaker as he instructed—and we children yelled the text after him at the top of our voices. And about the time when reckless R-13 stuffed balled-up paper into his mouthpiece: instead of the prepared text, crumpled paper shot out. R was punished, of course. His deed was nasty, of course, but we chuckled about it now—our whole triangle—and, I'll admit, I did, too.

*Of course, the discourse was not about "God's commandments" of the Ancients but about the commandments of the One State.

"And what if he had been an actual human—like the instructors of the Ancients? It would've been . . ." (a "b" fountain from the thick, smacking lips . . .).

The sun came through the ceiling and the walls; sun from above, from all sides, reflecting up from below. O was sitting on R's lap with minute droplets of sun in her blue eyes. I had somehow warmed up, recovered: $\sqrt{-1}$ was stifled, had ceased to stir . . .

"So, how then is that Integral of yours? Will we be flying off to enlighten those planet-dwellers soon, eh? Well, get on with it, get on with it! Otherwise, we poets will scribble so much that your Integral won't be able to lift off for the weight of it all. Every day from eight to eleven . . ." R shook his head, scratched the back of his head—the back of his head was like a squarish little suitcase attached from behind (I was reminded of that old painting "In the Carriage").

I brightened up: "So, you too are writing for the Integral? Well, tell me, what about it? What, at least, for example, did you write today?"

"Today—about nothing. I was busy with other things . . ." The "b" sprayed straight at me.

"What other things?"

R grimaced: "Thing things! Well, if you want to know, there was a conviction. I was waxing poetic on the occasion of a conviction. One idiot, one of our own poets . . . he sat among us for two years as though everything was normal. And then suddenly—get this—'I,' he says, 'I am a genius, a genius—above the law.' And blathered on like that . . . so you see, that's what . . . ugh!"

His thick lips hung, the lacquer was stripped from his eyes. R-13 leapt up, turned, and fixed his gaze somewhere on the other side of the wall. I watched his tightly locked little suitcase and thought: what is he now mulling over in that little suitcase of his?

There was a minute of awkward, asymmetrical silence. It was not clear to me what was going on, but there was something going on.

"Happily, the antediluvian times of the omnipotent Shakespeares and Dostoevskys—or whoever they were—have passed," I said loudly, on purpose.

R turned his face. Just as before, his words sprayed me, gushed from him, but it seemed to me that the joyful lacquer in his eyes was long gone.

"Yes, dear mathematician, happily, happily, happily! We are the happiest, arithmetical mean . . . what is it you people say: to integrate from zero to infinity, from the cretin to Shakespeare . . . that's it!"

I don't know why—it was a completely inappropriate moment—but I was reminded of that woman, her voice, and some kind of fine thread was extending itself between her and R. (What was this thread?) And again, $\sqrt{-1}$ took control. I opened my badge: 16:25. They had forty-five minutes left on their pink ticket.

"Well, time for me to go . . ." I kissed O, shook hands with R, and went to the elevator.

On the avenue, having already crossed to the other side, I looked around: there were gray-blue, opaque cages of lowered blinds in the light, sun-pervaded glass block of buildings—cages of rhythmical Taylorized happiness. On the seventh floor, my eyes found R-13's cage: he had already lowered the blinds.

Sweet O . . . Dear R . . . There is something about them that is also (why "also" I don't know, but let the words come as they will)—there is something about them that is not totally clear to me. But nonetheless: I, he, and O—we are a triangle, perhaps not equilateral, but a triangle nonetheless. We, in the language of our forebears (it may be that to you, my planetary readers, this language is more understandable), we are a family. And how good it is sometimes to relax for a short time in this simple strong triangle, to lock oneself away from all that . . .

KEYWORDS:

A Liturgy. Iambs and Trochees. The Cast-Iron Hand.

A solemn, bright day. On days like these you forget about all your weaknesses, imprecisions, sicknesses, and everything is crystal-fixed and eternal—like our new glass . . .

Cube Plaza. Sixty-six powerful concentric circles: the stands. And sixty-six rows: quiet, bright faces and eyes reflecting the radiance of the skies—or, maybe, the radiance of the One State. Crimson flowers, like blood: the lips of women. The soft garlands of children's faces in the first few rows, near the center of the action. Profound, strict, gothic silence.

According to descriptions that have been handed down to us, the Ancients experienced something like this during their "services." They, however, worshipped their absurd, unknown God whereas we worship a non-absurd one—one with a very precise visual appearance. Their God didn't give them anything except an eternal, torturous journey; their God didn't think up anything more clever than that. And there's no apparent reason why it sacrificed itself. We, on the other hand, make sacrifices to our God, the One State—calm, carefully considered, reasonable sacrifices. Yes, this was the solemn liturgy to the One State, a remembrance of the crusades—the years of the Two-Hundred-Year War—this was the grand celebration of the victory of the many over the one, the sum over the unit . . .

Here, one such sacrifice stood on the steps of the sun-drenched Cube. A white . . . and yet not—not white, but colorless—a glass face, glass lips. He was all eyes—black, absorbing, swallowing holes—with that terrible world but several minutes away. His golden badge and digits were already removed. His hands were bound with a purple ribbon (an old-fashioned custom: the explanation, apparently, is that in ancient times, when all this was not carried out in the name of the One State, the convicted, understandably, felt it within their rights to resist, and so their hands were usually fettered with chains).

But above, on the Cube, by the Machine: the immobile, metallic figure of Him whom we call the Benefactor. From here, from below, you couldn't make out His face: you could only see that it was described by severe, majestic, quadratic outlines. But then, His hands . . . Sometimes this very thing happens in photographs: the hands are placed too close, in the foreground—and they come out enormous, riveting your gaze, pushing everything into the background. These heavy hands, still calmly lying on His knees—it was clear: they were stone. And the knees only barely supported their weight . . .

And all of a sudden, one of these colossal hands slowly began to rise—a slow, cast-iron gesture—and from the stands, acknowledging the raised hand, a cipher walked up to the Cube. He was one of the State Poets, whose happy lot it was to adorn the celebration with his verses. And above the stands, divine, brass iambs began to thunder—about the madman with the glassy eyes who was standing up there on the steps, waiting for the logical conclusion to his craziness.

. . . A blaze. Inside the iambs, buildings are rocking and liquid gold is bursting upward, then tumbling down. Green trees are twisting in convulsions, dripping sap—then only the black crosses of their skeletons remain. Then Prometheus appears (referring to us, of course):

Suddenly, the fire in the machine, the steel,
And the chaos, by the Law, were brought to heel.

Everything was new and steeled: a steel sun, steel trees, steel people. Then suddenly some madman "the fire set free," and again everyone perished ...

I have, unfortunately, a bad memory for poetry, but I do remember one thing: he couldn't have chosen more instructive and beautiful images.

Again, the slow, severe gesture: a second poet approached the steps of the Cube. I even half-rose from my seat: was it possible? Yes: those thick African lips, it's him ... Why didn't he say something earlier about the honorable task before him? His lips were trembling, gray. I can understand it: in the face of the Benefactor, in the face of the whole assembly of Guardians. But really: to be so nervous ...

Sharp, rapid trochees—as though delivered with a sharp ax. About an unheard-of crime: about blasphemous poems, in which the Benefactor was called ... no, I won't even raise my pen to repeat it.

R-13, pale, went and sat down, not looking at anyone (I hadn't expected this shyness from him). In one negligible differential of a second, someone's face flashed past me—a sharp, black triangle—and immediately faded: my eyes and a thousand others were focused up above, toward the Machine. Up there, a third cast-iron gesture was made by the inhuman hand. And, fluttering in an invisible wind, the criminal walked, slowly—a step up, and another, and then a pace, the last of his life—and he, with his face to the sky, his head thrown back, stood on his very own final plot.

The Benefactor circled around the Machine, as gravely and stony as fate, and put His enormous hand on the lever.... There was neither a rustle, nor a breath: all eyes were on the hand. This must be a thrilling fiery whirlwind, to be the instrument, the potential force behind hundreds and thousands of volts. What a great charge!

An immeasurable second. The hand, applying the current, descends. The unbearably sharp blade of a beam flashes, then a barely audible crackle—like a tremor—in the pipes of the Machine. A prostrate body—suffused in a faint luminescent smoke—melting, melting, dissolving with horrifying quickness before our eyes. And then nothing: just a puddle of chemically pure water that only a minute ago swilled tempestuously and redly in his heart.

All this was straightforward; every one of us knew it already: it was the dissociation of matter, yes. It was the fission of the atoms of the human body, yes. And, moreover, each time it was like a miracle, it was like an affirmation of the superhuman might of the Benefactor.

Up above, in front of Him, were the flushed faces of a dozen female ciphers, their lips half-open from excitement, their flowers fluttering in the wind.*

According to old custom, a dozen women adorned the unif of the Benefactor—not yet dry from the spray—with flowers. With the majestic stride of a high priest, He slowly descended, crossing slowly among the stands—and, after Him, the soft white branches of female hands and a uni-million storm of cries arose. And then those same cries were raised in honor of the assembly of Guardians, invisibly present somewhere here, in our rows. Who knows: it may be that the Guardians were foreseen in the fantasy of the ancient person, which conceived of gentle-terrible "archangels," assigned to each person at birth.

Yes, there was something of the ancient religions, something as purifying as thunderstorms and gales, about the whole celebration. You, to whom it falls to read this—are you familiar with moments like these? If not, I am sorry for you.

---

*They were, of course, from the Botanical Museum. I personally do not see anything beautiful in flowers and the same goes for everything that belongs to the wild world, which was chased off long ago beyond the Green Wall. Only the rational and the useful are beautiful: machines, boots, formulas, food, etc.

KEYWORDS:

A Letter. A Membrane. My Shagginess.

That day, yesterday, was like the paper through which chemists filter their solutions: all suspended particles, everything that was superfluous, remained on the paper. And this morning I went downstairs thoroughly distilled, transparent.

Downstairs, in the vestibule, behind a small desk, the monitor was glancing at her timepiece and noting down the digits of entering ciphers. Her name was U . . . but then again, I'd better not give her digits, because I am afraid of the possibility that I'll write something bad about her. Though, in reality, she is a very respectable elderly lady. The only thing that you might dislike about her was that her cheeks droop somewhat—like fish gills (but, you might think: so what?).

Her pen squeaked and I saw myself on her page: "D-503." And next to it: a smudge.

Just as I was going to draw her attention to it, she suddenly lifted her head and dripped an inky sort of grin onto me: "There's a letter. Yes. You'll get it, my dear—yes, yes, it will get to you."

I knew: the letter, having been read by her, would still have to pass through the Bureau of Guardians (I think it would be redundant to explain this natural procedure) and it would get to me not later than 12:00. But I was bothered by that grin; an ink droplet had clouded my transparent solution. So much so that later, at the building site of the Integral, I simply could not concentrate and at one point I even made a mistake in my calculations, which never happens to me.

At 12:00 the pinkish-brown fish gills and the little grin appeared again and finally, the letter was in my hands. Not knowing why, I didn't read it there, but stuck it into my pocket and hurried to my room. I unfolded it, ran through it with my eyes, and then sat down . . . It was official notification that cipher I-330 had registered me and that today at 21:00 I was to go to her—to the address below . . .

No: after everything that has happened, after I very unambiguously indicated my attitude toward her . . . Furthermore, she couldn't have known: if I had gone to the Bureau of Guardians or not. You see, there was no way she could have known that I had been sick—well, that basically I wasn't able to go . . . And despite all that . . .

In my head, a dynamo spun and droned. The Buddha—yellow—lily of the valley—a pink half-moon . . . Yes, and then there was the fact that—the fact was: O wanted to come to me today. Could I show her this notification—regarding I-330? I don't know. She wouldn't believe it (yes, and how, really, could anyone believe it?), she wouldn't believe that it has nothing to do with me, that I am completely . . . And I know: it will be a difficult, absurd, absolutely illogical conversation . . . Please, anything but that. Let it resolve itself mechanically: I'll simply send her a copy of the notification.

I was sticking the notification in my pocket hurriedly—and I caught a glimpse of my horrible monkey hand. I was reminded of how she, I-330, on the walk that day, took my hand and looked at it. Surely, she doesn't actually . . .

And now it is fifteen minutes to 21:00. A white night. Everything is greenish-glassy. But it is a sort of different, fragile glass—not ours, not real—it is a fine glass shell and under this shell, things are spinning, flying, humming . . . And I would not be surprised if now the cupolas of the auditorium arose in round, slow smoke and the elderly moon inkily grinned—like that woman who sat behind the little desk this morning—and if all blinds were lowered immediately, and if behind those blinds ...

A strange feeling: my ribs felt something like iron twigs and they were obstructing—they were positively obstructing my heart, and tightening, so there wasn't enough space for it. I stood at the glass door with the golden digits I-330. She was bent over a table with her back to me, writing something. I walked in ...

"Here ..." I extended the pink ticket to her. "I received a notification today and I am now presenting myself."

"How precise you are! Give me a minute—will you? Have a seat; I am just finishing."

Again she looked down at the letter—and what was there behind her lowered blinds? What will she say—what will she do in the next second? How could I find out, calculate it, when the whole of her is from that other place, from the wild, ancient land of dreams?

I silently watched her. My ribs were iron twigs, tightly ... When she speaks, her face is like a rapidly glittering wheel: you can't make out the separate spokes. But, at that point, the wheel was immobile. And I saw a strange combination: her dark eyebrows hitched up high to the temples—a mocking, sharp triangle, pointing upward—and two deep wrinkles, from her nose to the corners of her mouth. And these two triangles somehow contradicted each other, imposing on her whole face this unpleasant, irritating X—like a cross. A face crossed out with a cross.

The wheel began to turn; the spokes merged ...

"So you didn't go to the Bureau of Guardians?"

"I was ... I couldn't. I was sick."

"Yes. Well, I thought so. Something was always going to prevent you—it didn't matter what." Sharp teeth, a smile. "And so, now you are in my hands. You do remember: 'Any cipher who does not declare themselves to the Bureau in the course of forty-eight hours is considered ...'"

My heart struck so hard that the twigs bent. Like a little boy—foolish, like a foolish little boy, I had been caught, and foolishly, I stayed silent. And I felt: I have been caught—by hand, by foot ...

She stood up and stretched lazily. She pressed a button and with a light crackle the blinds fell on all sides. I was severed from the world—alone with her.

I-330 was somewhere behind my back, near the closet. Her unif rustled and fell; I listened—all of me listened. And I was reminded of . . . it's gone—flashed past in one hundredth of a second . . .

Not long ago I had to calculate the curvature of a new model of street diaphragm (now these elegantly decorated diaphragms are on every avenue, recording street conversations for the Bureau of Guardians). And I remember: each was a concave, pink, quivering membrane; they were strange organisms, made up of only one organ—an ear. I was now this membrane.

Then the unsnapping of buttons, the collar, to the breast and further, lower. Glassy silk rustled on her shoulders, knees, the floor. I heard—which is clearer than seeing—one foot stepping from out of the heap of bluish-gray silk, then the other . . .

The tautly stretched membrane vibrated and recorded the quiet. No: it recorded the abrupt beating of a hammer on twigs in between endless pauses. And I heard (I saw): her, behind me, thinking for a minute.

After that: the doors to the closet. Then: some kind of lid banged and again, silk, silk . . .

"Well, here you go."

I turned around. She was in a light, saffron-yellow, ancient-style dress. This was a thousand times meaner than if she had been wearing nothing. Two sharp dots were smoldering with pink through the fine fabric—two coals through ash. Two gently rounded knees . . .

She sat on a low chair. On the four-sided little table in front of her was a flask with something poison-green in it and two tiny little glasses on stems. The corner of her mouth smoked from a slim paper tube: this was ancient smoking (I forget right now what it was called).

The membrane was still vibrating. The hammer beat—inside me—on the twigs, so burning-hot they were red. I distinctly heard each strike and . . . and what if suddenly she hears them, too?

But she calmly smoked, calmly looking at me, and carelessly flicked her ash on my pink ticket.

As cold-bloodedly as possible, I asked: "Listen, in that case—why ever did you register me? Why did you make me come here?"

It was as if she didn't hear me. She poured from the flask into the little glass, took a sip.

"Delightful liqueur. Would you like some?"

Only then did I get it: alcohol. Yesterday's lightning flashed: the stone hand of the Benefactor, the unbearable blades of the laser beams, but this time, instead, it was her in the Cube, with her head thrown back—body outstretched. I winced.

"Listen," I said, "you must know: anyone who poisons themselves with nicotine and alcohol, in particular, will be shown no mercy by the One State..."

Dark eyebrows, high up toward the temples, a sharp, mocking triangle: "To destroy the few quickly is more reasonable than to give the many an opportunity to ruin themselves—degeneration and all that. This is obscenely correct."

"Yes... obscenely."

"Yes, and if this little bunch of bald, naked truths is turned out onto the streets... No, imagine it yourself... well, for example, take my faithful admirer—yes, you know him—imagine that he threw off this whole lie of clothing, and stood there, in public, just as he was born... Ha!"

She laughed. But her lower, sorrowful triangle was clearly visible to me: two deep creases from the corners of her mouth to her nose. And for some reason, from these creases it became clear to me: that man—the twice-bent, stooping and wing-eared one—had embraced her. Just as she was right now... He...

Mind you, I am trying to relay my (abnormal) feelings at the time. Now, as I write this, I realize perfectly well: all this was just as it ought to have been, and he, like every honest cipher, has an equal right to joy. And it would be unjust... well, yes, all that is clear.

I-330 laughed very strangely and at great length. Afterward, she looked intently at me, inside: "The important thing is that I am completely peaceful with you. You are so sweet—oh, I am sure of that—and you wouldn't think of going to the Bureau and telling them that I drink liqueur and smoke. You will be sick—or you will be busy—or whatever. Furthermore: I am sure that you are going to drink this charming poison with me now . . ."

What an obnoxious, taunting tone. I definitely felt: now I hate her again. But, why "now"? I had hated her the whole time.

She downed the whole little glass of green poison, stood up—her whole pinkness shining through the saffron—took a few steps, and stopped behind my chair . . .

All of a sudden: a hand around my neck and then lips on my lips . . . no, somewhere even deeper, even scarier . . . I swear that this was completely unexpected to me, and, maybe, it was only because of this . . . I couldn't possibly have . . . Now I know this absolutely definitely: I could not have wanted what happened next.

Unbearably sweet lips (I suggest that this was the taste of the "liqueur") and a mouthful of burning-hot poison was poured into me—and then more—and more . . . I unfastened from the Earth and became an independent planet, furiously rotating, rushing down, down—according to some kind of uncalculated orbit . . .

I can describe this last scene only approximately, only by more or less close analogy.

The thought had somehow never even entered my head before, but, well, it goes exactly like this: we, on the Earth, are constantly walking over a bubbling, crimson sea of fire, hidden there, in the belly of the Earth. But we never think about it. But what if suddenly the fine crust of earth under our feet became glass, and suddenly we could see . . .

I became glass. I saw into myself, inside.

There were two of me. One me was the former, D-503, cipher D-503, but the other one . . . Before, he only just managed to stick his shaggy paws out of my shell, but now he has crawled out whole, the shell is cracked open, now shattered into pieces and . . . and what next?

With all my strength, clutching at straws and at the arms of the chair, I asked, in order to hear myself (the former me): "Where . . . where did you get this . . . this poison?"

"Oh, this? Just a doctor, one of my . . ."

" 'One of my'? 'One of my'—who?"

And the other me suddenly jumped out and began to yell: "I won't allow it! I want there to be no one except me. I will kill anyone who . . . Because I—you. I—you . . ."

I saw it: he grabbed her roughly with his shaggy paws, tore up the fine silk and sunk his teeth into her. I distinctly remember: it was his teeth.

I don't know how, but I-330 slipped away. And there she stood, her eyes covered by those damned impermeable blinds, leaning her back against the closet and listening to me.

I remember: I was on the floor, hugging her legs, kissing her knees. And I begged: "Now—right now—this very minute . . ."

Sharp teeth. The sharp mocking triangle of her eyebrows. She bent down, saying nothing, and unfastened my badge.

"Yes! Yes, my sweet—my sweet." I started to hurriedly throw off my unif. But I-330, still mute, brought the timepiece on my badge up to my very own eyes. It was five minutes to 22:30.

I grew cold. I knew what this meant: appearing on the street after 22:30. All my craziness immediately blew away. I—was me. One thing became clear to me: I hate her, hate her, hate her!

Without a good-bye, without a glance, I flung myself right out of the room. Somehow managing to attach my badge while running downstairs in leaps using the emergency stairway (I was afraid to meet anyone in the elevator). I leapt out onto the empty avenue.

Everything was in its place, so simple, normal, legitimate: glassy buildings, beaming with lights; a glassy, pale sky; a greenish, still night. But underneath all this quiet, chilly glass, the boiling, the crimson, the shagginess drifted inaudibly. And panting, I rushed, in order not to be late.

Suddenly I felt: my hastily pinned badge was unfastening—it had unfastened and was jingling on the glass sidewalk. I stooped to pick it up and in that second of silence: someone's tramping steps were behind me. I turned around: something small and curved turned the corner. So, at least, it had seemed to me.

I bolted at full throttle, the air whistling in my ears. At the entrance I stopped—it was one minute before 22:30 on the clock. I listened: there was no one behind me. It had all obviously been a ridiculous hallucination, the action of the poison.

The night was torturous. The bed underneath me rose, fell, and rose again—sailing along a sine curve. To myself, I kept suggesting: "At night, all ciphers are obliged to sleep; this is an obligation, just exactly like working during the daytime. Indeed it is necessary in order to work in the daytime. Not sleeping at night is criminally . . ." But all the same I couldn't, I could not.

I'm finished. I am not in any condition to fulfill my obligations before the One State . . . I . . .

KEYWORDS:

No, I Can't—Let This Record Be Without Keywords.

Evening. A light fog. The sky is covered with a golden milky fabric and you cannot see what's there: beyond it, higher up. The Ancients knew what was there, up above: their majestic, bored skeptic . . . "God." We know that above us is a crystal-blue, bare, obscene nothing. But I don't know what is up there anymore—I have learned too much. Knowledge that is absolutely certain it is infallible: it is belief. I had a firm belief in myself; I believed that I knew everything in myself. And then . . .

I am in front of the mirror. And for the first time in my life—yes, exactly—for the first time in my life, I see myself clearly, definitively, consciously. I see myself, with astonishment, like some kind of "him." I am him: black eyebrows that look like they've been struck through with a straight line; and a vertical wrinkle between them, like a scar (I don't know whether it was there before or not). Steely gray eyes encircled by the shadows of a sleepless night; and behind this steel . . . it turns out, I had never known what was there. And it is from "there" (this "there" is both here and infinitely far away at the same time), it is from "there" that I am looking at myself, at him. And I firmly know: this person with eyebrows that look like they've been struck through with a straight line, he is an outsider and alien to me, and I am meeting him for the first time in my life. But I am real. I—not he . . .

No: period. All this is junk, and all these ridiculous sensations are delirium—the result of yesterday's contamination . . . by the mouthful of green poison—or was it by her? It doesn't matter. I am recording this only to show how strangely entangled and dislodged human reason—so precise and sharp—can become. Reason, which has even been able to make infinity (something so frightening to the Ancients) into a digestible concept, by . . .

The intercom clicked and digits appeared: R-13. Well fine, I'm actually glad: being alone now was going to be . . .

20 MINUTES LATER

On the plane of a piece of paper, in a two-dimensional world, these lines are side by side, but in another world . . . I am losing my numerical touch: 20 minutes might have been 200 or 200,000. And it is so odd to record what just occurred between R and me—I am calmly and carefully considering each word. It is the equivalent of you sitting in a chair by your own personal bed, crossing one leg over the other, and, with curiosity, watching yourself, your own self, writhe around on that very bed.

When R-13 came in, I was completely calm and normal. With a feeling of sincere rapture, I started talking about how magnificently he succeeded to trochee-isize the verdict and that it was his trochees that had hacked the madman to pieces and destroyed him more effectively than anything else.

"And furthermore, if I was invited to make a schematic sketch of the Machine of the Benefactor, I would without fail—without fail—somehow draw your trochees into this sketch." I finished.

All of a sudden, I see: R's eyes are frosting, his lips are graying.

"What's with you?"

"What. What? Well . . . oh, I'm simply fed up: everyone, everywhere, can only talk about the verdict *this* and the verdict *that*. I just don't want to hear any more of it—that's all. No more!"

He frowned and rubbed the back of his head—his little suit-case with its strange, inscrutable contents. A pause. Then he found something in his little suitcase, dragged it out, started unfolding it, and, having unfolded it, his eyes lacquered with laughter, he leapt up.

"On the other hand, I *am* composing something for your Integral . . . and it is something! It is something!"

His former self: lips smacking, spraying, words gushing in a fountain.

"You see"—an "s" fountain—". . . that ancient legend about paradise . . . it, you see, was about us, about now. Yes! Think about that! Those two in paradise stood before a choice: happiness without freedom or freedom without happiness; a third choice wasn't given. They, the blockheads, they chose freedom—and then what? Understandably, for centuries, they longed for fetters. For fetters—you understand? That was the cause of world sorrow. For centuries! Until *we* figured out how to return to happiness again . . . No, wait—wait, listen! We and the ancient God are side by side, at the same table. Yes! We have helped God to conquer the devil definitively—it was this devil, you know, who urged people to violate what was forbidden and take a bite of that fatal freedom; he was the malicious snake. But our boot: on his head—*crrunch!* And there: paradise is restored. Again we are simple-hearted innocents, like Adam and Eve. No more confusion about good and evil: everything is very simple, heavenly, childishly simple. The Benefactor, the Machine, the Cube, the Gas Bell Jar, the Guardians—all these are good, all these are majestic, wonderful, noble, sublime, crystal-clean. Because they guard our non-freedom—that is, our happiness. Those Ancients would be discussing it, deliberating and racking their brains: is it ethical, is it unethical . . . et cetera. So there you go. What do you make of my heavenly little poem, eh? It will have a very serious tone to it too . . . do you see? Quite something, eh?"

Well, I couldn't have seen better. I remember, I thought: he has such a ridiculous, asymmetrical outward appearance and such a correctly thinking mind. And because of that, he is so dear to me—

to the real me (I still consider the former me to be the real me—all this recent stuff is, of course, sickness).

R apparently read all this on my forehead, hugged me around the shoulders, and laughed.

"Oh, you . . . Adam! . . . Yes, and, incidentally, regarding Eve . . ."

He rummaged in his pocket, pulled out a notebook, flicked through it.

"The day after tomorrow . . . No, after two days. O has a pink ticket for you. How is that for you? Same as before? Do you want her to . . ."

"Well, yes, of course."

"Then I'll tell her. She herself, you see, will be too shy . . . What an affair, I tell you! I'm just a regular pink ticket to her, but you . . . you're . . . And she won't say who this fourth person is who has crawled into our triangle. Who is it—confess, you sinner—hmm?"

Curtains drew open in me and there was a rustling of silk, a green flask, lips . . . And for no particular reason, at this inappropriate moment, these words broke loose from me (if only I had contained myself!): "Tell me—have you ever had the occasion to try nicotine or alcohol?"

R tucked up his lips and peered at me from under his brow. I heard his thoughts with total clarity: "My friend, you're a good friend . . . but really . . ." And his answer: "Well, how can I put it? Personally—no. But I did know one woman . . ."

"I-330!" I screamed.

"How . . . you—you also? With her?" He spilled laughter, choked, and would start spraying again at any time.

The mirror in my room was hung so that you had to look across the table in order to see into it. From here, in the chair, I could only see my forehead and eyebrows.

And then I (the real me) saw the jagged line of my eyebrows in the mirror, and I (the real me) heard a wild, repulsive cry: "What?! Also? No: what do you mean by 'also'? No—I demand to know."

Stretched African lips. Goggle eyes . . . I (the real me) firmly grabbed this other self (the wild, shaggy, heavily breathing self) by the scruff of the neck. I (the real me) said to R: "Forgive me, for the

Benefactor's sake. I am totally sick, not sleeping. I don't understand what's wrong with me ..."

The thick lips smirked fleetingly.

"Yes, yes, yes! I understand—I understand! I'm familiar with that . . . theoretically speaking. See you later!"

He got to the doorway, then bounced back to the table like a little black ball and tossed a book onto it: "My latest . . . I brought it especially—I almost forgot. See you later." The "s" spattered me and he rolled away.

I am alone. Or, more like: alone with that other "me." I am on the chair and I have crossed my legs. From some kind of "there," I watch, with curiosity, as I—yes, me—writhe around on the bed.

Why is it—really, why is it that for three whole years, O and I have lived so amicably, and suddenly now, with just one word about that woman, about I-330 . . . Can it be that all that craziness (love, jealousy, etc.) isn't only the stuff of idiotic ancient books? And to think that it involves me! Equations, formulas, figures, and . . . and then this—I don't understand any of it! Any of it. Tomorrow I will go to R and tell him that . . .

That's not true: I won't. Not tomorrow, not the day after—I won't ever go again to see him. I cannot and do not want to see him. End of story! Our triangle has collapsed.

I am alone. It is evening. A light fog. The sky is covered with a milky golden fabric; if only I knew what was up above—up high? And if only I knew: who I am, which one is me?

KEYWORDS:

The Delimiting of Infinity. An Angel.
Reflections on Poetry.

It seems to me that I am getting better, that I can get better. I slept excellently. None of those dreams or that other sickly phenomena. Tomorrow, sweet O will come to me and everything will be as simple, correct, and delimited as a circle. I am not afraid of that word "delimited": the worthiest human efforts are those intellectual pursuits that specifically seek the uninterrupted delimiting of infinity, the reduction of infinity into convenient, easily digestible portions—into differentials. The divine beauty of my medium—mathematics—is exactly that. And the comprehension of this very beauty is exactly what that I-330 woman is lacking. But that's of no relevance here, just an accidental mental association.

These thoughts are set to the rhythmical, metrical rumble of wheels of the subterranean rail. I am scanning the rumblings and R's poems (his book from yesterday) in my head. And I feel: behind me, someone is carefully bending over my shoulder and staring at the open page in front of me. Without turning around, in a little corner of my eye, I see: pink, outstretched wing-ears, a twice-bent . . . it's him! But I didn't want to bother him and so I pretended I hadn't noticed him. How he came to be here, I don't know; he hadn't been here when I entered the train—I don't think.

This incident, meaningless in itself, had an especially good effect on me. I'd even say: it strengthened me. How pleasant it was to feel someone's vigilant eye lovingly protecting you from the slightest mistake, from the slightest misstep. Sentimental as it may sound, that same analogy came into my head again: the "guardian angel" as imagined by the Ancients. How much has materialized in our lives that they only ever imagined . . .

At the moment when I had sensed a guardian angel about myself, behind my back, I had been taking pleasure in a sonnet entitled "Happiness." I think I'm not mistaken if I say that it is a thing of rarity in its beauty and depth of thought. Here are the first four lines:

> *Forever amorous two-times-two*
> *Forever amalgamated in passionate four*
> *The hottest lovers in the world—*
> *Inseparable two-times-two*

And it continues on about all this—about the wisdom and the eternal happiness of the multiplication table.

Every genuine poet is necessarily a Columbus. America existed for centuries before Columbus but it was only Columbus who was able to track it down. The multiplication table existed for centuries before R-13 but it was only R-13 who managed to find a new El Dorado in the virgin thicket of digits. Indeed: is there a place where happiness is wiser, more cloudless, than in this miraculous world? Steel rusts; the ancient God created an ancient human capable of mistakes—and, therefore, He made a mistake Himself. The multiplication table is wiser, more absolute than the ancient God: it never—you understand—it never makes mistakes. And there is nothing happier than digits, living according to the well-constructed, eternal laws of the multiplication table. Without wavering, without erring. The truth is one, and the true path is one; and this truth is two-times-two, and this true path is four. And wouldn't it be absurd, if these happily, ideally multiplying pairs started to think about some kind of freedom, by which I clearly mean—about making a mistake? I find it axiomatic that R-13 was able to capture this most fundamental, most . . .

Then I felt it—first at the back of my head, then on my left ear—the warm, gentle breath of the guardian angel. He obviously noticed that the book on my knees was already closed and my thoughts were far away. No matter, I was prepared right then to peel open the pages of my brain before him: this was a calm, gratifying feeling. I remember: I even glanced around and I insistently and pleadingly looked him in the eye, but he didn't understand— or didn't want to understand—he didn't ask me about a thing. It was left to me to do one thing: tell everything to you, my unknown readers (now you are as dear to me, and as close and yet unattainable to me as he was in that moment).

This was my thought path: from the parts to the whole. The part was R-13 and the majestic whole was our Institute of State Poets and Writers. I thought: how could it be that the utter silliness of their literature and poetry didn't fling itself into the eyes of the Ancients? The tremendous, splendid force of the artistic word was wasted absolutely in vain. It's pure comedy: anyone wrote about whatever he took it in his head to write. It's just as comic and ridiculous that the oceans of the Ancients beat stupidly against their shores, night and day, and that the millions of kilogram-meters contained in these waves were only expended as kindling for the feelings of lovers. We, from those amorous whispers of the waves, procured electricity. From the beast, gushing with rabid froth, we made a domestic animal. And that is exactly how we tamed and saddled the once-wild natural force of poetry. Now poetry is no longer a brazen nightingale call. Poetry is a state service; poetry is purpose.

How could we have loved the four rules of arithmetic at school so sincerely and tenderly without our famous Mathematical Norms? And as for the classical image of "thorns": the Guardians are the thorns around the rose, guarding the delicate State Flower from rough contact . . . Whose stone heart can remain indifferent before the sight of the innocent lips of a child, babbling, as if in prayer: *"A bad little boy a rose did grab. The steel spike of a thorn his hand did jab. You naughty child, go home, be quick. Ow, ow, ow, how that jab did prick . . ."* etc.? And the Daily Ode to the Benefactor? Who, having read that, doesn't bow down piously before the selfless labor of this Cipher of Ciphers? And the terrifying red of the Flowers of Judicial Verdicts? And the immortal tragedy *He Who Was Late for Work?* And the reference book *Stanzas on Sexual Hygiene?*

All of life in its complexity and beauty is forever minted in the gold of words.

Our poets don't soar in the empyrean anymore: they came down to earth; they keep step with us under the strict mechanical March of the Music Factory; their lyres play the morning buzz of electric toothbrushes and the menacing crackle of the spark in the Machine of the Benefactor, and the majestic echo of the Hymn of the One State, and the intimate peal of the crystal-sparkling latrine, and the thrilling sputter of falling blinds, and the joyful voices of a new cookbook, and the barely audible whisper of the street membranes.

Our gods are here, below, with us—in the Bureau, in the kitchen, in the workshop, in the latrine. Gods have become like us, ergo, we have become like gods. And to you, my unknown planetary readers, we will come to you, to make your life as divinely rational and exact as ours.

KEYWORDS:

A Fog. You. A Completely Ridiculous Incident.

At dawn, I awoke with a pink, strong firmament right in my eyes. All was good, round. This evening O is coming here. I am undoubtedly already healthy. I smiled and fell back asleep.

The morning bell. I get up and everything is totally different: through the glass of the ceilings and walls, all around, everywhere, it is foggy. Crazy clouds, some heavy, some lighter, are getting closer, and there is already no distinction between the earth and the sky, everything is flying, melting, falling with nothing to catch on to. There are no more buildings: the glass walls have dispersed in the fog, like crystal salts in water. If you look up from the sidewalk, the dark figures of people in buildings are like suspended particles in a delirious, milky solution—some low-hanging and some higher up, and others, higher still, on the tenth floor. And everything is billowing—as though some kind of inaudible fire was raging somewhere.

At exactly 11:45, I purposefully looked at my timepiece in order to catch hold of the digits—the digits, at least, would rescue me.

At 11:45, before going to the usual session of physical labor, in accordance with the Table of Hours, I ran over to my room. All of a sudden, the telephone rings and there is a voice, a long, slow needle into my heart: "Aha, you're at home? I'm very glad. Wait for me on the corner. We'll set our course for the . . . well, you'll see where."

"You know perfectly well that I'm going to work right now."

"And you know perfectly well that you'll do just what I tell you to do. See you in a minute. In two minutes."

Two minutes later, I was standing at the corner. It was a necessity to show her that I was governed by the One State, not by her . . . "You'll do just what I tell you to do." And you can tell she is sure of it: you can hear it in her voice. But, now, I will tell her how it really is.

Gray unifs, woven from the damp fog, hurriedly spirited by me and unexpectedly vanished into the fog. I couldn't tear myself away from my timepiece—I was the sharp, trembling second hand. Eight, ten minutes . . . three minutes to 12:00, two minutes to 12:00 . . .

Enough. I'm off to work—and already late. How I hate her. But it was a necessity that I show her . . .

On the corner in the white fog: blood—a slit made with a sharp knife—it was her lips.

"It seems I have kept you waiting. But then, it doesn't matter. You're late as it is."

How I hate—but then, yes, I was late as it was.

I looked silently at her lips. All women are lips, all lips. Some are pink and firmly round: a ring, a tender guardrail from the whole world. And then there are these ones: a second ago they weren't here, and just now—like a knife-slit—they are here, still dripping sweet blood.

She comes up close, leans on my shoulder, and we are one, she flows into me and I know: this was the necessary part. I know this with every nerve, with every hair, with every sweet and almost painful beat of my heart. And I submitted to this "necessity" with joy. A piece of iron probably submits just as joyfully to its unavoidable, precise laws and fastens itself to a magnet. A rock, thrown up, wavers for a second and then falls downward, headlong to the ground. And a man, after his agony, exhaling finally, for the last time, dies.

I remember: I smiled bewilderedly and said, for no reason: "Fog . . . very."

"You like fog?"

She used an ancient, long-forgotten pronunciation of "You," the "You" of the owner to the slave, and it entered me sharply, slowly: yes, I am a slave, and this was also a necessity, it was also good.

"Yes, good . . ." I said to myself aloud. And then to her: "I hate the fog. I am afraid of fog."

"That means you love it. You're afraid of it—because it is stronger than you. You hate it—because you are afraid of it. You love it—because you can't conquer it yourself. You see, you can only love the unconquerable."

Yes, that is true. And that was precisely why—it was precisely why I . . .

We walked in two—as one. Somewhere far away, through the fog, the sun sang almost audibly, filling everything with firmness, pearl, gold, pink, red. The whole world is one immense woman, and we are in her very womb, we are not yet born, we are joyfully ripening. And it is clear to me, it is indestructibly clear to me that everything was for my sake: the sun, the fog, the pink, the red, the gold were all for my sake . . .

I wasn't going to ask where we were going. It didn't matter: only to go, to go, to ripen, to fill everything with more and more firmness—

"Well, here we are . . ." I-330 stopped in front of some doors. "Someone I know here is on duty today, as it happens. I spoke about him that time, at the Ancient House."

I was far away and using only my eyes, while carefully protecting the ripening, I read the sign: "Bureau of Medicine." All was understood.

A glass room, full of golden fog. Glass ceilings, colored bottles, jars. Wires. Bluish sparks inside tubes.

And a super-thin little man. He looked just as though he had been cut out of paper, and it wouldn't have mattered which way he turned since he was all profile, sharply sharpened. His nose: a gleaming blade. His lips: scissors.

I didn't hear what I-330 said to him but I watched how she spoke it. I could feel something: I was smiling irrepressibly, blissfully. The blades of the scissor-lips gleamed, and the doctor said: "Yes, yes. I understand. A most dangerous illness—I don't know of any more dangerous . . ." He laughed, and with a super-thin paper-hand wrote something and gave the piece of paper to I-330; he then wrote something else and gave it to me.

This was certification that we were sick, that we were not able to appear at the workplace. I had stolen my work from the One State, I am a thief, I would soon be under the Machine of the Benefactor. But this was a distant, abstract concern, like something in a book . . . I took the piece of paper without hesitating a second. I— my eyes, lips, hands—knew: this was a necessity.

At the corner, we took an aero from a half-empty garage. I-330 sat behind the wheel, like before; she moved the starter to "forward," and we tore off from the Earth, setting sail. And everything was following us: the pinkly golden fog, the sun, the super-thin-bladed profile of the doctor, which was all suddenly so near and dear. Before, everything revolved around the sun; now I know that everything revolves around me—slowly, blissfully, squinting its eyes . . .

The old lady was at the gates of the Ancient House. That sweet, overgrown-with-ray-wrinkles mouth. It had probably overgrown again and had only opened just now, for the first time in a few days, to smile.

"Aha, Miss Prankster! Can't get to work like everybody else . . . no? Well, now, all right . . . If anything happens—I'll run up and let you know . . ."

The heavy, creaking, opaque door closed and just then, with great pain, my heart opened wide and then wider still: all the way open. Her lips: mine. I drank and drank, then broke away and silently looked into the eyes thrown open to me . . . and again . . .

The semidarkness of the room, the blue, the saffron-yellow, the dark-green Morocco leather, the golden smile of the Buddha, the twinkle of the mirror. And my old dream is so understandable now: everything is impregnated with golden pink sap, and it was about to overflow its edges, about to gush—

Ripened. And, inevitably, like the iron and the magnet with sweet obedience to their precise, immutable laws, I poured myself into her. There was no pink ticket, there were no calculations, there was no One State, there was no me. There were only gentle, sharp, clenched teeth and there were gold eyes thrown wide open to me—and through them I slowly went inside, deeper and deeper still. And silence—except in the corner, thousands of miles away, where drops were dripping into the sink. I was the universe, and eras and epochs passed as drop followed drop . . .

Having thrown on my unif, I bent down to I-330 and sucked her in with my eyes one last time.

"I knew this . . . I knew you . . ." said I-330, very quietly. Quickly getting up, she put on her unif and there was her ever-sharp smile-sting.

"Well, now, fallen angel. You, I'd say, are now lost. You're not afraid, are you . . . ? Well, then, goodbye! You will return alone. Right?"

She opened the mirrored door that was set into one side of the closet; she waited, looking at me over her shoulder. I obediently left. But I had hardly stepped across the threshold when suddenly I needed her to press up against my shoulder again—only for a second, on my shoulder, not more.

I flung myself back into the room—she would (probably) still be buttoning her unif in front of the mirror. I ran in and stopped. The antiquated ring on the key in the door of the closet is still swinging—I see it clearly—but I-330 isn't there. She couldn't have gone anywhere—there was only one way out of the room—but, nevertheless, she wasn't there. I ransacked everything, I even opened the closet and felt the colorful ancient dresses in there: no one . . .

It's a bit awkward, my planetary readers, to tell you about this completely improbable incident. But what can I do if everything was really like that? Wasn't the whole day, from the early morning, after all, full of improbable incidents? Wasn't all this just like the ancient sickness of dreaming? If so—does it really matter whether I describe one more absurdity, or one less? Besides that, I am sure, sooner or later, I will succeed in including each and every one of these absurdities in some sort of syllogism. This calms me and I hope it calms you, too . . .

. . . How fulfilled I am! If only you knew how filled to the full I am!

KEYWORDS:

"Mine." The Forbidden. A Cold Floor.

Still more about yesterday's occurrences. I was busy during the Personal Hour before bedtime so I could not write these records yesterday. It has all been practically carved into me and particularly—forever, I'm quite sure—that unbearably cold floor . . .

In the evening O was meant to be coming over—it was her day. I went down to the monitor to get blind-lowering permission.

"Are you all right?" asked the monitor. "There's something about you today . . ."

"I . . . I'm sick."

In reality, this was true: I, of course, am sick. All this is a sickness. And right then, it occurred to me: yes, I have certification . . . I felt for it in my pocket: yes, it rustled. Meaning that everything had happened, everything had actually happened.

I extended the little piece of paper to the monitor. I felt my cheeks burn and without glancing up, I saw: the monitor looking at me in surprise . . .

It's 21:30. The blinds are lowered in the room to the left of mine. In the room on my right, I see my neighbor: bent over a book, his bald patch, knobbly with hummocks, and his forehead, a huge, yellow parabola. I pace and pace in torment: how can I—after all that just went on with I-330—now . . . with O? And from my right side, I clearly feel eyes on me. I distinctly see the wrinkles on his forehead: a row of yellow, illegible lines—and, for some reason, it seems to me that these lines are about me.

In my room at 21:45: a joyful, pink whirlwind, a strong ring of pink arms around my neck. And then I feel: the ring weakening, weaker and weaker still, then unfastening, the arms let go . . . "You are not the same, you are not your former self, you aren't mine!"

"What is with her wild terminology: 'mine'? I never was . . ." And I stumbled. It occurred to me—it's true, I wasn't before . . . but now I . . . It seems I no longer live in our rational world, but in an ancient, delirious—a world of square roots of minus one.

Blinds fall. There, behind the right wall, my neighbor is letting his book fall to the floor, and in that last, instantaneous narrow chink between the blinds and the floor, I see: a yellow hand grab the book. And inside me, I feel: I would have used all my strength if only to catch hold of that hand . . .

"I thought—I had hoped to see you today on the walk. I have a lot to— I really need to tell you . . ."

Sweet, poor O! Her pink mouth is a pink half-moon with its small horns pointing downward. But I cannot exactly tell her everything that has happened—if only because it would make her an accomplice to my crime, since I know that she hasn't enough strength to go to the Bureau of Guardians and, consequently—

O was lying down. I slowly kissed her. I kissed that innocent little crease on her wrist, her blue eyes were closed, the pink half-moon slowly blossomed, came undone, and I kissed her all over.

Suddenly I clearly felt it: how empty and spent I was. I can't, I musn't do this. I should but I musn't. My lips immediately went cold . . .

The pink half-moon began to tremble, faded, spasmed. O threw the bedspread over herself and wrapped herself up with her face in the pillow . . .

I sat on the floor by the bed—what an awfully cold floor—I sat there and said nothing. The excruciating cold from below was creeping higher and higher still. I imagine it was like the tacit cold up there, in the blue, mute interplanetary expanses.

"Please understand, I didn't want . . ." I muttered . . . "I tried hard . . ."

It was true: I (the real me) hadn't wanted to! But still: how could I put that into words for her? How could I explain to her that the iron hadn't wanted to, but its laws were inescapable and precise—

O lifted her head from the pillow and, not opening her eyes, said: "Go away," but through the tears it came out as "gowi" and for some reason this ridiculous trifle cut right into me.

Totally permeated with cold, frozen, I walked out into the corridor. There, behind the glass, was a light, barely perceptible puff of fog. Toward nighttime, it ought to descend, and apply itself to everything. What will this night bring?

O slipped past me without a word, toward the elevator. The door banged.

"One second," I cried. I became scared.

But the elevator was already droning down, down, down . . .

She took R away from me.

She took O away from me.

And yet, and yet . . .

KEYWORDS:

The Bell Jar. The Mirrored Sea. I Will Burn Forever.

I had only just entered the Integral's hangar when I encountered the Second Builder. His face was as it always is: round and white, like a porcelain platter, and he talks as though he is carrying something unbearably delicious on his platter: "Well, since you deigned to be ill, here, without you, without your direction, yesterday, we had a sort of event."

"Event?"

"Oh, yes! The bell rang, we finished up, and we were all being let out of the hangar and then, imagine: one of the guards caught an unnumbered person. And how he broke in—I can't understand. They led him off to the Operation Room. There, they will drag the how and why out of him, dear fellow ..." (A smile—delicious ...)

In the Operation Room, our best and most experienced doctors work under the direct leadership of the Benefactor himself. There are various devices in the Operation Room including, most important, the famous Gas Bell Jar. This is used essentially as it was in that old-fashioned school experiment: a mouse is put under a bell jar; the air in the bell jar is more and more rarefied by an air pump ... and, well, et cetera. But, of course, the Gas Bell Jar is a significantly more perfect apparatus—with its application of different gases—and then also, it is not merely a mockery of a small defenseless animal but has a higher purpose: the matter of the security of the One State, in other words, the happiness of millions. About five centuries ago, when work in the Operation Room had only just begun, there were fools who compared the Operation Room with the ancient Inquisition, but you see, that was just absurd. It was like equating a surgeon doing a tracheotomy to a highway robber: they both might have the same knife in their hands and they are both performing the same action (slitting the throat of a living person)—and yet one is a benefactor and the other, a criminal, one is a + sign and the other is a − sign . . .

All this is totally clear within a single second, within a single rotation of the logical machine. But just when the cogs have hooked that minus sign, something else pops up: the key ring is still swinging in the keyhole of the closet. The door, it was clear to see, had only just banged shut, but she, I-330, was gone: disappeared. The machine couldn't crank this over. Was it a dream? But even now, I still feel it: an inexplicable, sweet hurting in my right shoulder— I-330 pressed up against my right shoulder, next to me in the fog. "Do you like fog?" Yes, the fog and . . . I love everything, and everything is firm, new, astounding, everything is good . . . "Everything is good," I said aloud.

"Good?" His porcelain eyes goggled roundly. "That is, what is good about any of this? If that unnumbered person had managed to . . . it could have been . . . they are all around us, all the time, they are here, near the Integral, they . . ."

"But, who are *they*?"

"How should I know? But I feel them—you know? All the time."

"Have you heard? It seems some kind of operation has been invented—the excision of the imagination." (A few days ago, I had myself heard something of this nature.)

"Yes, I know—but what about it?"

"Well, let's just say that if I was in your shoes, I would go and ask for this operation to be performed on me."

On the platter, something distinctly revealed itself as lemon-sour. Dear man, the mere suggestion that he might have an imagination pains him ... But then, a week ago it probably would have pained me, too. But now—now, no: because I know that I have one and that I am sick with it. And I also know that I don't want to recover from it. I don't want to recover and that's that. We climbed up the glass steps. Everything underneath us, below, was as clear as the palm of my hand.

You, the readers of these records, no matter who you are, the sun is still above you. And if you've ever been sick like I am now, then you know what the sun is like—what it can be like. You know that in the morning, the sun is rosy, transparent, warm gold. And the air itself is a little rosy, all steeped in the sun's gentle blood. Everything is alive: stones are living and soft; iron is living and warm; people are alive and each and every one is smiling. It may happen that an hour later everything might disappear and an hour later, that rosy blood might drain away, but for now everything is alive. And I can see: something is pulsing and flowing through the glass essence of the Integral. I can see: the Integral is contemplating its great and terrifying future, its heavy cargo of inescapable happiness, which it will carry up there, up to you, the unknown, you, who eternally search and never find. You will find you will be happy—you are obliged to be happy—and you haven't much longer to wait.

The hull of the Integral was almost ready; the elegant, elongated ellipsoid made from our glass—everlasting, like gold, and supple, like steel. I saw: they were strengthening the glass body from the interior with transverse ribs and a frame of longitudinal stringers; in the stern they were laying the foundations for a gigantic rocket engine. Every three seconds, a combustion; every three seconds, the mighty tail of the Integral will disgorge flames and gases into cosmic space—and it will soar, soar—the fiery Tamerlane of happiness ...

I saw: people below, bending, straightening, turning, like the levers of one enormous machine, on the beat, rhythmically and rapidly, according to Taylorist mechanics. Pipes glittered in their hands: they were slicing away with fire, soldering the glass walls, the joints, the ribs, and the gussets together with fire. I saw transparent glass monster cranes slowly gliding along glass rails and, just like the people, obediently turning, bending, pushing their load into the belly of the Integral. And all this was one: a humanized, perfect people. This was a higher and more stupendous beauty, harmony, music . . . As quick as I could, I went downstairs to them, to be with them!

And here I was, shoulder to shoulder, fused with them, carried away by the steel tempo . . . Rhythmical movements; firm, round, ruddy cheeks; foreheads, mirror-smooth, not clouded by the folly of a single thought. I swam through the mirrored sea. I relaxed.

And suddenly a person placidly turned to me: "Well, then, everything okay—you're better today?"

"What do you mean, better?"

"Well, it's just that—you weren't here yesterday. We were, you know, thinking—that something dangerous . . . you . . ." His forehead beamed, his smile, boyish and innocent.

Blood surged to my face. I couldn't—I couldn't lie to such eyes. I said nothing, sinking . . .

Above, the porcelain face, shining in round whiteness, pushed down through a hatch.

"Hey, D-503! Could you . . . come up here? The frame's become rigid here, you see, with the consoles and the junction features creating stress on the quadrilateral . . ."

Not listening to the rest, I dashed headlong to him above—I had shamefully saved myself by fleeing. I was so dazzled by the sparkling glass steps under my feet that I didn't have the strength to lift my eyes, and with each step everything seemed more hopeless: this was no place for a criminal, contaminated like me. I will no longer be able to pour myself into the precise mechanical rhythm, I cannot swim with the mirror-placid sea. I will burn forever, rushing about, eternally trying to find a little corner where I can hide my eyes, until, finally, I find the strength to walk through those—

And an icy spark went through me: I—never mind me; I don't matter. But it would have to involve her too and she would also be . . .

I clambered out of the hatch and onto the deck and stopped: I didn't know where to go now, I didn't know why I was here. I looked up. There, the worn-out midday sun was ascending dully. Below was the Integral, gray-glassed, inanimate. The rosy blood had drained away and it was clear to me that all this had only been my imagination, that everything was as it had always been, and yet it was also clear that . . .

"Hey! 503? What's wrong? Are you deaf now? I've been calling you and calling you . . . what's wrong with you?" This was the Second Builder—right into my ear. He must have been shouting for a while.

What's wrong with me? I have lost my rudder. My motor is at full throttle, the aero is trembling and tearing along, but rudderless. I don't know where I am racing to: downward to the ground, or now upward to the sun, to the fire . . .

KEYWORDS:

Yellow. A Two-Dimensional Shadow. An Incurable Soul.

I haven't entered anything in these records for several days. I don't know how many: all days are one. All days are the same yellow color, like desiccated, incandescent sand, and there is not a tatter of a shadow, not a drop of water—it is yellow sand without end. I can't go on without her but she, ever since she disappeared at the Ancient House . . .

Since then, I've only seen her once, on the walk. It was two, three, four days ago—I don't know when: all days are one. She flashed past and for a second filled this yellow, empty world. That two-fold S was hand in hand with her (only as high as her shoulder), and there was that super-thin paper-doctor, and someone else, a fourth (I only remember his fingers: they flew out of his sleeve, like bundles of beams, exceptionally thin, white, and long). I-330 lifted her hand and waved at me; behind someone's head I saw her leaning over to the finger-beam man. The word "Integral" was audible; the whole foursome glanced over at me; and then they were lost in the gray-blue sky, and again there was only the yellow, desiccated path.

In the evening that day she had a pink ticket for me. I stood in front of the intercom, and with affection and then with spite, I prayed it to click, to make those digits appear on the white panel as soon as possible: I-330. Doors banged and the pale, the tall, the pink, and the dark-complexioned came out of the elevator; blinds fell all around me. She wasn't here. Hadn't come.

And, maybe, at this very minute, at exactly 22:00, as I write this, she has closed her eyes and is leaning on someone's shoulder like she did mine and uttering those same words: "Do you like . . . ?" But who to? Who is he? Is it that man with the finger-beams, or the lippy, spraying R? Or S?

S . . . Why do I hear his flat, puddle-squelching footsteps behind me all day, every day? Why is he behind me all day, every day—like a shadow? It's up ahead, beside me, behind me, this gray-blue, two-dimensional shadow: everyone walks through it, steps on it, but it is nevertheless invariably here, nearby—fastened to me with an invisible umbilical cord. It may be that this umbilical cord is her, I-330? I don't know. Or it may be that they, the Guardians, already know about it all, know that I . . .

Suppose someone told you: your shadow sees you, it sees you all the time. Do you understand? Suddenly you experience a strange sensation: the hands at your sides feel like someone else's and you are aware of how absurdly you're swinging your arms and how out of step you are. Then suddenly I can barely resist turning around to look—but looking back at anything is forbidden; my neck is locked. And I run and run, faster and faster, and at my spine, I feel it: the shadow is behind me, going faster and faster, and there is nowhere to flee, nowhere . . .

My room. I am at last alone. But then there's something else: the telephone. I pick up the receiver: "Yes, I-330, please." And again from the receiver there is a light noise, someone's footsteps along a corridor, past the door of her room, and they're saying nothing . . . I throw down the receiver—I can't stand it, can't stand any more. So I go to her.

That was yesterday. I ran over there and for the whole hour between 16:00 and 17:00, I wandered around the building in which she lives. Ciphers go past me, in rows. Thousands of feet were raining down in strokes, the million-footed Leviathan, heaving, was swimming past. But I, alone, am weathering the storm on an uninhabited island, and I'm searching, searching with my eyes through the gray-blue waves.

Any minute, from somewhere, anywhere: the sharp, mocking angle of her eyebrows, raised toward her temples above the dark windows of her eyes—and there, inside them, fires will be burning and shadows will be moving. I'll be instantly inside, in there, and I'll address her intimately, unavoidably intimately: "You know perfectly well—I cannot be without you. So why all this?"

But she says nothing. Suddenly, I hear the silence, instantly, I hear the Music Factory and I understand: it is already past 17:00 and everyone is long gone, I am alone, I am late. A glass desert, flooded with yellow sun, surrounds me. And, as if on the surface of water, I see: overturned, sparkling walls, suspended upside down from a glassy meniscus and I, too, am overturned, idiotically suspended upside down by my feet.

It is imperative that I immediately, this very second, go to the Bureau of Medicine to obtain certification that I am sick, otherwise they'll get me and—well, maybe that would be for the best. By staying here and calmly waiting until they see me and convey me to the Operation Room—everything would be over immediately, immediately everything would be expiated.

A light rustle, and the twice-bent shadow was in front of me. Without looking, I felt how rapidly his two steel-gray gimlets drove themselves into me, and I smiled with all available strength and said something (something, anything, needed to be said): "I . . . need to go to the Bureau of Medicine."

"What's the matter? Why ever are you standing here?"

I was totally ablaze with shame, absurdly suspended by my feet, upside down. I said nothing.

"Follow me," S said sternly.

I obediently followed, swinging my extraneous arms, which seemed to belong to someone else. I couldn't raise an eye and I walked, the whole time, in a wild, turned-on-its-head world: there were machines of some kind, their foundations on top of them, and there were people with feet glued antipodally to the ceiling, and below them, the sky was contained in the thick glass of the sidewalk. I remember: how very offensive it all was, that for the last time in my life I was having to see it all this way—overturned, unreal. But I couldn't raise an eye.

We stopped. There were steps before me. One step up and I'll see: figures in white doctor's aprons and an enormous mute Bell Jar . . .

With effort, a kind of spiral torque, I finally tore my eyes away from the glass below my feet—and suddenly the golden letters "Medicine" splashed in front of me . . . Why had he led me here and not to the Operation Room, and why had he spared me? But, at that moment, I wasn't thinking of these things: with one leap over the steps, the door solidly banged behind me and I exhaled. Yes: it was as though I hadn't breathed since dawn, as though my heart hadn't struck a single beat—and it was only now that I exhaled for the first time, only now that the floodgates of my chest opened . . .

There were two of them: one was shortish, with cinder-block legs, and his eyes, like horns, tossed up the patients; the other one was skinny and sparkling with scissor-lips and a blade for a nose . . . I had met him before.

I flung myself at him as though he were kin, straight into the blade, and said something about being an insomniac, the dreams, the shadows, the yellow world. The scissor-lips flashed and smiled. "How awful for you! By the looks of it, you've developed a soul."

A soul? That strange, ancient, long-forgotten word. We sometimes said "heart and soul," "soulful," "lost souls," but a "soul"—

"This is . . . this is very grave," I babbled.

"It's incurable," incised the scissors.

"But . . . what specifically is at the source of all this? I can't even begin . . . to imagine."

"Well, you see . . . it is as if you . . . you're a mathematician, right?"

"Yes."

"Well, take, for instance, a plane, a surface, like this mirror here. And on this surface—here, look—are you and I, and we are squinting at the sun, and see the blue electrical spark in that tube. And watch—the shadow of an aero is flashing past. But it is only on this surface for just a second. Now imagine that some heat source causes this impenetrable surface to suddenly grow soft, and nothing slides across it anymore but everything penetrates inside it, into that mirror world, which we used to look into as curious children—children aren't all that silly, I assure you. The plane has now become a volume, a body, a world, and that which is inside the mirror is inside you: the sun, the whirlwind from the aero's propeller, your trembling lips, and someone else's trembling lips. So you see: a cold mirror reflects and rejects but this absorbs every footprint, forever. One day you see a barely noticeable wrinkle on someone's face—and then it is forever inside you; one day you hear a droplet falling in the silence—and you can hear it again now . . ."

"Yes, yes, exactly . . ." I grabbed his hand. I could hear the faucet in the sink slowly dripping its droplets in the silence. And I knew that they would be inside me forever. But still, why—all of a sudden—a soul? I never had one—never had one—and then suddenly . . . Why doesn't anyone else have one, but me?

I squeezed harder on the skinny hand: I was terrified to let go of this lifeline.

"Why? And why don't we have feathers or wings but just scapulas, the foundation of wings? It's because we don't need wings anymore—we have the aero; wings would only be extraneous. Wings are for flying, but we don't need to get anywhere: we have landed, we have found what we were seeking. Isn't that so?"

I nodded my head in dismay. He looked at me, laughed sharply, javelinishly. The other one, hearing this, stumpily stamped through from out of his office, tossed the skinny doctor up with his hornlike eyes, and then tossed me up, too.

"What's the problem? What, a soul? A soul, you say? Damn it! We'll soon get as far as cholera. I told you"—the skinny one was horn-tossed again—"I told you, we must, everyone's imagination—everyone's imagination must be . . . excised. The only answer is surgery, surgery alone . . ."

He struggled to put on some enormous X-ray glasses, and walked around for a long time looking through my skull bone at my brain, and making notes in a notebook.

"Extraordinary, extraordinarily curious! Listen to me, would you agree . . . to be preserved in alcohol? This would be, for the One State, an extraordinarily . . . this would aid us in averting an epidemic . . . If you, of course, don't have any particular reasons not . . ."

"You see," the other one said, "cipher D-503 is the Builder of the Integral, and I am certain that this would interfere . . ."

"Ah," he mumbled and lumped off to his cabinet.

And then we were two. A paper-hand lightly, tenderly lay on my hand. A face in profile bent toward me and he whispered: "I'll tell you a secret—it isn't only you. My colleague is talking about an epidemic for good reason. Think about it; perhaps you yourself have noticed something similar in someone else—something very similar, very close to . . ." He looked at me intently. What is he hinting at—at whom? It can't be that—

"Listen . . ." I leapt from my chair. But he had already loudly begun to talk about something else: ". . . And for the insomnia, and your dreams, I can give you one recommendation: walk more. Like, for instance, tomorrow morning, go for a walk . . . to the Ancient House, for example."

He punctured me again with his eyes and smiled thinly. And it seemed to me: I could clearly and distinctly see something wrapped up in the fine fabric of his smile—a word—a letter—a name, a particular name . . . Or is this again that same imagination?

I was only barely able to wait while he wrote out my certification of illness for today and tomorrow, then I shook his hand once more and ran outside.

My heart was light, quick, like an aero, and carrying, carrying me upward. I knew: tomorrow held some sort of joy. But what would it be?

KEYWORDS:

Through the Glass. I Died. Corridors.

I am utterly perplexed. Yesterday, at the very moment when I was thinking that everything had been untangled, that I had found all the X's, a new unknown quantity arose in my equation.

The origin of the coordinates for this whole story is, of course, the Ancient House. The X, Y, and Z axes that emerge from this point have been the coordinates of my world in recent days. I walked on foot along the X axis (Fifty-ninth Avenue) to the origin of the coordinates. Yesterday's colorful whirlwind was inside me: upside-down buildings and people, my torturously extraneous arms, the flashing scissors, the sharply dripping droplets in the sink—these things had happened, once upon a time. And they were lacerating my flesh, energetically rotating in there, behind the surface that had been melted by some heat source, where the "soul" resides.

In order to fulfill the doctor's recommendation, I purposefully chose to walk, not along the hypotenuse, but along the two perpendiculars. And here I was on the second perpendicular: a section of the circular street at the foot of the Green Wall. From the boundless green ocean behind the Wall, a wild tidal surge of roots, flowers, twigs, leaves was rolling toward me, standing on its hind legs, and had it flowed over me I would have been transformed from a person—from the finest and most precise of mechanisms—into ...

But, happily, between me and this wild, green ocean was the glass of the Wall. Oh, the great, divinely bounding wisdom of walls and barriers! They may just be the greatest of all inventions. Mankind ceased to be wild beast when it built its first wall. Mankind ceased to be savage when we built the Green Wall, when we isolated our perfect, machined world, by means of the Wall, from the irrational, chaotic world of the trees, birds, animals ...

Through the glass—foggy and dim—I saw the stupid muzzle of some kind of beast, his yellow eyes, obstinately repeating one and the same incomprehensible thought at me. We looked at each other for a long time, eye to eye, through the mineshafts from the surface world to that other world, beyond the surface. But a thought swarmed in me: what if he, this yellow-eyed being—in his ridiculous, dirty bundle of trees, in his uncalculated life—is happier than us?

I waved my hand, the yellow eyes blinked, moved backward, and disappeared into the leaves. Poor being! How absurd: he being happier than us! It may be that he is happier than me, yes; but I, of course, I am an exception, I am sick. And, even I ...

I can already see the dark-red walls of the Ancient House and the sweet, overgrown, old-woman mouth. I rush to the old woman as fast as my legs could carry me: "She here?"

The tightly sealed mouth opened slowly: "And who is that— she?"

"Oh, well, ah, who? Well, I-330 of course ... We were here together, remember, on the aero ..."

"Ah—right ... okay-okay-okay ..."

Her wrinkles were rays around her mouth and her yellow eyes emitted sly rays too, probing into me, deeper and deeper. And finally: "Well, fine, okay ... she is here, she came through here not long ago."

She's here, I saw: at the old woman's foot was a shrub of silver-bitter wormwood (the courtyard of the Ancient House is thoroughly preserved in its prehistoric appearance—it is a museum, after all).

The wormwood had extended a branch toward the hand of the old woman and the old woman was stroking the branch on her lap. There were yellow streaks of sun. And in a blink: I, the sun, the old woman, the wormwood, the yellow eyes—we were all one, we were firmly connected by veins of some sort, and through these veins runs one communal, tempestuous, majestic blood . . .

I am now ashamed to write about this, but I promised in these records to be candid to the end. So here's what happened: I stooped down and kissed the overgrown, soft, mossy mouth. The old woman wiped her lips and began to laugh.

For some reason I went straight—at a run through the familiar, half-dark, echoing rooms—to the bedroom. I grabbed the door-knob as soon as I was at the door and suddenly: what if she isn't alone? I stood and listened closely. But I only heard: a knocking around—not in me, but somewhere near me—it was my heart.

I went in. A wide, undisturbed bed. The mirror. Another mirror on the door of the closet and there, in the keyhole: the key with the antiquated key-ring. And nobody.

I quietly called out: "I! Are you here?" I said, and then again even more quietly, with closed eyes, not breathing, as though I was kneeling in front of her: "I! Sweetness!"

Quiet. Only the hurried dripping of water from the faucet into a white teacup in the sink. I cannot now explain why but this was not pleasant for me: I forcefully turned off the faucet and walked out. She is not here: that is clear. And that means she is in some other "apartment."

I ran down the wide, twilight staircase, pulled at one door, the next, and then a third: locked. Everything was locked, except for the one, "our" apartment, and there was nobody in there . . .

All the same, I went up there again—I myself don't know why. I walked slowly, with difficulty: the soles of my feet had suddenly become cast-iron. I distinctly remember the thought: it is a mistake that the force of gravity is a constant. Therefore, all my formulas . . .

Then—an explosion: a door slammed all the way downstairs, someone rapidly stamped along the flagstones. I—light again, lighter than ever—flung myself at the banister and leaned over to cry out everything, with one word, with one cry, "You!"

And I was numb: below, inscribed on the dark square of the shadow from the window frame, S's head flew by flapping its pink wing-ears.

A lightning flash: there was only one naked conclusion, without a basis (I still don't know the basis of this conclusion). And it was: I must not—by any means—be seen by him.

On tiptoes, pressing against the wall, I slid upward to the unlocked apartment.

A second's pause at the door. He was dully stamping up here. If only for that door! I pleaded with the door, but it was wooden: it started to creak and then howled. I passed through the whirlwind of green, red, the yellow Buddha, and I was in front of the mirror on the door of the closet: my pale face, my eyes listening hard, my lips . . . and I can hear—through the noise of my blood—the door creaking again . . . It is him, it's him.

I grab at the key in the door of the closet and the key-ring swings. This reminded me of something—yet another instantaneous, naked conclusion without a basis—or more likely, it was a splinter of a conclusion: that time when I-330—I quickly open the door to the closet and I am inside, in the darkness. I shut it tight. I take one step—the floor is rocking under my feet. I slowly, softly start swimming downward. There was a darkening in my eyes, I died.

⋅ ⋅ ⋅

Later, when it came to writing down all these strange events, I rummaged through my memory and through my books, and now I understand it, of course: this was the condition of temporary death, familiar to the Ancients, but, as far as I know, completely unknown among us.

I have no concept of how long I was dead, probably five to ten seconds overall, but after some time I was resurrected and opened my eyes: it was dark and I could feel descent, descent . . . I put my hand out to grab hold and I was scratched by a rough wall quickly slipping up and away. There was blood on my finger and it was clear that all this was not a game of my sick imagination. But what was it then?

I heard my trembling breathing like a dotted line (I am ashamed to admit to this—but everything was so unexpected and inexplicable). A minute—two, three—all in descent. Finally, a soft bump: whatever it was that was falling from under my feet was now motionless. In the darkness I groped around and found some sort of handle, pushed on it, and a door opened into dim light. I saw: a smallish square platform quickly fly up behind me. I dashed at it, but it was too late: I was stranded here . . . wherever this "here" was—I didn't know.

A corridor. A thousand-pound silence. There were lamps along the rounded vault of the ceiling, in an endless, twinkling, flickering, dotted line. It looked a bit like the "tubes" of our subterranean rail, but only much narrower and not made from our glass but from some kind of ancient material. Caves flashed through my mind, where people had apparently saved themselves in the time of the Two-Hundred-Year War . . . Never mind: I have to move forward.

I walked, I would guess, about twenty minutes. I turned right. A wider corridor, brighter lamps. There was a kind of vague drone. It may be machines, it may be voices—I didn't know anything but that I was next to a heavy, opaque door and the drone was coming from it.

I knocked, and I knocked again—louder. Things quieted down behind the door. Something clanked, the door slowly, heavily opened to me.

I don't know which of us was more dumbfounded . . . my blade-nosed, skinny doctor stood in front of me.

"You? Here?" And his scissor blades slammed together. But I—it was as though I had never known even one human word—I was mute. I looked at him and didn't understand anything of what he was saying to me. It must have been something about me having to leave: because he quickly forced me back to the end of this brighter corridor with his planar, paper-thin stomach, then turned me around and pushed me at the back.

"If you please . . . I wanted to . . . I thought that she, I-330 . . . But behind me . . ."

"Stand here." The doctor cut me off and disappeared.

Finally! Finally she is somewhere nearby. She is here—so it does, after all, matter where "here" is. The familiar, saffron-yellow silk, a smile-sting, lowered blinds for eyes . . . My lips, hands, knees are trembling and in my head is the silliest thought: "Vibrations produce sound. A tremble must make a sound. Why, then, isn't it audible?"

Her eyes uncovered themselves to me, opened wide and I went inside . . .

"I could not stand it any longer! Where were you? Why?" I didn't tear my eyes away from her for a second, I was talking as if I were delirious—rapidly, unconnected (and it may be that I was only thinking it all). "A shadow was behind me . . . I died—in the closet . . . Because that man, your . . . says with his scissors that I have a soul . . . and it's incurable . . ."

"An incurable soul! My poor dear!" I-330 burst out laughing. Her laughter splashed me, the delirium passed, and everything sparkled, our chuckles were tinkling, and how . . . how good everything was.

The doctor appeared from around the corner again—the miraculous, wonderful, skinny doctor.

"Well." He stopped next to her.

"Everything's fine, everything's fine! I'll tell you later. He accidentally . . . Tell them that I will be back in . . . about fifteen minutes . . ."

The doctor flashed back around the corner. She waited. A muffled bang of the door. Then slowly, slowly, deeper and deeper I-330 plunged a sharp, sweet needle into my heart, pressing up to me with her shoulder, her arm, every part of her, and we walked off together, together as a twosome—a onesome . . .

I don't remember where things contracted into darkness but in the darkness we went up steps, endlessly and silently. I didn't see it but I knew: she walked just like I did—eyes closed, blind, head thrown back, teeth biting lips while listening to the music of my barely audible tremble.

I regained consciousness in one of the countless nooks of the courtyard of the Ancient House by some kind of fence, made of earth, and the naked, rocky ribs and yellow teeth of a collapsed wall. She opened her eyes and said: "The day after tomorrow at 16:00." She left.

Had all this really happened? I don't know. I will find out the day after tomorrow. The only real evidence: there is torn skin on my right hand, at the tips of my fingers. But today, at the Integral, the Second Builder assured me that he himself had seen me accidentally touch the polishing wheel with these fingers—and that was the whole reason for it. That may be true, indeed. Very possibly. I don't know—I don't know anything.

KEYWORDS:

Logical Jungles. Wounds and Plaster. Never Again.

Yesterday I lay down—and I sank at once into the depths of a dream, like a capsized and overladen ship. A muffled, heaving mass of green water. And slowly I am rising to the surface from the depths and somewhere in the middle deepness, I open my eyes: my room, a still-green, stiffened morning. A stripe of sunshine went into the mirrored door of my closet—and then into my eyes. This interferes with any precision in fulfilling the hours of sleep prescribed by the Table of Hours. The best thing would have been to open the closet door. But it was as if I was in a cobweb and there was a cobweb in my eyes, I didn't have the strength to get up . . .

All the same I got up, opened it, and suddenly I saw: I-330 behind the mirrored door, disentangling herself from her dress, all pink. I was now so used to such utter improbabilities that, as far as I remember, I didn't get surprised at all and I didn't ask a thing: I went into the closet, slammed the mirrored door behind me, and, panting—quickly, blindly—I greedily united with I-330. I can see even now: coming through a slit in the door, into the darkness, there was a sharp sun-ray fracturing like lightning on the floor, on the wall of the closet, and higher up—and this cruel, sparkling blade fell on I-330's outstretched, bare neck ... and there was something so scary about this for me that I couldn't restrain myself and I screamed—and then I opened my eyes.

My room. The stiffened morning, still green. A stripe of sunshine on the door of the closet. I am in bed. A dream. But my heart is still beating energetically, quivering, gushing, and the tips of my fingers and my knees are aching. It had all undoubtedly happened. But I don't know: which is dream and which is reality. Irrational quantities are sprouting through everything solid, usual, and three-dimensional, and instead of hard, polished planes, something gnarled and shaggy is surrounding me ...

It will still be a while until the bell rings. I lie and think, and uncoil an extraordinarily strange logical chain.

To every equation, to every formula in the surface world, there is a corresponding curve or mass. We don't know the corresponding masses to irrational formulas, to my $\sqrt{-1}$—we haven't ever seen them ... But the very horror of it all is that these masses—invisible masses—do exist. They necessarily, inevitably must exist because mathematics is like a screen on which the whimsical, prickly shadows of irrational formulas cross before us. Mathematics and death: neither makes mistakes. And if these masses are not evident in our world, on the surface, then it's inescapable: they must have their own entire, enormous world there, behind the surface ...

I jumped up without waiting for the bell, and ran around the room. My mathematics—until now, the only solid and stable island in my entire gone-crazy life—had also become detached, was floating, spinning. What, I mean, what is this absurd "soul"? Is it as real as my unif, as my boots (even though I cannot see them right now since they are behind the mirrored door of the closet)? And if boots are not a sickness—why is a "soul" a sickness?

I searched for and did not find the exit from this wild logical thicket. These were the same unknown and terrible jungles as those others, beyond the Green Wall, with extraordinary, incomprehensible, beings who speak without words. I felt as though I was seeing something through a sort of thick glass: it was infinitely vast and simultaneously infinitely small, it was scorpion-like with its hidden but nagging minus-pinch—it was $\sqrt{-1}$ . . . But perhaps it was nothing other than my "soul" and like the legendary scorpion of the Ancients, it was voluntarily stinging itself with all that it could . . .

The bell. Day. All this hasn't died and hasn't disappeared but has been covered up by the light of day; like visible objects that don't die but, toward night, are covered by the nightly darkness. In my head there is a light, wavering fog. Through the fog, I see: long glass tables; sphere-heads are chewing in time, slowly and silently. From a distance, through the fog, a metronome is tapping, and under the regular caress of this music, I count to fifty, mechanically, together with everyone: the fifty mandatory masticatory motions to each bite. I go downstairs, mechanically, on the beat, and I write my name down in the exit book, as everyone does. But I feel: I live separately from everyone else, alone, fenced in by a soft, sound-muffling wall, and behind this wall is my world . . .

But here is the thing: if this world is mine alone, then why is it in these records? Why are these absurd "dreams," closets, and endless corridors here? It is with regret that I see, instead of an orderly and strict mathematical epic poem in honor of the One State—I see some kind of fantastic adventure novel emerging from me. Ah, if only this was really only some sort of novel, and not this new life of mine: full of X's, $\sqrt{-1}$, and descents.

But it may be that this is for the best. It is highly likely that you, my unknown readers, are mere children in comparison with us (after all, we were bred by the One State, and consequently we have achieved the utmost pinnacle of human potentiality). And, like children, you will only swallow this bitter thing I am giving you if it is thoroughly coated with a thick adventuresome syrup.

EVENING

Is this feeling familiar to you: you are tearing along in an aero, in a blue upward spiral, the window is open, a whirlwind is whistling in your face, and there is no Earth, you forget all about the Earth, the Earth is as distant as Saturn, Jupiter, and Venus? That is how I live these days, with a whirlwind in my face—I have forgotten about the Earth and I have forgotten about sweet, pink O. But the Earth still exists, and sooner or later I must land on it again. But I shut my eyes before the days when that name is written into my Table of Sex Days—the name O-90 . . .

This evening the distant Earth reminded me of itself.

In order to fulfill the doctor's orders (I sincerely, sincerely, want to recuperate), I wandered around the glassy, straight-line deserts of the avenues for a whole two hours. In accordance with the Table of Hours, everyone was in the auditorium, except me . . . This was, essentially, an unnatural sight. Imagine this: a human finger, cut off from the whole, from the hand—a separate human finger, stooping, bent down, skipping, running along a glass sidewalk. This finger is me. And the strangest, most unnatural thing of all is that the finger doesn't want to be on the hand, with the others, at all. It wants to be alone, like (oh, all right, I have nothing left to hide), it either wants to be alone or to be with that woman again, pouring my whole self into her through our shoulders or the interlaced fingers of our hands . . .

I was returning to my building after the sun had started setting. An evening, pink ash was on the glass of the walls, on the gold of the spire of the Accumulator Tower, and in the voices and smiles of every passing cipher. Isn't it strange: the rays of the extinguishing sun fall at the very same angle as those that light up the morning, but everything is completely different in this light, this pinkness is different—it's so quiet and a little bitter-ish—but in the morning it will be ringing and fizzy again.

Downstairs, in the vestibule, U, the monitor, pulled a letter from underneath a heap of envelopes covered with pink ash and gave it to me. I will repeat: she is a very respectable woman, and I am sure that she has the best of intentions toward me. And yet, every time I see those hanging, fish-gill cheeks, I find it somehow unpleasant.

Stretching out her dry hand with the letter, U sighed. But this sigh only slightly swayed the curtain that separates me from the world: I was entirely projected onto the envelope trembling in my hands, in which—I didn't doubt—was a letter from I-330.

Then there was a second sigh, so blatant, twice-underlined, that I tore myself away from the envelope and saw: through bashful eyes under lowered venetian blinds, between the gills, was a tender, smothering, blinding smile. And then: "Poor you, poor, poor . . ." A triple-underlined sigh and a barely perceptible nod toward the letter (the contents of the letter would have been known to her, naturally, as it is her duty to read them).

"No, really, I'm . . . Why do you say that?"

"No, no, my dear. I know you better than you know yourself. I have scrutinized you for a long time. And I can see that you need someone to take you by the hand and walk you through life, someone who has studied life for many years . . ."

I feel: all pasted over by her smile—it was plaster that was meant to cover the imminent wounds from this letter trembling in my hands. And finally—through the bashful venetian blinds—very quietly: "I will think about it, my dear, I'll think about it. And be calm—if I feel up to it—no, no, I must first think about it a bit . . ."

Great Benefactor! Don't tell me that I am meant to . . . don't tell me she is saying that—

In my eyes there was a shimmering, there were thousands of sinusoids, and the letter was shuddering. I walk closer to the light, to the wall. There, the sun is dying down—on me, on the floor, on my hands, on the letter—everything was thick with dark pink, sad ash.

The envelope ripped open. Eyes straight to the signature. Then a wound—it was not I-330, not I-330, it was . . . O. Then another wound: a blurred smudge on the bottom right-hand corner of the page where a drop had fallen . . . I can't stand smudges—whether it was the ink or from . . . it didn't matter what it was from. And I know that, before now, this unpleasant stain would have been simply unpleasant to me, unpleasant to my eyes. But why then does this grayish speck now make everything turn leaden and darker, like a raincloud? Or—is this again my "soul"?

The Letter:

You know . . . or perhaps, you don't know—I don't write as well as I should—but anyway, you will know it now. For me, without you, there is no day, no morning, and no spring. R, to me, is only . . . well, that's not important to you. In any case, I am very grateful to him: if I had been alone without him these last few days I don't know what I would have . . . Over these last few days I have lived what seems like ten, maybe twenty years. And it is as if my room is not four-cornered, but round and endless—around and around, everything is one and the same, and there is not a door anywhere.

I cannot stand life without you—because I love you. And I can see, I understand: you don't need anyone anymore, anyone on earth, except that woman, that other woman, and, you see, it is exactly because I love you that I should—

I only need two or three more days to glue myself back together from these pieces into a resemblance of the former O-90—then I will go and remove my name from your list, and things should get better for you, things for you should be good. Never again will I bother you. Forgive me.

O

Never again. That, of course, would be better: she is right. But why do I, why do I—

KEYWORDS:

Infinitely Small of the Third Order.
From Underneath Eyebrows. Over the Parapet.

There, in the strange corridor with the vibrating dotted line of dim lamps . . . Or no, no—not there: later, when I was with her in that forsaken corner in the courtyard of the Ancient House, she said: "The day after tomorrow." This "day after tomorrow" is today and everything is on wings—the day is flying. And our Integral is now winged, too: they finished the construction of the rocket engine, and today started it up and let it idle. What magnificent, powerful salvos; for me, each of them was a salute to her honor, to the one and only, in honor of today.

Before the action began (= the blast), a dozen ciphers from our hangar were standing around and gaping under the barrel of the engine. Afterward, exactly nothing of them remained, except some crumbs and soot. I write this here with pride because the rhythm of our labor did not falter for even a second because of this—no one even flinched. We and our machines continued our straight-lined and circular movements with the same old precision, as if nothing had happened. A dozen ciphers are barely one hundred millionth part of the mass of the One State and, according to practical calculations, this is infinitely small of the third order. Arithmetically illiterate compassion was only something the Ancients knew; to us, it is amusing.

And it is amusing to me that yesterday I could ponder over some sorry, insignificant speck, some smudge, and even write about it in these pages. This is that same "softening" of the surface which should be amber-hard like our walls (there was an ancient saying, "like being up against a brick wall").

It's 16:00. I didn't take an extra walk: I couldn't be sure that she wouldn't decide, at any moment, when everything is sparkling in the sun, to come . . .

I am almost alone in the building. I can see far into the distance through the sun-flooded walls: there are rooms, hanging in the air, empty, mirrorly repeating one another to the right, to the left, and below. Only a gaunt gray shadow is slowly crawling up the bluish stairway, sketched in sunny ink. I can already hear its footsteps. Now I can see it through the door. I feel it: a plaster-smile pasted on me as it goes past, to the other stairway, and continues upward . . .

The intercom clicked. I threw my whole self at the narrow white panel and . . . and it was some unfamiliar male cipher (it started with a consonant). There was a buzzing and the elevator door banged. In front of me was a forehead, sloppily pulled aslant over a pair of eyes . . . what a very strange effect: it was as if he were speaking from that place, from underneath his eyebrows, where his eyes were.

"A letter to you from her" (this, from underneath his eyebrows, from under the overhang). "She requests that you—without fail—do everything it says."

From underneath his eyebrows, from under the overhang, he looked around. Yes, yes, there is no one, nobody is here, well, give it to me, then! Looking around once more, he thrust the envelope at me and left. I was alone.

No, I was not alone: a pink ticket fell from the envelope and there it was, though hardly discernible—her scent. It's her, she is coming, coming to me. Quick—the letter, I must read it all with my own eyes, so I can actually believe it . . .

What? It is not possible! I read it again, hopping through the lines: "The ticket . . . and you must lower the blinds, as if I was actually there with you . . . It is absolutely necessary that they think that I . . . I am very . . . very sorry . . ."

The letter: torn into shreds. My mangled, broken eyebrows appear in the mirror for a second. I took up the ticket, about to do the same to it as I had done to her letter and—

"She requests that you—without fail—do everything it says."

My hands weakened, unclenched. The ticket fell onto the table. She is stronger than me, and it looks as though I will do exactly what she wants. But then again . . . then again, I don't know. We will see—this evening is still far off. The ticket lay on the table.

My mangled, broken eyebrows appear in the mirror. Why don't I have a doctor's certificate today? I would have gone for a walk and walked around the whole of the Green Wall without stopping and then fallen into bed, to the depths . . . But I must be off to auditorium 13, I must screw myself up tightly so that for two hours—for two hours I do not stir . . . though I need to scream and stamp my feet.

The lecture. It was very strange that the voice from the glittering apparatus was not metallic, as usual, but a kind of soft, shaggy, mossy voice. It was female—what she might have looked like in the flesh flickers through my mind: a petite thing, a little hook of an old woman, like the one at the Ancient House.

The Ancient House . . . suddenly everything rushes up like a fountain from below and I have to screw myself up so tightly, with all my strength, so I don't flood the whole auditorium with a scream. The soft, shaggy words go right through me, and there is only one thing from it all that stays with me: something to do with children and child-breeding. I am like a photographic negative—everything is imprinted on me with a sort of foreign, strange, meaningless precision. A golden crescent: the reflection of light on the loudspeaker. Underneath it is a child—a living illustration—reaching for the crescent; the hem of its microscopic unif is pushed into its mouth; a little fist, tightly squeezed, with its thumb (a very little one, I suppose) shoved inside; and a light, chubby shadow, the crease on its wrist. These things imprinted themselves on me, like they would on a photographic negative. Then its naked foot stretched out over the edge, a pink fan of toes was stepping into the air—and then—then toward the floor—

And a female scream flapped up to the stage with the invisible wings of a unif, grabbed the child with her lips—by its chubby wrist-crease—and shifted it to the middle of the table, then left the stage. I was imprinted again: a pink half-moon mouth with its small horns turned downward and blue saucer-eyes filled to the brim. It was O. And I felt as though I was before some sort of well-proportioned formula; I suddenly sensed the necessity and legitimacy of this insignificant event.

She had been sitting a little bit behind me and to the left. I turned around to look: she obediently drew her eyes away from the table with the child and her eyes pointed to me, into me. And again: I, she, and the table on the stage were three points, and a line was being drawn between these points—a projection of inevitable but as yet unforeseen events.

Then home, along the streets, green and dusky but sharp-sighted with streetlamps. I hear something: I am ticking like a clock. And the hands of this clock are now proceeding over some digit: I am about to do something from which there is no turning back. She needs someone to think that she is at my place. But I need her and I don't care about her "needs." I don't want to be someone else's blinds. And that's all there is to it.

Behind me there is a familiar, puddle-squelching gait. I don't look around but I already know who it is: S. He will follow me all the way to the door of my building and then he'll probably stand below on the sidewalk with his gimlets screwing upward toward my room until my crime-hiding blinds fall . . .

He, my guardian angel, had put an end to the matter. I was decided: I wouldn't do it. I was decided.

When I climbed up to my room and turned on the lights, I couldn't believe my eyes: O was standing by my table. Or, more accurately, she was hanging there: like an empty dress hanging after being taken off. Underneath her dress it seemed she was missing a spring; her arms and her legs were springless and her voice, hanging there, was springless, too.

"I . . . about my letter. Did you get it? Yes? I need to know your answer—I need to know right now."

I shrugged my shoulders. I looked at her blue, brimming eyes with pleasure—as if everything was all her fault—and I lingered over my answer. I struck her with my words, one by one, with a certain pleasure, saying: "Answer? What . . . You are right. Without a doubt. About everything."

"So, that means . . ." There was the slightest tremble coating her smile, but I could see it. "Well, that's very good! I will now—now I'll go."

And she stayed hanging over the table. Downcast eyes, legs and arms. I-330's crumpled pink ticket was still on the table. I quickly unfurled this manuscript—my "WE"—covering the ticket with its pages (it may be that I was hiding it from myself more than from O).

"Look. I'm writing everything down. It's already ninety-nine pages long . . . Something very surprising is emerging."

A voice—a shadow of a voice: "But remember . . . when you were on page seven and I . . . I let a teardrop fall on it—and you . . ."

Inaudible, hasty droplets brimming over blue saucers, down her cheeks and words, hastily brimming over, too: "I can't anymore, I must go now . . . I won't ever come here again, never. But the only thing I want . . . All I need is a baby from you—give me a baby and I will go, I'll go!"

I could see: she was all atremble under her unif, and I could feel myself also start to—I put my hands behind me and smiled: "What? Now you're after the Machine of the Benefactor?"

And back at me with another word-torrent over a dam: "Fine! But, you see, I would still get to feel—get to feel it inside me. And even if I only get to see it for a few days . . . Just to see its little wrist-crease, just here—like that baby on the stage. Just for one day!"

The three points: I, she, and that chubby crease of the little fist on the table . . .

In childhood, I remember we were once taken to the Accumulator Tower. At the very top level, as I bent over the glass parapet and saw the people-dots below, my heart ticked sweetly: What if I . . . ? At that thought I only clutched the handrails even tighter. But now I am jumping over the edge.

"That's what you want? In complete knowledge of the fact that you would . . ."

Her eyes closed, as though directly facing the sun. A wet, glistening smile.

"Yes, yes! That's what I want!"

I snatched the ticket—I-330's ticket—out from under the manuscript and ran downstairs to the monitor. O grabbed at my arm, yelling something, but I only understood afterward, once I'd returned, what she had been saying.

She was sitting on the edge of the bed, hands tightly clutched together on her lap.

"That was . . . was that her ticket?"

"What difference does it make? Yes—it was hers."

Something crystallized. Most likely, O had simply stirred slightly. She was sitting, hands on her lap, saying nothing.

"Well? Quick let's . . ." I roughly squeezed her arm and red spots (tomorrow's bruises) formed on her wrists, right on the chubby, childlike crease.

That was the last of it. With a flick of the switch, all thoughts went out. Then with darkness and sparks, I was over the parapet, on my way down . . .

KEYWORDS:

A Discharge. The Material of an Idea. The Cliff of Zero.

It was a discharge—that's the most suitable word for it. Now I see that it had been just like an electrical discharge. Over the last few days my pulse had been getting drier, quicker, and more strained as the poles drew toward each other. There was a dry crackle. Another millimeter later: an explosion. And then, silence.

I am now very quiet and empty inside like a building after everyone has left, and you are lying alone, sick, and you can hear the distinct metallic rapping of your thoughts so clearly.

It may be that this "discharge" has finally cured me of my torturous "soul" and that I have become one of us again. At the very least, without all that sickliness, I can now mentally picture O on the steps of the Cube, I can picture her inside the Gas Bell Jar. And if she names my name, there, in the Operation Room, let her. In my final moment I will piously and gratefully kiss the punishing hand of the Benefactor. I have the right to receive punishment according to my relationship to the One State—and I will not cede this right. None of us ciphers should ever dare to refuse this, our single, only—and, as such, valuable—right.

. . . Thoughts rapping quietly, metallically, distinctly: a mysterious aero carries me to the blue heights of my favorite abstractions.

And here in this cleanest sharp air, I see my rationale about my "rights" burst with a light pop, like a pneumatic tire. And I can see clearly that these ideas about "rights" were merely a throwback from a ridiculous superstition of the Ancients.

There are clay ideas and there are ideas that have been carved out of gold or out of our precious glass over the ages. And in order to determine the material of an idea, you need only drip strong-acting acid on it. Even the Ancients knew one such acid: *reductio ad finem*. That is what they called it, apparently. But they were afraid of this poison and they preferred to see anything, be it a clay sky or a toy sky, rather than a blue nothing. We—may the Benefactor bless us—are adults, and don't need toys.

So, take the idea of "rights" and drip some acid on it. Even the most adult of the Ancients knew: the source of a right is power, a right is a function of power. Take two trays of a weighing scale: put a gram on one, and on the other, put a ton. On one side is the "I," on the other is the "WE," the One State. Isn't it clear? Assuming that "I" has the same "rights" compared to the State is exactly the same thing as assuming that a gram can counterbalance a ton. Here is the distribution: a ton has rights, a gram has duties. And this is the nat-ural path from insignificance to greatness: forget that you are a gram, and feel as though you are a millionth part of the ton . . .

You, voluptuous, ruddy Venusians, you, smoke-blackened black-smiths of Uranus: I hear your grumble in my own blue silence. But listen: everything that is great is simple. Listen: only the four rules of arithmetic are steadfast and eternal. And it is only the code of morals that resides within these four rules that is great, steadfast, and eternal. This is the ultimate wisdom; this is the apex of the pyramid that people clambered up—red with sweat, kicking and wheezing—for centuries. And from this apex we look down to the bottom and see insignificant worms still churning up something that survives in us from our ancestors. They all look identical from this apex: an unlawful mother, O; a murderer; and that madman who dared to throw his poems at the One State. Their sentences are also the same: an untimely death. This is the very justice that peo-ple who lived in stone houses, lit by the rosy, innocent rays of the morning of history, could only dream about; their "God" punished those who disparaged the Holy Church in exactly the same way as he punished those who committed murder.

You, Uranians, as severe and black as ancient Spaniards (who were wisely capable of burning offenders at the stake): you are silent. I have a feeling that you are with me. But I can hear pink Venusians murmuring something about torture, punishment, and about the return to barbarian times. My dears: I pity you that you are not capable of philosophically mathematical thinking.

Human history goes up in circles, like an aero. The circles are different—some golden, some bloody—but they are all divided into 360 degrees. They start at zero and progress to 10, 20, 200, 360 degrees, and return to zero again. Yes, we have returned to zero. Yes. But to my mathematically reasoning mind, something is clear: this zero is completely different and new. We departed from zero to the right then we returned to zero from the left, and so: instead of plus zero, we are at minus zero. Do you understand?

This zero looks like a silent, colossal, narrow, knife-sharp cliff to me. In the ferocious, shaggy darkness, having held our breath, we cast off from the black, midnight side of the Zero Cliff. For centuries, we sailed and sailed, each of us a Columbus, we rounded the whole circle of the Earth, and finally, hooray! Ahoy and everyone's up the mast: ahead of us is a different, as yet unknown side of the Zero Cliff, lit up by the aurora polaris of the One State, an azure mass, the sparks of a rainbow, the sun ... hundreds of suns, billions of rainbows ...

It is only the thickness of a knife that separates us from that other, black side of the Zero Cliff. The knife is the most durable, immortal, the most genius thing that man created. The knife was the guillotine; the knife is the universal means of solving all knots; and along the blade of a knife lies the path of paradox—the single most worthy path of the fearless mind ...

KEYWORDS:

The Duty of the Author. The Ice Swells.
The Most Difficult Love.

Yesterday was her day and again she didn't appear, and again I got an unintelligible note from her that clarified nothing. But I am calm, completely calm. If I perform absolutely everything just as the note dictates, if I carry the ticket to the monitor and then lower the blinds and sit in my room alone, then it is not, of course, it is not because I don't have the strength to go against her wishes. How silly! Of course not! It is merely that the blinds separate me from all those plastering, therapeutic smiles and I can write these very pages in peace, for one thing. And second: without her I am afraid I will lose perhaps the only single key to figuring out those unknown quantities (the story of the closet, my temporary death, and all that). And I now feel myself duty-bound to figure them out, even simply as the author of these records, never mind the fact that all unknowns are, in a larger sense, man's natural enemy. *Homo sapiens* is only man, in the fullest sense of the word, when his grammar contains no question marks, only exclamation marks, commas, and periods.

And so today, at 16:00, directed explicitly by what I consider to be my authorly duty, I took an aero and went off to the Ancient House again. There was a powerful evening wind. The aero punched through the thicket of air with difficulty; transparent branches whistled and lashed. The city below looked made of pale-blue blocks of ice. All of a sudden, a cloud appears, a quick, slanted shadow. And the ice turns leaden and swollen and, like when standing on the banks of a river in the springtime, you anticipate—any moment now—a cracking, a surging, a twirling, a bolting away. But then the moment passes, and the next does too, and the ice is still, and instead, you yourself are swelling, your heart is beating more anxiously and frequently. (But why am I writing about this, and where do these strange sensations come from? There's no such thing as an icebreaker that could break the most transparent and most durable crystal that is our life.)

There was no one at the entrance to the Ancient House. I walked around and saw the old woman-gatekeeper near the Green Wall: her hand was stuck against her forehead, she was looking upward. Up above the Wall: the sharp black triangles of some kind of bird were cawing and throwing their breasts at the solid barrier of electrical waves and then being flung backward, only to try flying over the Wall yet again.

I see: slanting, quick shadows across her dark face, overgrown with wrinkles, and a quick glance at me.

"No, no, no one is here! That's right! And there's no reason for you to go up there. Yes . . ."

But why is there "no reason"? And what is this strange attitude—am I merely someone else's shadow? Well, maybe you and everyone else are my shadows! Didn't I populate these pages with all of you? Not long ago they were just four-cornered, white deserts. Without me, would you have ever been seen by all those that I am leading through the narrow footpaths of these written lines?

I didn't actually say any of this to her, as you would expect. I know from my own personal experience: it is very cruel to pierce a person with doubts of his three-dimensional reality and suggest any kind of other reality. I just dryly pointed out to her that her task was to open the door and she let me into the courtyard.

Empty. Quiet. There is a wind over there, behind the walls, far away, just like there was that day when we, side by side, a twosome, a onesome, emerged from the depths, from those corridors—if this had really happened after all. I walked under some stone arches where my footsteps were smacking the gray vaults above and then falling behind me as though another person was treading behind me, at my heels. Yellow walls with redbrick pimples watched me through the dark square lenses of their windows; they watched as I opened the singing doors of sheds, as I looked into corners, down blind alleys and backstreets. I went through a gate in a fence into a vacant lot. These were monuments to the Two-Hundred-Year War: the naked stone ribs and the yellow bare-toothed jawbones of walls coming up from the soil; an ancient oven with vertical pipes; a ship fossilized forever among splashes of stone-yellow and brick-red.

An impression, indistinct, as though delivered through the thickness of water, at depth: I had seen these yellow teeth before. I started searching around. I was falling into holes, stumbling over stones, rusty paws were grabbing at my unif as sharply salted drops of sweat crawled down my forehead into my eyes ...

Nowhere! I couldn't find that exit from below anywhere. The exit from the corridors—it just wasn't here. But then, perhaps that's a good thing: further proof that it was all just one of my "dreams."

Tired, covered with dust and some kind of cobweb, I opened the gate to return to the main courtyard when suddenly from behind: a rustle, squelching footsteps. In front of me stood the pink wing-ears and the twice-bent smile of S.

He, narrowing his eyes, screwed his gimlets into me and asked: "Taking a walk?"

I said nothing. My arms became extraneous.

"So, tell me, are you feeling better now?"

"Yes, thank you. It seems I am returning to normal."

He released me—raising his eyes upward. His head tilted upward and I noticed his Adam's apple for the first time.

An aero buzzed up in the air, not high—about fifty meters up. I recognized it as the apparatus of the Guardians with its slow, low flight and the lowered black proboscis of its observing tube. But there weren't just two or three of them as usual, but somewhere between ten and twelve of them (unfortunately, I have to be limited to an approximate figure).

"Why so many today?" I mustered the courage to ask.

"Why? Well . . . A genuine doctor will start treating a person who is still healthy; someone who might become sick tomorrow, the day after tomorrow, in a week's time. It's prophylaxis!"

He nodded his head and flopped off along the stone slabs of the courtyard. Then he turned and said, over his shoulder: "Be careful!"

I was alone. Quiet. Empty. Far off, above the Green Wall, birds and wind were rushing about. What did he mean by that?

My aero quickly glided along an airstream. Faint, heavy shadows from the clouds cast themselves below, and the pale-blue cupolas, the cubes of glass ice, turned leaden and swollen.

EVENING

I opened my records to deliver to their pages a few, as I see it, useful thoughts (for you, readers) about the great Day of the One Vote, which is approaching rather soon. And I realized: I can't write right now. I can't stop listening to how the wind flaps its dark wings over the glass of the walls; I can't stop looking around in anticipation. Of what? I don't know. And when those familiar brownish-pink gills appeared in my room, I was very glad, and said so clean-heartedly. She sat down, chastely straightened the pleats of her unif that fell between her knees, immediately pasting smiles all over me—in small dollops over each of my cracks—and I felt good, strongly connected.

"So, when I went into class today"—she works in the Children-Rearing Factory—"there was a caricature of me on the wall. Yes, yes, I swear to you! They depicted me as sort of fishlike. Maybe I really do . . ."

"No, no, no, come now," I hurried to say. (Up close, in actuality, it was clear that there was nothing there resembling gills at all, and that it was completely inappropriate when I mentioned the gills before.)

"Yes, well, ultimately, it's not important. But, you see, it was the deed itself. Of course, I called the Guardians. I love children very much and I consider this kind of cruelty to be the most difficult and highest love—you know what I mean?"

Absolutely! This intersected with my thoughts so well. I couldn't restrain myself and I read her an excerpt from Record Twenty, beginning with: ". . . Thoughts rapping quietly, metallically, distinctly . . ."

Without looking, I saw how the brownish-pink cheeks quivered and then moved toward me, closer and closer, and then her dry, hard, sort of prickly fingers were in my hands.

"Give—give this to me! I will duplicate it and make the children learn it by heart. We need this—not just your Venusians—but us, too—now, tomorrow, and the day after tomorrow."

She glanced over her shoulder and said very quietly: "Have you heard? They're saying that on the Day of the One Vote . . ."

I leapt up: "What—what are they saying? What about the Day of the One Vote?"

My cozy walls had vanished. For a second, I felt as though I'd been thrown out there, outside, where a giant wind is rushing about on wings and the slanting, dusky clouds are getting lower and lower . . .

U wrapped my shoulders with her outstretched arms, hard and firm (though I noticed: the bones of her fingers were shaking in resonance with my agitation).

"Please sit down, my dear, don't worry. It doesn't matter what they're saying . . . And if you need me, I'll stay close by you that day. I will leave my children at school with someone else and I will be with you, because evidently you, my dear, you are also a child, and you need . . ."

"No, no." I waved. "Not a chance! Then you'll really think that I really am some sort of baby—that I can't cope by myself . . . Not a chance!" (I'll admit: I had other plans with regards to that day.)

She smiled and the unwritten subtext of her smile was obvious: "Oh, what a stubborn boy!" She then sat down. Her eyes were lowered. Her hands chastely arranged the pleats of her unif that had fallen between her knees—and then, she was on to something different: "I think . . . that I should make up my mind . . . for your sake . . . But I ask you not to hurry me. I still need to think about it a bit . . ."

I wasn't hurrying her. Though I did realize that I should be happy at the prospect—that there is no greater honor than to improve someone's evening years with yourself.

. . . Wings, wings, all night long. I am walking around with my hands protecting my head from these wings. And then there is a chair. But the chair is not one of our contemporary ones, but an ancient model, made of wood. Alternating the movement of its feet like a horse (the right one forward—the left one backward; the left one forward—the right one backward), the chair runs up to my bed, climbs up into it—and I make love to the wooden chair (uncomfortable, painful).

It is astonishing: it must be possible to concoct some sort of means of treating this dream-disease or making it rational—useful, even.

KEYWORDS:

A Frozen Wave. Everything Is Perfecting. I Am a Microbe.

Imagine yourself standing on the shore: waves rhythmically rising, rising, and then suddenly they stay there, they set, they freeze. That is how terrifying and unnatural it was when our Table-appointed walk got tangled unexpectedly, it got muddled up and stopped. The last time that something like this happened was 119 years ago, according to the *Chronicles,* when, in the very midst of the walk, with a whistle and smoke, a meteorite fell from the sky.

We were walking as we always do, like the warriors of Assyrian monuments: thousands of heads with two united, integrated legs and two integrated, sweeping arms. At the end of the avenue, where the Accumulator Tower was sounding threateningly, we came upon a quadrilateral: guards at the front, behind, and on the sides; three ciphers in unifs in the middle with their golden badges already removed—and everything was terrifyingly clear.

The enormous dial at the pinnacle of the Tower was a face: bending over through the clouds and spitting down seconds, waiting indifferently. And at exactly 13:06, a commotion occurred in the quadrilateral. All this was quite close to where I stood; I could see the minute details and I clearly remember a thin, long neck and the tangled mess of light blue veins on his temples, like rivers on the geographical map of a small, unknown world, and this unknown world was a young cipher by the looks of him. He must have noticed someone in our row: he got up on his tiptoes, extended his neck, and stopped. One of the guards cracked him with the bluish spark of an electrical whip; he yelped thinly, like a puppy. And then there was a distinct crack, approximately every two seconds—a yelp—a crack—a yelp.

We continued walking rhythmically, like Assyrians, and looking at the graceful zigzag of the sparks, I thought: everything in human society is boundlessly perfecting—just as it should. The whip of the Ancients was such an ugly implement—but look how much beauty . . .

But then, like a nut coming off an engine at full throttle, a thin, stubbornly supple female figure ripped away from our row with a scream: "Enough! Stop it!" and threw herself right into the quadrilateral. This was like the meteor 119 years ago: the whole walk froze and our rows, like the gray crests of waves, were bound by an unexpected frost.

For a second I saw her as an outsider, like everyone else: she was already not a cipher—she was only a person; she existed only as the metaphysical substance of insult, inflicted toward the One State. But one of her movements—a turning, a curve to the left—and it was suddenly clear to me: I know, I know this supple, whiplike body—my eyes, my lips, my hands know her. At that moment I was absolutely sure of it.

Two guards moved to cut her off. For a second, one clear reflective patch of street was visible but their trajectory was cutting through to it and in a second they would catch her . . . My heart stalled and then stopped and I threw myself at this patch without considering whether it was: possible, impossible, ridiculous, rational . . .

I felt thousands of eyes on me, wide with horror, but this just gave more reckless, joyful strength to the wild, hairy-handed person that had torn itself from me, and he ran all the faster. But after two steps, she turned around. Before me was a trembling, freckle-spattered face with ginger eyebrows . . . Not her! Not I-330.

A mad, gushing joy. I wanted to scream something like: "There she is! Get her!" But I hear only my own whisper. And a heavy hand on my shoulder. I'm being held, led, I attempt to explain to them...

"Listen, but you see, you must understand that I thought that it..."

But how could I explain everything about myself, everything about my sickness, as I have done in these records? I piped down and went along submissively ... A leaf, torn from its tree by an unexpected gust of wind, falls obediently, but along the way it twists, clinging to each familiar branch, shoot, and twig: that is how I clung to each mute sphere-head, to the transparent ice of the walls, to the light blue needle of the Accumulator Tower stuck up into the clouds.

At the moment when blank curtains were definitively prepared to separate me from the whole wonderful world, I saw, in the near distance: a familiar colossal head was gliding over the mirrored street, flapping his pink arm-wings. A familiar flattened voice: "I consider it my duty to bear witness to the fact that cipher D-503 is sick and not able to regulate his feelings. And I am certain that his enthusiasm was natural indignation..."

"Yes, yes." I latched on. "I even screamed: 'Get her!'"

From behind, over my shoulder: "You didn't scream anything."

"Yes, but I meant to—I swear to the Benefactor, I meant to."

For a second, I was riveted by his gray, cold, gimlet eyes. I don't know if he saw that I was telling the (almost) truth, or if he had some secret purpose in taking mercy on me at this point, but as soon as he had written a short note and given it to one of the ciphers holding me, I was free again—that is, rather, I was included again in the well-constructed, infinitely stretching Assyrian rows.

The quadrilateral containing the freckled face and the temples with the geographical map of light blue veins was hidden behind the corner, forever. We walk—one million-headed body—with a humble joy in each of us, similar, I imagine, to what molecules, atoms, and phagocytes experience. The Christians of the ancient world (our only predecessors, as imperfect as they were) also understood this: humility is a virtue and pride is a vice; "WE" is divine, and "I" is satanic.

So here I am, in step with everyone now, and yet I'm still separate from everyone. I am still trembling all over from the agitation I endured, like a bridge after an ancient train has rumbled over it. I am aware of myself. And, of course, the only things that are aware of themselves and conscious of their individuality are irritated eyes, cut fingers, sore teeth. A healthy eye, finger, tooth might as well not even be there. Isn't it clear that individual consciousness is just sickness?

It may be, after all, that I am not a phagocyte, calmly going about its business of devouring microbes (with light blue temples and freckles). It may be that I am a microbe, and maybe I am one of thousands among us, still pretending, like me, to be phagocytes . . .

What if today's essentially irrelevant occurrence—what if all this is only the beginning, only the first meteorite in a whole series of rumbling, burning rocks, spilling through infinity toward our glass paradise?

KEYWORDS:

Flowers. The Dissolution of a Crystal. If Only.

They say that there is a kind of flower that blooms only once a century. Then couldn't there be one that flowers only once every thousand years—or once every ten thousand years? Maybe there are and we just don't know it because today is itself that once-in-a-thousand-year moment.

Intoxicated with bliss, I walk down the staircase to the monitor and abruptly, before my eyes, everywhere around me, thousand-year buds silently burst open. Everything is blooming all around me: chairs, boots, golden badges, electric lamps, someone's dark shaggy eyes, the faceted columns of the banisters, a handkerchief dropped on the steps, the little monitor desk, and, over that little desk, the tender brown-spotted cheeks of U. Everything is unusual, new, tender, pink, moist.

U takes my pink ticket, and over her head, through the glass of the wall, the moon hangs from an invisible branch, light blue and fragrant. I point to it with my finger and say triumphantly: "The moon—do you get it?"

U looks at me and then at the digits on the ticket and I see that familiar, very charmingly chaste gesture: adjusting the pleats of her unif between the corners of her knees.

"You have, my dear, an abnormal, sickly look about you—since abnormality and sickliness are the same thing. You are ruining yourself—and no one will tell you so."

This "no one," of course, equates with the cipher on the ticket: I-330. Sweet, marvelous U! You, of course, are right: I am imprudent, I am sick, I have a soul, I am a microbe. But what if blooming is a sickness? What if it is painful when a bud bursts? And don't you think that spermatozoids are the most frightening of all microbes?

I am upstairs in my room. I-330 is in the wide bowl of the chair. I am on the floor, hugging her calves, my head on her knees; we are saying nothing. Silence, a pulse . . . I am a crystal, and I am dissolving in her, in I-330. I feel it clearly, totally: a melting, the melting of the polished facets that confine me in space. I am disappearing, dissolving in her knees, in her. I am becoming ever smaller and simultaneously ever wider, ever bigger, ever unbounded. Because she is not she, but the universe. And for a second I am one with this chair by the bed, suffused with joy. The grandly smiling old woman at the doors of the Ancient House, the wild jungle beyond the Green Wall, some kind of silver wreckage dozing like the old woman against a black background, and the slamming of a door in the far distance—all this is within me and together with me, listening to the beating of my pulse and flying through this blissful second . . .

With a ridiculous, muddled flood of words, I attempt to tell her that I am a crystal and that there is a door inside me and that I feel like a happy chair. But such nonsense comes out that I stop. I am just embarrassed and suddenly . . .

"Sweet I, I'm sorry! I can't understand it at all—I'm talking such nonsense . . ."

"How do you know that nonsense isn't a good thing? If human nonsense had been nurtured and developed for centuries, just as intelligence has, then perhaps something extraordinarily precious could have come from it."

"Yes . . ." (I think she is right—how could she not be, right now?)

"And for one of your nonsenses in particular, for what you did yesterday on the walk—I love you even more—even more."

"But why have you tortured me, why haven't you come to see me, why did you send your pink tickets, why did you make me do . . ."

"Well, maybe I needed to test you. Maybe I needed to know that you would do everything that I wanted you to do—that you are totally mine?"

"Yes, totally!"

She took my face—all of me—into her palms and raised up my head: "So, tell me, how are those 'duties of the honest cipher' going? Hmm?"

Sweet, sharp, white teeth: a smile. There, in the wide bowl of the armchair, she is like a bee: both a sting and honey are inside her.

Yes, duties . . . I mentally flick through my recent records: it's true, there aren't any thoughts anywhere about what, essentially, I was supposed to have gone and done . . .

I say nothing. I smile rapturously (and probably goofily, too), I look at her pupils, skipping from one to the other, and in each of them I see myself: I am tiny, millimeterly, confined in these tiny, iridescent dungeons. And then, once again: bees, lips, the sweet pain of blooming . . .

In each of us ciphers, there is an invisible, quietly ticking metronome, and we can tell time with a precision of within five minutes without looking at a clock. But at that point in time, the metronome in me had stopped; I didn't know how much time had passed and, alarmed by this, I grabbed my badge with its timepiece from under my pillow . . .

Thank the Benefactor: twenty minutes to go! But minutes are laughably short, dock-tailed, and they are running away on us while I have so much to tell her—everything, all about myself, about the letter from O, about that awful evening when I gave her a child and something about my childhood years, about the mathematician Pliapa, about $\sqrt{-1}$, and about how I cried bitterly that first time at the Day of the One Vote because there was a spot of ink on my unif.

I-330 raised her head, leaned on her elbow. Two long, sharp lines at the corners of her mouth, the dark angle of her raised eyebrows: a cross.

"Maybe, on that day . . ." She stopped, and her eyebrows grew darker still. She took my hand and squeezed it hard. "Say you won't forget me; will you remember me forever?"

"Why are you like this? What are you talking about, I, my sweet?"

I-330 said nothing and her eyes were already looking past me, through me, far away. I suddenly heard the wind slapping against the glass with its gigantic wings (I imagine this was happening all that time, but I had only just heard it), and, for some reason, I was reminded of the piercing birds above the Green Wall.

I-330 shook her head—shedding something. She brushed up to me with her whole self—just like an aero springing when it touches down for that second before actually landing.

"Now, hand me my stockings. Quick!"

The stockings had been flung on my table, on the open page of my records (page 193). In our haste, I brushed against the stack of paper, and the pages spilled and couldn't be put back in order—but, more to the point, if they were put back in order, then it wouldn't be the real order anyway; there would still be thresholds, iambs, and X's.

"I can't do this," I said. "You're here, right now, near me, and yet it's as though you're behind an ancient, opaque wall: I can hear rustlings and voices through the wall but cannot make out the words, I don't know what is there. I can't stand it. You are always not quite telling me everything—you haven't once told me where I was that day when I found myself at the Ancient House, what those corridors were, and why the doctor—or perhaps none of it ever happened?"

I-330 laid her hands on my shoulders, slowly, and penetrated my eyes deeply.

"You want to know everything?"

"Yes, I want to. I have to."

"And you won't become too afraid to follow me anywhere, all the way—wherever I may take you?"

"Yes, wherever!"

"Good. I promise you, when the holiday is over, that is, if ... Oh, yes, and how is your Integral? I always forget to ask—is it almost done?"

"No. What do you mean by 'that is if'? Again: that is if what?"

She (already at the door): "You'll see for yourself ..."

I am alone. The only thing that remains of her is a barely audible scent, something like that sweet, dry, yellow dust from beyond the Green Wall. And another thing: question-hooks, like those that the Ancients used for fishing (the Prehistoric Museum), were firmly lodged in me.

... Why did she suddenly ask about the Integral?

KEYWORDS:

The Limits of a Function. Easter. Everything Crossed Out.

I am like a machine being driven to excessive rotations: the bearings are incandescing and, in a minute, melted metal will begin to drip and everything will turn to nothing. Quick: get cold water, logic. I am pouring it over myself by the bucketload but the logic sizzles on the hot bearings and dissipates elusive white steam into the air.

Well, one thing is clear: in order to establish the true value of a function, one must take it to its limits. And it is clear that yesterday's ridiculous "dissolution into the universe," taken to its limits, is death. Because death is exactly that: the ultimate dissolution of my self into the universe. And hence, if "L" signifies love and "D" signifies death, then $L = f(D)$—that is, love is a function of death ...

Yes, exactly, exactly. That is why I am afraid of I-330, I struggle with her, I don't want—but how can "I don't want" and "I want" coexist in me? And the most hideous part of this is: I want yesterday's blissful death again. The hideousness of it is that, even now, when the logical function has been integrated, when it is obvious that it is implicitly composed of death, I still want her, my lips, my hands, my breast, every millimeter of me ...

Tomorrow is the Day of the One Vote. She will be there, of course, and I will see her, but only from afar. From afar—that will be painful, because I need her, I am uncontrollably drawn toward her, her hands, her shoulders, her hair . . . But I actually want this pain—bring it on.

Great Benefactor! What absurdity to want pain. Who doesn't understand that pain is negative, a component that decreases the sum that we call happiness? And, consequently . . .

Well, you see, there are no more "consequentlies." Pure and bare.

EVENING

Through the glass windows of the building: a windy, feverishly pink, uneasy sunset. I have turned my chair around so this pinkness is not in front of me and I'm flicking through my records. And I can see: I forgot again that I am not writing this for myself but for you, my unknowns, whom I love and pity, for you who are still plodding along in distant centuries, below.

So, on to the Day of the One Vote, a great day. I have always loved it, since childhood. I imagine it is something like the day the Ancients called "Easter." I remember that the day before it, we would make mini-hour-calendars for ourselves and we would cross out the hours with such glee, one by one. One hour closer was one hour less to wait . . . If I could be sure that no one would see it, I would (I cross my heart) carry one of these mini-calendars around with me even now, and I would follow it to see how many hours were left until tomorrow, when I will see, though from far away . . .

(An interruption: they brought me a new unif, straight from the workshop. According to custom, we are all given new unifs for tomorrow. In the corridor, there are footsteps, joyous cries, noise.)

I continue. Tomorrow I will see all the same sights that repeat themselves from year to year and are newly exciting every time: the mighty chalice of unanimity, the reverentially raised hands. Tomorrow is the day of the annual election of the Benefactor. Tomorrow, once again, we will offer the Benefactor the keys to the unshakable stronghold of our happiness.

It goes without saying that this does not resemble the disordered, disorganized elections of the Ancients, when—it seems funny to say it—the result of an election was not known beforehand. Building a government on totally unaccounted-for happenstance, blindly—what could be more senseless? And yet still, it turns out, it took centuries to understand this.

It is hardly necessary to say it but in this, as in everything else, there is no place for chance and unexpected events are not possible. And the election itself is more symbolic in nature: to remind us that we are a unified, mighty, million-celled organism, that we—using the words of the "Evangelists" of the Ancients—are one Church. Because the history of the One State does not know a single instance in which, on this day of rejoicing, even one voice dared to disturb the magnificent unison.

They say that the Ancients conducted elections in some kind of secrecy, hiding like thieves; several of our historians even confirm that they appeared at the election festivities completely masked. (I imagine this fantastic, gloomy spectacle: nighttime, a square, figures in dark cloaks stealing along a wall; the crimson flame of torches cowering in the wind . . .) Why would all this mystery be necessary? Even today it is not understood conclusively; the likeliest explanation is that elections were connected to some sort of mystical, superstitious, maybe even criminal rites. For us, there is nothing to hide and nothing to be ashamed of: we celebrate election day in the daytime, openly and honestly. I see everyone vote for the Benefactor; everyone sees me vote for the Benefactor—and it couldn't be any different, since "I" and "everyone" are the unified "WE." As ennobling, sincere, lofty, and furthermore expedient as this is, so the Ancients' thievish "mystery" was cowardly. And if you even suggest the impossible, that is, that there could be some dissonance in the usual homophony, then the invisible Guardians are here, among our ranks: at any moment, they can stop ciphers who are falling into error and save them from their next false step—and save the One State from them. And then, one last thing . . .

Through the left-hand wall I can see: a woman hurriedly unbuttons her unif in front of the mirrored door on the closet. And for a second, in dimness: eyes, lips, two sharp pink knots. Then the blinds fall, and instantaneously everything is like it was yesterday, and I don't know what this "one last thing" means and I don't want to think about it, I don't want to! I want only one thing: I-330. I want her to be with me, each minute, every minute, alone with me. And what I wrote just now about the One Vote is all irrelevant, not what I meant, and I want to cross it all out, tear it up, and throw it out. Because I know (call it blasphemy): the only holiday is when I am with her, when she is near me, side by side. Without her, tomorrow's sun will only be a little tin circle and the sky will be tin, painted blue, and I myself will be . . .

I grab the telephone receiver: "I-330, is that you?"

"Yes, it's me. How late is it?"

"Is it too late? I wanted to ask you . . . I want you to be with me tomorrow. My sweet . . ."

I say "my sweet" very quietly. And for some reason a moment this morning at the hangar flashed through my mind: for a joke they had put a timepiece under the hundred-ton hammer. There was a swing, a gust of wind in my face, and then: a hundred-ton-tender touch of the delicate timepiece.

A pause. It seemed to me that I could hear there—in I-330's room—someone whispering. Then her voice: "No, I can't. You'll see: I would have . . . No, I can't. Why? Tomorrow you'll see."

NIGHT

KEYWORDS:

Descent from the Skies.
The Greatest Catastrophe in History.
An End to the Known.

Before the proceedings began, when everybody stood up and the solemn, slow canopy of the Hymn, the hundreds of pipes of the Music Factory and the millions of human voices swayed above our heads . . . I forgot everything for a moment. I forgot the alarming thing I-330 had said about today's holiday; I forgot, seemingly, about her altogether. I was now that same little boy that once cried about the tiny and barely noticeable spot on his unif. Even if no one here sees the indelible black spots on me now, I know that the criminal that I am has no place among these wide-open, honest faces. Ah, if only I'd stand up right now and choke and scream out everything about myself. Then there would be an end to it—bring it on! Just for one second to feel clean and mindless, like this baby-blue sky.

All eyes were raised up high: to the morning blueness, chaste, not yet dried of its nighttime tears. There, above, was a dot, barely visible, sometimes dark, sometimes clothed in rays of light. It was Him, descending from the skies to us, the new Jehovah on his aero, as wise and kind and cruel as the Jehovah of the Ancients. He was getting closer with every minute and He could probably see us already: a million hearts offered up to Him on high. And I joined

Him mentally, to see all this from above: the concentric circles of the tribunal contoured with fine, light-blue dotted lines like the circles of a cobweb strewn with microscopic suns (our shining badges); and the white, wise Spider would now sit at the center of it—the Benefactor, clad in white—who wisely binds us by our hands and feet with His benefactorly threads of happiness.

His magnificent descent from the skies was complete. The brass of the Hymn fell silent, everyone sat down and right then I understood: the whole delicate cobweb is drawn tight and quivering, and on the verge of ripping should anything unlikely happen . . .

Rising slightly, I looked around and my glance was met by affectionate, anxious eyes, all skipping from face to face. One cipher raised a hand and signaled to another with a hardly perceptible wiggle of his fingers. Then came a finger signal reply. And another . . . I understood: they were the Guardians. I understood: they are anxious about something, the cobweb is drawn tight, quivering. And inside me, like a radio receiver tuned to the same frequency, there was a corresponding quiver.

A poet was reading a pre-election ode on the stage but I couldn't hear a word of it—only the rhythmical swinging of the hexametric pendulum, which was bringing us ever closer to the appointed hour. And I was feverishly flicking through the rows of faces, one after the other—like pages—but I still couldn't see the one I was specifically looking for; and I must find it as quickly as possible because in a moment the pendulum would tick again and then—

It's him. Of course. Pink wing-ears rush along by the stage and a running body, reflected as the dark, twice-bent loops of the letter "S," is gliding across the glistening glass; he was heading somewhere through the intricate passages between the tribunals.

S and I-330: there is some kind of thread (between them, I mean. There has always been some kind of thread between them, to my mind; I still don't know what kind but one day I will untangle it). I snagged him with my eyes; he was a little ball rolling away with a thread trailing behind him. Then he stopped, he . . .

Like a strike of high-voltage lightning: I was pierced and tied up in a knot. In our row, all of forty degrees away from me, S had stopped and bent over. I saw I-330, and, next to her, the repulsive, African-lipped, and smirking R-13.

My first thought was to fling myself over there and scream at her: "Why are you with him today?! Why didn't you want to be with me?!" But my hands and feet were strongly entangled in the invisible, beneficial cobweb; clenching my teeth, I sat like I was made of iron, not taking my eyes off her. Even now I can feel the sharp physical pain in my heart. I remember thinking to myself: if there can be physical pain from a non-physical cause, then it is clear that . . .

A conclusion, unfortunately, eluded me. I seem to recall that something about a "soul" flashed past and some senseless ancient phrase flew by: "a tortured soul." And I froze: the hexameter had fallen silent. Something was starting to happen . . . what was it?

The customary five-minute pre-election break. The customary pre-election silence. But this wasn't the usual prayerly, reverential silence: this was like ancient times, before the invention of the Accumulator Tower, when the untamed sky still raged with "thunderstorms." This was like the moment before an ancient thunderstorm.

The air was transparent cast-iron. It made you feel like you had to breathe with your mouth stretched wide open. My hearing, strained to a painful extent, was recording: a mouse-gnawing, uneasy whisper somewhere behind me. Not raising my eyes, I can still see those two—I-330 and R—next to each other, shoulder to shoulder, and those strange, shaggy hands that I hate so much are trembling on my knees . . .

Everyone held the timepieces of their badges in their hands. One. Two. Three . . . five minutes . . . and from the stage, a slow, cast-iron voice: "I ask those who vote 'Yes' to please raise your hands."

If only I could look him straight in the eye, like before, with devotion: "Here I am, my whole self. My whole self! Take me!" But I couldn't now summon the courage. With effort, as if all my joints had rusted, I raised my hand.

The rustling of millions of hands. Someone's stifled "Ah!" And I could feel that something had already started and it was falling headlong, but I didn't understand what it was, and I didn't have the strength to—I didn't dare look . . .

"Who says 'No'?"

This was always the most magnificent moment of the holiday: everyone continues to sit, immobile, joyfully bowing their heads to the beneficial yoke of the Cipher of ciphers. But now, to my horror, I heard another rustling: a very light sound, like a sigh, but more audible than the brass pipes of the Hymn earlier. It's like the last sigh of a person's life—barely audible—and yet everyone's faces blanch on hearing it, and cold drops appear on their foreheads . . .

I raised my eyes and . . .

In the hundredth part of a second, the hairspring of a clock, I saw: thousands of hands wave up—"No"—and fall again. I saw I-330's pale face, marked with a cross and her raised hand. My vision darkened.

Another hairspring; a pause; quiet; a pulse. Then—as though signaled by some sort of crazy conductor—the whole tribune gave out a crackle, screams. A whirlwind of soaring unifs on the run, the figures of the Guardians rushing about in panic, someone's heels in the air in front of my very eyes, and, next to the heels, someone's wide-open mouth, bellowing an inaudible scream. For some reason, this cut into me more sharply than anything else: thousands of soundlessly howling mouths, as though on a monstrous movie screen.

And, also on the screen, for a second, somewhere below me, I saw the whitened lips of O: she stood, pressed against the wall of a passage, shielding her stomach with arms folded in a cross. And then she was gone—washed away—or I just forgot about her, because . . .

This is not on a screen anymore—it is inside me myself, inside my squeezed heart, in my throbbing temples. Above my head to the left, R-13 suddenly leapt onto a bench: sputtering, red, and mad. In his arms was a pale I-330, with her unif ripped from shoulder to breast—blood on white. She clung tightly to his neck, and with gigantic bounds from bench to bench—repulsive and deft, like a gorilla—he carried her to the top.

It was like a fire incident in ancient times—everything became crimson—and there was only one thing to do: jump and catch up with them. I can't myself explain now where I got the strength for it, but I thrashed through the crowd like a battering ram—over someone's shoulder—over benches—and I was nearly there—and then I grabbed R by the collar: "Don't you dare! Don't you dare, you . . . Get!" (Thankfully, my voice wasn't audible, since everyone was yelling for themselves, everyone was running.)

"Who? What is all this? What?" R turned, trembling, his lips spattering—he probably thought that he had been grabbed by one of the Guardians.

"What? Right now— You can't, I won't allow it! Let her go—right now!"

But he only smacked his lips angrily, shook his head, and ran on further. And then I—I am extremely ashamed of recording this but I think I must nonetheless, I must, I must record everything, so that you, my unknown readers, can learn the history of my sickness in its entirety—then I swung and hit him on the head. You hear that? I hit him! I remember it distinctly. And I also remember: a feeling of some sort of liberation, a lightness in my whole body from having delivered this blow.

I-330 quickly crawled down out of his arms.

"Go away!" she screamed at R. "Can't you see? He . . . Go away, R, go away!"

R, baring white, African teeth, spattered some word into my face, dived off, and disappeared. And I picked I-330 up into my arms, tightly squeezing her to me, and bolted.

The heart inside me was beating, it was enormous, and such a tempestuous, hot—such a joyful wave was unleashed with each beat. And so what if something had been smashed into smithereens—it doesn't matter! Just to carry her like this, carry her, carry her . . .

EVENING. 22:00

It is with difficulty that I hold this pen in my hand: such is the immense fatigue after all the head-spinning events of this morning.

Can it be true that the safeguarding, age-old walls of the One State have caved in? Can it be true that we are again shelterless in the savage state of freedom—like our distant predecessors? Can it be true that there is no Benefactor? "No" . . . on the Day of the One Vote . . . "No"? I am ashamed, pained, and scared for them. But who are "they"? And who am I: "they" or "we"? How will I know?

So: there she was, sitting on a bench, being warmed by the sun on the very highest tribunal, to which she had been carried. From her right shoulder down, the beginning of a miraculous, incalculable curve is exposed; and there was the finest, little red snake of blood. It was as though she didn't notice the blood or her exposed breast . . . no, it was more than that: she saw it all but this was exactly what she needed right now—if her unif had been buttoned up, she would have ripped it open herself, she would have . . .

"And tomorrow . . ." She is breathing greedily through gritted, sparkling, sharp teeth. ". . . And tomorrow—who knows what happens? Do you get it? I don't know and no one knows—it's all unknown! You understand, that this is the end to the Known? This is the new, the improbable, the unpredictable."

Down below, there is frothing, rushing, screaming. But all that is far away, and getting farther away because she is looking at me, she is slowly pulling me into her through the narrow, golden windows of her pupils. She does this for a long time, saying nothing. And it reminds me for some reason of that time when I looked through the Green Wall and I saw someone's strange, yellow pupils, and how birds were hovering above the Wall (or was that on a separate occasion?).

"Listen: if nothing happens tomorrow, nothing in particular— I will take you back there—you understand?"

No, I don't understand. But I am nodding my head, saying nothing. I have dissolved, I am infinitely small, I am a dot . . .

When all is said and done, this dotty state has its logic (these days): there are more uncertainties in a dot than anything else; it only takes a push or a jiggle for it to turn into thousands of different crooked lines, hundreds of shapes.

I am scared of being jiggled: what will I turn into? And I'm thinking that everyone is the same as me, scared of the smallest movement. Here, now, as I write this, everyone is sitting, taking refuge in their glass cages and waiting for something. In the corridor you can't hear the usual buzzing of the elevator at this hour, you can't hear the laughter, the footsteps. Occasionally I see: people walking along the corridors on their tiptoes, in twos, looking around, whispering . . .

What will tomorrow bring? What will I turn into tomorrow?

KEYWORDS:

The World Exists. A Rash. 105 Degrees.

Morning. Through the ceiling: the sky has its usual strong, round, and red-cheeked appearance. I think I would have been less surprised if I had seen some unusual quadrilateral sun overhead, people in multicolored clothing made of bestial wool, and opaque stone walls. Could it be that the world—our world—still exists? Or is this just inertia, the generator is turned off but the gears are still rumbling and spinning: two rotations, three rotations, and it will freeze on the fourth . . .

Are you familiar with this strange condition? It is night and you have fallen asleep and then you open your eyes in the blackness and suddenly: you have become lost and you start to feel around quickly, quickly looking for something familiar and solid—the wall, the lamp, the chair. I felt around just like that in the *State Gazette*—quickly, quickly—and here is what I found:

YESTERDAY, THE LONG AND IMPATIENTLY AWAITED DAY OF THE ONE VOTE TOOK PLACE. FOR THE 48TH TIME THE BENEFACTOR, WHO HAS PROVEN HIS UNSHAKABLE WISDOM MANY TIMES OVER, WAS UNANIMOUSLY CHOSEN. THE CELEBRATION WAS CLOUDED BY A SLIGHT

DISTURBANCE WROUGHT BY THE ENEMIES OF HAPPINESS, WHICH, NATURALLY, DEPRIVES THEM OF THE RIGHT TO BECOME BRICKS IN THE FOUNDATIONS OF THE ONE STATE, RENEWED YESTERDAY. IT IS CLEAR TO EACH OF US THAT TAKING THEIR VOICES INTO ACCOUNT WOULD BE AS RIDICULOUS AS TAKING THE ACCIDENTAL COUGHS OF SICK PEOPLE IN A CONCERT AUDIENCE AS A PART OF A MAJESTIC, HEROIC SYMPHONY . . .

Oh, the wisdom of it! Can it be, after all, in spite of everything, that we are saved? Could there be any objections to this most crystalline syllogism?

And then, these two lines:

TODAY AT 12:00 THE JOINT SESSION OF THE ADMINISTRATIVE BUREAU, THE BUREAU OF MEDICINE, AND THE BUREAU OF GUARDIANS WILL TAKE PLACE. IN THE COMING DAYS AN IMPORTANT STATE ACT WILL BE EFFECTED.

Yes, the walls are still standing—here they are—I can feel them with my hands. And the strange feeling that I am lost, that I don't know where I am, that I have lost my way, has already gone, and it's not half-surprising that I see a blue sky, a round sun, and everyone, as usual, going off to work.

I walked along the avenue especially purposefully and loudly, and it seemed to me that everyone else was doing the same. But here at the crossroads, I turn the corner and I see: everyone is sort of strangely skirting around a space at the corner of the building— as though some sort of pipe had burst in the wall and cold water was spraying everywhere, making it impossible to walk along the sidewalk.

Five, ten paces more and I was also drenched with the cold water, rocked and knocked off the sidewalk . . . On the wall, approximately two yards up, written on a square piece of paper, the incomprehensible poison-green letters:

MEPHI

And underneath it, an S-like curved spine and wing-ears transparently fluttering in rage or anxiety. He was stretching his right hand up, and his left arm, behind him, was helpless like a hurt, broken wing. He was jumping up to tear down the piece of paper but couldn't as he was just not close enough.

Everyone who was passing by probably had the same thought: "If I ... me, one of many ... go up and help him ... won't he think that I am guilty of something and that is the reason I want to ...?"

I admit: I had that very same thought. But I remembered how many times he had been my real guardian angel, how many times he had saved me and so I dared to go up, reach up my arm, and tear down the piece of paper.

S turned around and quickly-quickly his gimlets were into me, to my depths, where he found something. Then he raised his left eyebrow and with this eyebrow, nodded at the wall, where "MEPHI" had hung. And the tail of his smile flashed at me—it was actually rather cheerful, to my surprise. But then again, what's there to be surprised about anymore? Given the choice of the agonizingly slow-rising temperature of the incubation of an illness or a rash with a 104-degree fever, a doctor will always prefer the latter: at least the illness is clearly present. The "MEPHI," which broke out on the wall today, is a rash. I can understand this smile ...*

On my way down to the subterranean rail, there was another white piece of paper on the immaculate glass of the steps: "MEPHI." And down inside, it was on the wall, on the bench, and on the mirror of the train car (glued, apparently, in haste)—that same white, terrifying rash was everywhere.

In the silence: the distinct humming of the wheels, like the noise of feverish blood. Someone was touched on the shoulder—he winced and dropped his bundle of papers. And to the left of me was another cipher reading one and the same, one and the same, one and the same line, over and over again, in his newspaper, and the newspaper is trembling just noticeably. And I feel as though everywhere—in wheels, hands, newspapers, and eyelashes—there

---

*I should say that I only discovered the exact grounds of this smile after many days, after being filled to the brim with events both strange and unexpected.

is a pulse, it's getting faster and faster, and maybe today, when I go down to that place with I-330, the black line on the thermometer will reach 102, 104, 106 degrees . . .

In the hangar was the same silence, like the buzzing of a distant, invisible propeller. The machines say nothing, frowning, standing still. And only the cranes glide, vaguely audible, as if on their tip-toes, stooping, grabbing light blue blocks of frozen air with their pincers and loading them into the flank cisterns of the Integral: we are preparing for its test flight.

"Well, then, will we finish loading within the week?"

This was me to the Second Builder. His face was porcelain, painted with sweet blue and tender pink little flowers (eyes, lips), but today they were somehow off-color, washed out. We consider this question aloud, but I suddenly cut off in mid-word and stand, mouth agape: high up, under the cupola, on the light blue block raised by the crane, was a barely noticeable, little white square—a glued scrap of paper. And I was shaking all over—maybe, from laughter—yes, I could hear myself laughing (have you ever done that, heard yourself laughing?).

"No, okay, listen . . ." I say. "Imagine that you are in an ancient airplane, the altimeter shows five thousand meters and the wing breaks off, you're like a tumbler pigeon falling, and on your way down you are calculating: 'Tomorrow . . . from twelve to two I will . . . from two to six . . . six o'clock is dinnertime . . .' Well, isn't that funny? And, can you see, that's exactly what we're doing?!"

The little light blue flowers stir, goggling. What if I am made of glass and he can see that in three or four hours' time . . .

KEYWORDS:

No Keywords of Any Kind Are Possible.

I am alone in infinite corridors—those very corridors. A mute, concrete sky. Somewhere water is dripping on stone. A familiar, heavy, opaque door and, from behind it, a dull drone.

She said that she would come out and get me at exactly 16:00. But 16:00 passed five, ten, fifteen minutes ago: no one is here.

For a second, I am the former me, who is frightened that the door might open. Still, five more minutes and if she doesn't come out . . .

Water is dripping somewhere nearby. Nobody here. With miserable delight, I feel: saved. I slowly walk back along the corridor. The flickering dotted line of little lamps on the ceiling grows dimmer and dimmer . . .

All of a sudden, behind me, the door hastily clatters, a rapid tramp softly ricochets off the ceiling, off the walls, and she, gliding toward me, lightly panting from running, breathes through her mouth: "I knew that you would be here, that you would come! I knew you—you . . ."

The javelins of her eyelashes move apart, letting me inside and . . . How can I explain what this ancient, ridiculous, miraculous rite does to me, when her lips touch mine? What formula could express this whirlwind that clears my soul of everything except her? Yes, my soul, yes . . . laugh if you want to.

She slowly lifts her eyelids with some effort and slowly manages words: "No, enough . . . afterward. Now we should go."

The door opens. There are steps, worn and old. An intolerably colorful uproar, a whistle, daylight . . .

· · ·

Almost twenty-four hours have passed since then; everything has partly settled inside me but nevertheless it is extraordinarily hard for me to give even the most approximately exact description. It is as if a bomb had exploded in my head and I am surrounded by: piles after piles of open mouths, wings, cries, leaves, words, stones . . .

I remember, my first thought was: quick, go back, fast as you can. It was clear that while I had been waiting in the corridor, they had somehow blown up and destroyed the Green Wall and everything had darted over and swamped our city, which until now had been unsoiled with that lower world.

I must have said something of the sort to I-330. She burst out laughing: "No, not at all! It is simple—we have come out beyond the Green Wall . . ."

Then I opened my eyes wide and I was face-to-face, in actuality, with the very thing, which no living person today had seen until now—other than through the cloudy glass of the Wall, which weakened, obscured, and reduced it by a thousand times.

The sun . . . it wasn't our sun, evenly distributed along the mirrored surfaces of the streets: it was live splinters and incessantly jumping dots, blinding your eyes and spinning your head. And the trees were like candles jutting right up into the sky; like spiders on gnarled paws squatting on the earth; like mute, green fountains . . . And everything is crawling, stirring, rustling and a sort of rough, little tangle rushes up underfoot and I am riveted, I can't take one step because it is not level under my feet—do you understand? It was not level but sort of repulsively soft, yielding, living, green, bouncy.

I was deafened by it all and I choked—that's perhaps the most appropriate word for it. I stood, seizing on to some sort of swinging bough with both hands.

"Don't worry, don't worry! This is only the beginning, it will pass. Be brave!"

Next to I-330, against the head-spinningly jumping green lattice, someone's very fine, paper-thin profile . . . no, not just someone's, I know this person. I recognize: the doctor. No, no, I understand everything very clearly now. And I also understand: the two of them are taking me under the arms and dragging me forward, laughing. My legs are wobbling, sliding. Cawing, moss, hummocks, knots, trunks, wings, leaves, a whistle . . .

And the trees dispersed—a bright clearing . . . people in the clearing . . . or, I don't know what they were—maybe "beings" is more accurate.

This is the most difficult part. Because at this point we depart from the confines of the believable. And it is clear to me now why I-330 was always stubbornly silent about this: I wouldn't have believed it anyway—even from her. It's also possible that tomorrow I won't believe myself—or these records of mine.

In the clearing, stirring around a naked, skull-shaped rock, was a crowd of three hundred, four hundred . . . persons—I suppose "person" is the word, it's difficult to say anything else. And just like at the tribunals when, in the general mass of faces, you take in only those that are familiar to you, at first I could only see our gray-blue unifs. And then—a second later—among the unifs, completely distinct and simple: jet-black, chestnut, golden, dark-bay, roan, and white people—yes, by the looks of them, they were people. They were all without clothes, and they were all covered with short, shining fur like the kind that you can see on the stuffed horses at the Prehistoric Museum. But the females had faces just exactly like— yes, yes, exactly like—those of our own women: tenderly pink and not overgrown with hair, and their breasts, likewise, were free of hair—big, firm, beautiful geometrical forms. The males were only hairless on part of their faces—like our ancestors.

This was unbelievable to such an extent, unexpected to such an extent, that I stood calmly—I can positively assert that I stood calmly—and looked on. Like a set of scales: once you have completely filled up one cup, you can put as much of anything into it and the arrow won't move anyway . . .

Suddenly I am alone: I-330 is not with me anymore. I don't know how she disappeared or where she has gone. There are only those satiny furs, shining in the sun around me. I grab someone by the hot, firm, jet-black shoulder: "Listen, for the Benefactor's sake— you haven't seen—where did she go? She was here, just now—just a second ago . . ."

Shaggy, stern eyebrows turned to me: "Sh, sh, sh! Quiet!" And it nodded shaggily over to the middle of the clearing, where the yellow, skull-like rock stood.

There she was, on top, above all the heads, above everyone. The sun was coming from that same direction right into my eyes and the whole of her—against the blue linen of the sky—was a sharp, coal-black silhouette on blue. Clouds were flying a little higher up, but it was as if the rock, not the clouds, but she herself on the rock with the crowd behind her in the clearing, were all inaudibly gliding, like a ship, and the light earth underfoot was floating away . . .

"Brothers . . ." It was her. "Brothers! You all know that there, in the city behind the Wall, they are building the Integral. And you know that the day has arrived when we will destroy this Wall— every wall—so that the green wind can blow from pole to pole— the whole Earth over. But the Integral is taking these walls up there, to the thousands of new Earths, to those that will whisper to you tonight with their fires through the black night leaves . . ."

Around the rock: waves, foam, wind . . . "Down with the Integral! Down!"

"No, brothers: not that. The Integral should be ours. On the day when it first casts off into the sky—we will be on it. Because the Builder of the Integral is here with us. He forsook the Wall and he came here with me, to be among us. All hail the Builder!"

In a blink, I am somewhere up high and underneath me are heads and heads, and gaping, screaming mouths, and arms pouring upward and then falling. This was exceptionally strange, intoxicating: I felt myself above everyone, I was myself, a separate thing, a world; I stopped being a component, as I had been, and I became the number one.

And then I was put down next to the rock itself: a creased body, happy and crumpled, as though released from a lover's clutches. The sun, a voice from above, and a smile from I-330. A golden-haired, herb-smelling woman, all satiny-gold, appears. In her hands is a cup, seemingly made of wood. She drinks from it with her red lips and gives it to me, and I drink greedily, with closed eyes, in order to quench the fire: I am drinking sweet, prickly, cold sparks.

And then the blood inside me, and the whole world, is going a thousand times faster; the light Earth is flying like a bit of fluff. And everything is lighter, simpler, clearer to me.

And now I see the familiar, enormous letters—MEPHI—on the rock, and for some reason this is just as it should be, this is the simple, sound thread, connecting everyone. I see the crude sketch of a winged youth with a transparent body (it was also on the rock, I think), and there is a blinding, red-hot coal in place of his heart ... And again, I understand this coal ... or rather, I feel it—just as I was feeling but not hearing each word (she is talking from above, on the rock). And I feel that everything is breathing together and everyone has somewhere to fly to, like those birds above the Wall that time ...

From behind, from the densely breathing thicket of bodies came a loud voice: "But all this is pure madness!"

And, it seems, I leapt onto the rock (yes, I think it was me). From there I could see the sun, the heads, and a green, toothed saw against the blue and I cried out: "Yes, yes, exactly! And we must all go crazy, it is essential that we all go crazy—as soon as possible! It is essential—I tell you!"

I-330 is next to me; her smile is two black lines from the edges of her mouth upward at an angle; and there is a piece of coal inside me, and it is, for an instant, light, almost painless, beautiful ...

After that, I'm left with only stray, embedded fragments:

A bird, slowly, lowly passing by. I see it is alive, like me. It turns its head to the right, to the left, like a person, and then screws its black round eyes into me.

Another fragment:

A spine of shining fur, the color of old elephant bones. A dark, transparent insect with tiny wings climbing along the spine and the spine quivers to drive the insect away, then quivers again . . .

And another:

The shadow of leaves is a weave, a lattice. In this shadow, people are lying around and munching on something that looks like the legendary food of the Ancients: long, yellow fruit and a piece of something dark. A woman puts one of these in my hand and I find it funny: I don't know if I can eat it.

One more:

A crowd, heads, feet, hands, mouths. Faces spring out for a second—and disappear, like popping bubbles. One second, transparent wing-ears flash past (but perhaps it just seemed that way to me).

I squeeze I-330's hand as hard as I can. She looks around: "What's wrong?"

"He is here . . . I thought I saw . . ."

"Who is he?"

"S . . . Here, just now—in the crowd . . ."

Coal-black, thin eyebrows, hitched up to the temples, a sharp triangle, a smile. And it isn't clear to me why she is smiling: how can she smile?

"You don't understand, I-330, you don't understand what it would mean if he or any of his people were here."

"How funny! As if it would occur to someone there, behind the Wall, that we are here. Remember, you yourself—did you ever think that this was possible? They're looking for us there—and let them! You are delirious."

She smiles lightly, joyfully, and I smile; the Earth, drunk, joyful and light, is floating . . .

KEYWORDS:

Both of Them. Entropy and Energy.
The Opaque Part of the Body.

Okay: if your world looks like the world of our distant ancestors, then imagine for yourself that one day you stumble upon a sixth or seventh part of the world—some sort of Atlantis in the ocean— and there you find far-fetched labyrinth-cities, people swooping through the air without the help of wings or aeros, and rocks you can lift up with a mere glance ... Basically, the sorts of things that wouldn't even enter your head, even if you were suffering from the dream-sickness. Well, that's how it was for me yesterday. Because, you must understand, not one of us has ever, since the end of the Two-Hundred-Year War, been behind the Wall—but I already told you that.

I know: my duty to you, unknown friends, is to recount the finest details of the strange and unknown world that was revealed to me yesterday. But at the moment I am in no state to return to this. Everything is new, new, new—a sort of downpour of events—and one of me is not enough to collect it all. I am stretching out the flaps of my unif and cupping my hands and yet whole bucketfuls still flow past me, and only drops end up on these pages ...

At first, I overheard loud voices behind my door and I recognized I-330's flexible, metallic voice. But there was another, almost as rigid as a wooden ruler—it was the voice of U. Then the door swung open with a crack and they both shot into my room. Just like that: they shot in.

I-330 put her hand on the back of my chair and smiled over her right shoulder at U, with all her teeth. I wouldn't like to stand in the way of that smile.

"Listen," I-330 said to me, "this woman seems to have made it her goal to protect you from me, as if you were a small child. Is this—with your permission?"

And then, the quivering gills: "Yes, he is a child. Yes! And that's why he doesn't see that you, with him, that all this is only so that . . . that all this is a farce. Yes! And it is my duty . . ."

For an instant, the broken, jagged line of my eyebrows was in the mirror. I leapt up and, straining to contain my other self with his trembling hairy fists, straining to shove each word out through my teeth, I screamed at her point-blank, right into her gills: "Th-thissss very second—get out! Get out!"

The gills swelled brick-redly, then sank, and grayed. She opened her mouth to say something and then, saying nothing—slammed it and left.

I threw myself at I-330: "I cannot forgive—I will never forgive myself for this. She dared to . . . to you? . . . You don't think that I think that . . . that she . . . This is all because she wants me to be registered to her, but I . . ."

"Fortunately she won't manage to be registered to you now. And if there are thousands like her, it doesn't matter. I know that you will believe me and not those thousands. Because, well, after yesterday's . . . I am beholden to you, just like you wanted. I am in your hands. At any moment, you could . . ."

"What, at any moment I could . . . what?" And then I understood. Blood was gushing into my ears and cheeks and I cried: "What are you talking about?! Never talk like that! You of all people should understand that that was the former me but now I'm . . ."

"Who knows who you are . . . A person is a novel: you don't know how it will end until the very last page. Otherwise, it wouldn't be worth reading to the very end . . ."

I-330 was stroking my head. Her face was not visible to me, but I could hear in her voice that she was looking far into the distance and her eyes had caught onto a cloud, floating inaudibly, slowly, who knows where to . . .

Suddenly she pushed me aside with her hand, firmly and tenderly.

"Listen: I came to tell you that these might be the last days before . . . Did you know? All auditoriums were shut down today."

"Shut down?"

"Yes. And I walked past and saw them in the auditorium buildings preparing something. There are tables and medics in white."

"But what does this mean?!"

"I don't know. For the meantime no one knows. And that's the worst of it. I just feel—they've turned on the current, the sparks are running, and if not today, then tomorrow . . . But perhaps they won't succeed."

A long time ago I had ceased understanding who "they" were and who "we" were. I'm not sure if I want "them" to succeed or not. Only one thing is clear to me: I-330 is now walking along a fine line, and any second now . . .

"But this is madness," I say. "You against the One State. It is the same as stopping up the muzzle of a gun with your hand thinking it will hold back the gunshot. This is pure madness!"

A smile.

" 'Everyone must go crazy—as soon as possible.' Someone else said that yesterday. Do you remember that? Over there . . ."

Yes, it is in my records. And, consequently, it was, in fact, real. I say nothing and look at her face where the dark cross is particularly distinct.

"I-330, my sweet . . . while it isn't too late . . . Do you want me to give up everything, forget everything and we can go off together, behind the Wall, to be with those people . . . whoever they are?"

She shook her head. Through the dark windows of her eyes, there, inside her, I saw that the wood-fire was blazing, the sparks and tongues of the fire ascended and there were piled heaps of dry, pitch-black wood. And it was clear to me: it was too late, my words were already redundant . . .

She stood up, about to leave. If these are the final days, if they are the final minutes . . . I grabbed her by the hand.

"No! Just a little longer—for the Benef . . . for the sake of . . ."

She slowly lifted my hand up to the light—the hairy hand, which I so hated. I wanted to pull it away, but she held it firmly.

"Your hand . . . See, you don't know—and few know this—that various women from here, from our city, have occasionally loved those on the other side. You probably have a few drops of sunny forest blood in you. Maybe that's why I also . . . you . . ."

A pause. How strange: my heart is racing so wildly from this pause, from this emptiness, from this nothingness. And I cry: "Aha! You aren't leaving yet! You aren't leaving—until you have told me about them—because you love . . . them—but I don't even know who they are or where they come from. Who are they? The half we lost? The H_2 and the O, which make up H_2O—streams, seas, waterfalls, waves, and storms all require that these halves are joined together . . ."

I distinctly remember each of her movements. I remember how she picked up a glass triangle from my table and the whole time I was speaking she pressed its sharp rib into her cheek. A red mark appeared on her cheek, then ripened to a pinkness and disappeared. And, amazingly, I cannot recall her words—especially the beginning—I only recall various separate images and colors.

I know the beginning was about the Two-Hundred-Year War. And then: red on green grass, on dark mud, on the blue of snow and red puddles that never dried up. Then yellow grass, burnt by the sun and naked, yellow, disheveled people and disheveled dogs and, just nearby, the swollen cadavers of dogs, or maybe of people . . . This, of course, was behind the walls: because the city was already conquered, and our modern petroleum food was available there.

And from sky to ground there were black, heavy drapes and the drapes were swaying: slow pillars of smoke, above the forests, above the villages. A dull wail: a black, infinite procession was being driven into the city—to be saved by force and taught happiness.

"You knew almost all this?"

"Yes, almost."

"But what you didn't know, and few do, is that a small group of them survived and stayed to live there, behind the walls. Naked, they went off into the woods. They learned from the trees, the beasts, the birds, the flowers, the sun. They grew hair all over, but under their fur, they harbored hot, red blood. It's worse for you: you are overgrown with numbers, numbers crawl all over you, like lice. You all need to be stripped of everything and be driven out naked into the forest. Let it teach you to shiver from fear, from joy, from mad rage, from the cold and to pray to the fire. And we, MEPHI, we want . . ."

"No, wait—'MEPHI'? What are the 'MEPHI'?"

"MEPHI? That is the ancient name for he who . . . You remember: there, on the rock, the image of the youth . . . ? Or, no: I'd better explain this to you in your own language, you'll get it faster . . . So: there are two forces in the world, entropy and energy. One tends toward blissful peace, to happy equilibrium, and the other toward destruction of equilibrium, toward torturously constant movement. Entropy: our, or more accurately, your ancestors, the Christians, worshipped it like it was God. But we, anti-Christians, we . . ."

And in that moment, there was a barely audible whisper of a knock on the door and into the room jumped that same flat-face with the forehead pulled down over his eyes—the one who had brought me notes from I-330 more than once.

He ran right up to us and stopped, breathing heavily through his nose—like it was an air pump—and he couldn't get out a word: he must have run with all his might.

"Well? What happened?" I-330 grabbed him by the arm.

"They are coming—here . . ." the air pump finally panted. "The Guardians . . . with that man. You know, what's his . . . the sort of hunchbacked one . . ."

"S?"

"Yes, yes! They are not far off—in the building. They'll be here in a second. Quick, quick!"

"Nonsense! There's still time . . ." She laughed with sparks and joyful flame-tongues in her eyes.

This was either ridiculous, reckless bravery or this was something I had yet to understand.

"I-330, for the sake of the Benefactor! Don't you see—this is . . ."

"For the sake of the Benefactor?" A sharp triangle, a smile.

"Well, for my sake, then . . . I beg you."

"Ah, but I still have one matter to discuss with you . . . Well, fine, then—tomorrow . . ."

She nodded cheerfully (yes: cheerfully) at me; the other man also nodded, thrusting himself forward from under his overhanging forehead for a second. And I was alone.

Quickly: to my desk. I unfurled my notes and picked up my pen so that they would find me hard at work for the good of the One State. And suddenly every hair on my head was alive, separate, and stirring: what if they pick up one of these pages and read some of these recent records?

I was sitting at the desk, not moving, and I saw how the walls were shaking, how the pen in my hand was shaking, the letters were fluttering, merging . . .

Should I hide them? But where? Everything is glass. Should I light it on fire? But they would see me from the corridor and the neighboring rooms. And I couldn't, anyway; I wouldn't have the strength to destroy this excruciating and possibly most precious piece of myself.

In the distance, down the corridor: voices and footsteps. I just managed to grab a bunch of pages and slip them under myself. Now I was rooted here to the chair, which was oscillating with its every atom, and, under my feet, the decks were pitching up and down . . .

Scrunched up into a little ball, huddled under the overhang of my own forehead, somehow, from under my brow, I stole a look: they were walking from room to room, beginning on the right-hand end of the corridor, and coming closer and closer. Some ciphers were sitting, frozen stiff, like me; others were leaping up to greet them and widely flinging open their doors—those lucky ciphers! If only I could also . . .

"The Benefactor is the most enhanced disinfectant, a necessity for humankind, and it has the effect of preventing peristalsis in the organism of the One State . . ." I dispensed this complete nonsense with my lurching pen and leaned over my desk lower and lower while a crazy blacksmith hammered in my head. And with my back I heard the doorknob rattle. Wind fanned in and the chair underneath me began to dance . . .

Only then did I summon the strength to tear myself away from my page and turn toward those who had entered the room. (It is so hard to perform farce . . . oh, who was it today that said something about farces?) S was first into the room: sinister, silent, his eyes rapidly drilling wells into me, into my chair, into the shuddering pages under my hand. Then, a second later: a few familiar, everyday faces at my threshold. One stood out from the rest with her swelling, pink-brown gills . . .

I recalled everything that had happened in this room half an hour ago and it was clear to me what she would now do . . . My whole being was beating and pulsing in the (fortunately, opaque) part of my body under which I had hidden my records.

U walked up to him, to S, carefully tugged on his sleeve, and softly said: "This is D-503, the Builder of the Integral. You've heard of him, perhaps? He is always like this, at his desk . . . Never sparing himself a moment."

. . . I never what? What a miraculous, astounding woman.

S started to slide toward me, leaned over my shoulder, over the table. I shielded what I had written with my elbow, but he yelled severely: "I request that you show me what you have there immediately!"

I gave him the piece of paper, ablaze with shame. He read it through and I saw how a smile crawled from his eye and scampered down his face and, slightly stirring its little tail, settled down somewhere into the right corner of his mouth . . .

"Somewhat ambiguous, but still . . . Okay then, you can continue. We won't bother you any longer."

He began to shuffle—as if across water—to the door, and with each of his steps, my arms, legs, and fingers gradually returned to me, my soul equally distributed itself throughout my body again, and I breathed . . .

The last thing: U held back in my room, walked up to me, and leaned to my ear with a whisper: "You're lucky that I . . ."

Incomprehensible: what did she mean by that?

In the evening, later, I found out: they had taken three ciphers off with them. However, as with all occurrences, no one would talk about it aloud (the instructive influence of our invisible, ever-present Guardians). Conversations, for the most part, concerned the rapid fall of the barometer and the change of weather.

KEYWORDS:

Threads on a Face. Sprouts. Antinatural Compression.

It's strange: the barometric pressure is falling, but there is still no wind, just silence. There is a storm up above that has already begun but it is still inaudible to us. Clouds rush along at full steam. There are only a few of them so far: separate, jagged fragments. It is as if some city up above has been overthrown and there are pieces of wall and tower flying down, growing bigger before your eyes with horrifying speed, drawing ever closer. But there are days to go—days of flying through pale-blue infinity—before they crash down to the ground, to us, down here.

It is silent down here. Fine, mysterious, almost invisible threads in the air. They are brought here each autumn from that other place, behind the Wall. They float along slowly and then you suddenly feel something foreign and invisible on your face. You want to wave it away but no, you can't, there isn't any way of getting rid of it . . .

You feel many more of these threads if you walk near the Green Wall as I did this morning. I-330 indicated that she wanted to see me at the Ancient House, in that "apartment" of ours. [I could already make out, from afar, the opaque and red*] mass of the Ancient House when I heard someone's small footsteps and frequent breathing behind me. I looked around and saw O, who had chased up to me.

She seemed altogether special somehow, consummately and firmly round. Her arms, the cups of her breasts, and her whole body, which were all so familiar to me, had become round and stretched her unif. The fine material would split open at any moment—into the sun, into the light. An image comes to me: in springtime over there, in the green thickets, new sprouts fight their way through the earth just as stubbornly—to yield branches and leaves and to blossom as quick as they can.

She said nothing for several seconds, her blues shining into my face.

"I saw you then, on the Day of the One Vote."

"I saw you, too . . ." And just then I recalled how she stood below me, in the narrow thoroughfare, pressing against the wall, and covering her stomach with her hands. I looked, not meaning to, at the round stomach under her unif.

It was obvious that she noticed this as she stood all roundly pink with her pink smile: "I am so happy—so happy . . . I am full—you see—full to the brim. These days I walk around and hear nothing that goes on around me. I just listen to my insides, inside myself . . ."

I said nothing. There was something foreign on my face and it was bothering me—I couldn't free myself of it in any way. And suddenly, unexpectedly, her blues still shining, she grabbed my hand and I felt her lips on my hand . . . It was the first time in my life I had experienced it. It was some kind of ancient caress that had been unknown to me until this moment, and the shame and pain it caused was such that I (perhaps, even roughly) snatched my hand away.

"Listen—you've gone out of your mind! And so much so that in

---

*This fragment is missing from the most reliable Russian manuscript of *We* in existence. A very good translation of *We*, completed by B. Cahvet Duhmal in 1929 and given the title *Nous Autres*, has it as *"J'apercevais déjà de loin la masse opaque et rouge,"* from which this English translation was derived.—*trans.*

general you ... What are you so happy about? Could you possibly have forgotten about what's in store for you? It may not be right away but in a month, in two months ..."

She was extinguished; all her circles caved in, buckled. And inside me, in my heart, was an unpleasant, pain-inducing compression, associated with the feeling of pity. (The heart is nothing other than an ideal pump. It sucks liquid through—compressions and contractions are utterly absurd in the technical sense—and so it is clear that this "love," "pity," and the rest, which are said to bring about these compressions, are essentially absurd, unnatural, and sickly too.)

Silence. The cloudy green glass of the Wall was on the left. The dark-red mass was ahead. And these two colors, appearing together, their equal action and reaction, gave me what seemed to me to be a brilliant idea.

"Wait! I know how to save you. I will deliver you from this business of seeing your own child and then dying. You will be able to feed it—you understand—you will watch it grow in your arms and become round and ripen like fruit."

She started to shake all over and clutched at me.

"You remember that woman ... that day, a while ago, on our walk? Well, see, she is here, now, at the Ancient House. Let's go see her and I will make sure to arrange it all immediately."

I could already picture the two of us leading her along the corridors—and then there she'd be, among the flowers, the grasses, the leaves ... But she stepped backward, away from me, and the little pink horns of her half-moon trembled and curved downward.

"You mean—*that* woman?" she said.

"Well, I mean ..." I became embarrassed for some reason. "Well, yes: *that* woman."

"And you want me to go to her—so that I can ask her—so that I ... Don't you dare mention this again!"

Hunching over, she quickly walked off. Then it was as if she remembered something. She turned around and screamed: "And so what if I die?! It's none of your business—isn't it all the same to you?"

Silence. Pieces of blue wall and tower are falling from above and growing bigger before my eyes with horrifying speed—but they have yet hours and, perhaps, days to go, flying through infinity. Invisible threads are slowly floating around and settling on my face and, try as I might, I can't shake them off, I can't get rid of them.

I walk slowly to the Ancient House. With an absurd, torturous compression in my heart . . .

KEYWORDS:

The Final Number. Galileo's Mistake.
Wouldn't It Be Better?

Here is my conversation with I-330 yesterday in the Ancient House (amid the multicolored noise that stifles the logical progress of thought: the red, the green, the bronze-yellow, the white, the orange colors . . . All the while, under the smile of the snub-nosed ancient poet, frozen in marble).

I am reproducing this conversation letter for letter because it seems to me that it has enormous, critical meaning for the fate of the One State and more: for the fate of the universe. And also because here, you, my unknown readers, may find some justification for my . . .

I-330, immediately, without any preparation, dumped everything on me: "I know that the Integral's first test flight is the day after tomorrow. On that day—we will take it into our own hands."

"What? The day after tomorrow?"

"Yes. Sit down, stay calm. We can't afford to lose a minute. Among the hundreds who were taken at random by the Guardians yesterday, there were twelve MEPHI. And if we let two or three days go by then they will be killed."

I said nothing.

"They will be sending electrical engineers, mechanics, doctors, and meteorologists to you to observe the progress of the test. And on the dot of twelve—remember that—when they ring the dinner bell and everyone goes through to the cafeteria, we will stay behind in the corridor, lock everyone in the cafeteria—and the Integral is ours . . . You understand that this is necessary—at all costs. The Integral will be a weapon in our hands, which will help everything immediately, quickly, painlessly . . . Their aeros . . . ha! They will simply be an insignificant swarm of midges against a hawk. And then: if it is unavoidable, we might have to direct the barrels of the motors downward and they will have only one thing left to do . . ."

I leapt up.

"This is pointless! This is ridiculous! Isn't it clear to you yet: you are starting what is called—a revolution!"

"Yes, a revolution! Why is it ridiculous?"

"Ridiculous—because revolutions aren't possible. Because our—I am talking, not you—our revolution was the last. And there cannot be any more revolutions . . . Everyone knows that . . ."

A mocking, sharp triangle of eyebrows: "My sweet, you are a mathematician. More than that, you are a philosopher of mathematics. So then, tell me: what is the final number?"

"What is that? I . . . I don't understand: which final number?"

"Well—the last, the highest, the biggest . . ."

"But, I-330—that is ridiculous. The number of numbers is infinite; which final one do you want?"

"Well, which final revolution do you want then? There isn't a final one. Revolutions are infinite. Final things are for children because infinity scares children and it is important that children sleep peacefully at night . . ."

"But what is the point—whatever is the point in all this—for the Benefactor's sake? What can the point be if everyone is already happy?"

"Let's suppose . . . Well, okay then, say you're right. Then what comes next?"

"How funny. A perfectly childish question. Tell a child something—explain it completely, to the very end, and they will always ask, without fail: What happens next? Why?"

"Children are the only brave philosophers. And brave philosophers are, inevitably, children. And that's just it—we must always think like children with their what-happens-nexts."

"Nothing happens next! Period. Throughout the universe, all over, uniformly distributed . . ."

"Aha! Uniform, all over! That's exactly it—entropy, psychological entropy. To you, to a mathematician, isn't it clear that it's the differences—the differences—between temperatures, it's in thermal contrast that life lies. And if everywhere, throughout the whole universe, there are bodies of equal warmness or equal coldness . . . You have to bang them together—to create fire, explosion, inferno. And that's what we are doing—banging things together."

"But, I-330, come on, don't you see? Our ancestors did exactly that at the time of the Two-Hundred-Year War . . ."

"Oh, and they were right—they were a thousand times right. They made only one mistake. Afterward they believed that they were the final number—which doesn't exist in the natural world, it just doesn't. Their mistake was the mistake of Galileo: he was right that the Earth moves around the sun, but he didn't know that the whole solar system itself moves around some other center. He didn't know that the real, not the relative, orbit of the Earth is not just a naïve circle . . ."

"And you—the MEPHI?"

"But we—we know, meanwhile, that there is no final number. Though we might forget it too. Yes—it's highly probable that we will forget it when we grow older—and everyone inevitably grows older. And then, unavoidably, down we will go like autumn leaves from a tree . . . just like all of you, the day after tomorrow when . . . No, no, my sweet—not you yourself. You are on our side, of course, you are on our side!"

She was blazing, whirling, glittering, and I had never yet seen her like this. She hugged me with her whole self and I disappeared . . .

Finally, looking me solidly and firmly in the eyes: "So remember—twelve."

And I said: "Yes, I will remember."

She left. I was alone in the midst of the tempestuous, discordant uproar of blue, red, green, bronze-yellow, orange . . .

Yes, at 12:00 . . . Suddenly, I had a ridiculous sensation that something foreign had settled onto my face, something that I couldn't get rid of however I tried. Suddenly it was yesterday morning again and U was screaming those words into I-330's face . . . Why? What is this absurdity?

I rushed to get outside—back to my room, back as quick as I could . . .

Somewhere behind me I heard a piercing squeak above the Wall. And ahead, against the setting sun, everything was made of crimson, crystallized fire: the orbs of the cupolas, the enormous, blazing cube-buildings, and the spire of the Accumulator Tower, frozen lightning in the sky. And to all this—all this impeccable, geometrical beauty—I myself, with my own hands, am supposed to . . . Isn't there a way out or another way?

I went past some auditorium (I don't remember its number). Inside, benches were stacked in heaps; in the middle, there were tables covered with sheets of snow-white glass; and there was a spot of pink, sunny blood on the white. Some unknown and very terrifying tomorrow is hidden in all this. It just goes against nature for a thinking and seeing being to live among these irregularities and unknown X's. It is as if someone blindfolds you and then makes you walk around like that and you feel your way around, stumbling, and you know that there is an edge somewhere very nearby and that it would only take one step for the only thing left of you to be a flattened, mangled piece of meat. Isn't that just about the same thing I'm going through?

. . . But what if you didn't wait for it to happen—but jumped headfirst over the edge? Wouldn't that be the single most correct action, immediately untangling everything?

KEYWORDS:

The Great Operation. I Forgave Everything.
The Crashing of Trains.

We are saved! At the very last moment, when it seemed that there was nothing left to latch on to, when it seemed that everything was over . . .

Okay: it's as if you had climbed up the steps to the terrible Machine of the Benefactor and, with a heavy clang, you were covered by the bell-glass, and for the last time in your life, as quick as you can, you swallow the blue sky with your eyes . . .

And suddenly: it was all only a dream. The sun is pink and happy. And the wall—what a joy to stroke the cold wall with your hand! And the pillow—you could revel endlessly in the depression that your head makes on the white pillow . . .

That is approximately what I experienced when I read the *State Gazette* this morning. It was all a bad dream and it is over now. How fainthearted I am, how inconstant, that I was already considering self-inflicted death. Now I'm embarrassed to read through the last few lines I wrote yesterday. But it doesn't matter: just let them remain as a memory of the unbelievable, of that which could have been and that which will never be . . . yes, never!

On the first page of the *State Gazette* the words were shining:

BE JOYFUL!

FOR HENCEFORTH YOU ARE PERFECT! UNTIL THIS DAY, YOUR OWN OFFSPRING—MECHANISMS—WERE MORE PERFECT THAN YOURSELVES.

IN WHAT WAY?

EVERY SPARK IN A DYNAMO IS THE SPARK OF THE PUREST REASON; EVERY MOTION OF THE PISTON IS AN IMMACULATE SYLLOGISM. BUT DOES THAT SAME INFALLIBLE REASON NOT EXIST IN YOU?

THE PHILOSOPHY OF CRANES, PRESSES, AND PUMPS IS COMPLETE AND CLEAR, LIKE A COMPASS-DRAWN CIRCLE. BUT ISN'T YOUR PHILOSOPHY UP TO THE STANDARD OF A COMPASS?

THE BEAUTY OF A MECHANISM IS IN ITS STEADFAST, PRECISE, AND PENDULUM-LIKE RHYTHM. BUT THEN YOU, WHO HAVE BEEN NURTURED BY TAYLORIST SYSTEMS FROM CHILDHOOD, HAVEN'T YOU GROWN UP TO BE PENDULUM-PRECISE?

WITH ONE EXCEPTION: MECHANISMS DON'T HAVE IMAGINATIONS.

HAVE YOU EVER SEEN AN INANELY DREAMING AND DISTANT SMILE BREAK ACROSS THE PHYSIOGNOMY OF A PUMP CYLINDER WHILE IT WAS AT WORK? HAVE YOU EVER HEARD OF A CRANE, IN THE NIGHT-TIME, IN THE HOURS ALLOCATED FOR REPOSE, TURNING OVER IN AGITATION AND SIGHING?

NO!

BUT YOU—BLUSH AS YOU WILL!—THE GUARDIANS SEE YOU AND YOUR SMILES AND SIGHS WITH INCREASING FREQUENCY. AND—LOWER YOUR EYES!—THE HISTORIANS OF THE ONE STATE HAVE TENDERED THEIR RESIGNATIONS IN ORDER NOT TO HAVE TO RECORD SUCH SHAMEFUL EVENTS.

BUT IT IS NOT YOUR FAULT: YOU ARE SICK. THE NAME OF THIS SICKNESS:

IMAGINATION.

THIS IS THE WORM THAT GNAWS BLACK WRINKLES ONTO YOUR FOREHEAD. THIS IS THE FEVER THAT CHASES YOU, AND YOU RUN OFF INTO THE DISTANCE EVEN THOUGH THIS "DISTANCE" BEGINS WHERE HAPPINESS ENDS. IT IS THE LAST BARRICADE ON THE PATH TO HAPPINESS.

BUT BE GLAD: IT HAS BEEN DETONATED ALREADY.

THE PATH IS CLEAR.

THE MOST RECENT DISCOVERY OF STATE SCIENCE IS THE LOCATION OF THE IMAGINATION: THE PATHETIC CEREBRAL NODULE IN THE REGION OF THE PONS VAROLII. CAUTERIZE THIS NODULE WITH X-RAYS THREE TIMES AND YOU ARE HEALED OF YOUR IMAGINATION.

FOREVER.

YOU WILL BE PERFECT, YOU WILL BE MACHINE-EQUAL. THE PATH TO ONE-HUNDRED-PERCENT HAPPINESS IS CLEAR. HURRY, ALL OF YOU—YOUNG AND OLD—HURRY TO UNDERGO THE GREAT OPERATION. HURRY TO THE AUDITORIUMS, WHERE THEY ARE PERFORMING THE GREAT OPERATION. ALL HAIL THE GREAT OPERATION! ALL HAIL THE ONE STATE! ALL HAIL THE BENEFACTOR!

. . . You, if you could have read this for yourself, not here in my records, which seem like an ancient, whimsical novel . . . If you could have held in your hands, like I held in mine, this shaking newspaper page still smelling of ink . . . If you could have known, like I did, that all this is a very real actuality, if not today's then tomorrow's . . . Wouldn't you be feeling the exact same thing as I am now? Wouldn't your head be spinning like mine is now? Wouldn't these same terrifying, sweet, icy needles be running through your spine and arms? Wouldn't you feel like a giant, like Atlas—and that if you straightened yourself up you would hit your head on the glass ceiling?

I grabbed the telephone receiver: "I-330 . . . Yes, that's right: I-330," and then, chokingly, I yelled: "You're at home, right? Have you read . . . you're reading it now? Now, this really is, this really is . . . This is astounding!"

"Yes ..." A long, dark silence. The receiver was just audibly humming, thinking about something ... "I must see you today without fail. Yes, at my place after 16:00. Without fail."

Sweet! What a dear sweetheart! "Without fail." I could feel: I was smiling and there was no way to stop myself, and I would carry this smile through the streets like a streetlamp, high overhead ...

There, from outside, the wind blew at me. It twisted, whistled, lashed. But it only increased my joy. Wail and howl away—it doesn't matter. You cannot bring down these walls now. And so what if cast-iron, flying clouds are coming down overhead—let them! You won't darken the sun. We, Joshuas, sons of Nun, have affixed its chain to the zenith forever.

A dense bunch of Joshuas stood on the corner, their foreheads adhered to the glass of a wall. Inside there was a person lying on a blinding-white table. Under a white sheet, two bare soles set up a visible yellow angle. White medics bent over toward his head and a white arm extended a syringe full of something.

"And you—why don't you go in?" I asked of no one in particular or, perhaps, of everyone.

"Well, what about you?" Someone's sphere turned to me.

"I will ... later. First I have to ..."

I walked off, somewhat embarrassed. I actually needed to see her, I-330. But I couldn't answer why it had to be "first."

The hangar. The Integral glimmered, sparkled with pale-bluish iciness. In the engine room, the dynamo was buzzing affectionately, repeating one and the same word, over and over endlessly—a familiar sort of word, a word I probably use. I bent over and stroked the long, cold pipe of the engine. Sweet ... what a darling sweetheart. Tomorrow you will come alive, tomorrow, for the first time in your life, you will shake with the fiery, burning eruption in your womb ...

How would I have looked at this powerful glass monster if everything had stayed like it was yesterday? If I had thought that tomorrow at 12:00 I would betray it ... yes, betray it ...

A cautious tap on my elbow, from behind. I turned around: it was the flat platter face of the Second Builder.

"You already know," he said.

"What? The Operation? Yes, it's something, isn't it? How—everything, everything is suddenly . . ."

"No, no, not that. The test flight has been changed to the day after tomorrow. All because of this Operation . . . We rushed and strived, all for nothing . . ."

"All because of the Operation . . ." Funny, limited person. He can't see anything past his own plate. If only he knew that if it wasn't for the Operation, then tomorrow, at 12:00, he would be stuck in the frame of the glass cage, thrashing around and climbing the walls . . .

My room. 15:30. I walk in and see U. She is sitting at my desk—bony, straight, and hard—having established her right cheek in her palm. She must have been waiting for a long time because when she jumped up to greet me, there were five little dents on her cheek from her fingers and thumb.

For a second, that unfortunate morning reappeared to me: just there, next to the table, she stood behind I-330, infuriated . . . But the second passed and was now clouded by today's sun. The same thing happens sometimes when, on a bright day, you walk into your room and absentmindedly flick the light switch. The light comes on but it's as if it wasn't even there—so silly, pathetic, redundant . . .

Extending my hand to her without thinking, I forgave everything. She grabbed both my hands, squeezing them tightly, prickling them, and, quivering anxiously, with cheeks hanging like ancient jewelry, she said: "I've been waiting . . . I only need a minute . . . I just wanted to say how happy I am, how glad I am for you! You see, tomorrow or the day after tomorrow, you will be totally healthy, you will be born again . . ."

I saw some paper on the table: the last two pages of yesterday's records. They lay where I had left them that evening. If she had seen what I had written there . . . But, it doesn't matter anyway. No, it is all history, now so distant that it's funny, like looking through binoculars backwards . . .

"Yes," I said, "and you know, as I walked along the avenue just now, there was a person in front of me, and he was casting a shadow onto the street. And, you see, the shadow was gleaming. And, I think, well actually, I'm sure, that tomorrow there will be absolutely no shadows, not one person will have one, not one thing will have one, and the sun will go through everything..."

She, tenderly and sternly: "What an imagination! I wouldn't even let the schoolchildren talk like that..."

And she went on about the children and how she drove them to the Operation immediately, in a herd, and about how they had had to bind them up, and about the fact that "you have to be cruel, yes, cruel, to be kind," and that she, it seems, is finally deciding whether to...

She arranged the gray-light-blue fabric between her knees and stopped talking, then quickly smothered me all over with her smile and left.

And, thankfully, the sun had not yet stopped today. The sun was still running, and it was already 16:00. I knock on her door—and my heart knocks...

"Enter!"

I go straight to the floor, by her chair, hugging her knees, my head thrown back, looking into her eyes—alternately, at one and then at the other—and seeing myself in each of them, in miraculous captivity...

On the other side of the wall, there was a storm, there were clouds hardening into cast-iron: let them! Crowded, tempestuous words were brimming over the edges of my head and I was flying out loud together with the sun, off somewhere... Well, now we know where I'd be flying. And there are planets following me: flame-spurting planets, densely populated with fiery singing flowers; and mute, blue planets, where rational rocks are united into organized societies—they are planets like our Earth that have reached the summit of absolute, one-hundred-percent happiness...

And suddenly, from above me: "You don't think that this summit of happiness is really just that—the uniting of rocks into an organized society?"

And a triangle, sharper and sharper, darker and darker: "...And as for happiness... Really? After all, desire is torturous, isn't it? And so it's clear that happiness happens when there are no more desires, not one ... What a mistake, what ridiculous prejudice, that until now, we have been putting a plus sign in front of absolute happiness. It is, of course, a minus sign—a divine minus."

I remember muttering, distractedly: "Absolute minus. 273 degrees ..."

"Minus 273—exactly. Rather cool, but doesn't this prove that we are indeed at the summit?"

Like before, long ago, she was somehow speaking for me, using me, developing my thoughts to their full extent. But there was something terrible in this—I couldn't stand it—and with strain, I dragged a "no" out of myself.

"No," I said. "You ... are joking ..."

She burst out laughing, loudly—too loudly. Quickly, in a second, she laughed herself up to some sort of edge—and stepped back, stepped down. A pause.

She stood up. Put her hand on my shoulder. Looked slowly at me for a long time. Then drew me to herself and then there was nothing left at all: only her sharp, hot lips.

"Good-bye!"

This was from far away, from above, and it reached me slowly, maybe, one or two minutes later.

"What do you mean, 'Good-bye'?"

"Well, you're sick, you committed crimes because of me—and it was torturous for you, wasn't it? And now you can have the Operation—and you can cure yourself of me. So this—this is good-bye."

"No," I cried.

A mercilessly sharp black triangle on the white: "What? You don't want happiness?"

My head broke apart; two logical trains had collided, piling on top of each other, crushing, splitting ...

"Well, what then? I'm waiting. Choose: the Operation and its hundred-percent happiness or ..."

"I can't go on without you, I can't, I must not be without you," I said, or only thought it—I don't know which—but I-330 heard it.

"Yes, I know," she answered. And then, her hands still holding me by the shoulders, and her eyes not letting mine go: "In that case—until tomorrow. Tomorrow at twelve. Remember?"

"No. It's put off for one more day . . . The day after tomorrow . . ."

"Even better for us. At twelve. The day after tomorrow . . ."

I walked alone along the dusky street. The wind twirled, carrying and chasing me like a piece of paper. Fragments of cast-iron sky were flying down, flying down through infinity—but they have a day or two to go . . . Oncoming unifs grazed against me but I walked alone. It was clear to me: everyone was saved, but there was to be no saving me, I don't want saving . . .

KEYWORDS:

I Don't Believe. Tractors. A Human Sliver.

Do you believe that you will die? Yes, people are mortal and if I am a person, then, of course ... But that's not what I mean. I know that you know this. I am asking: has it ever happened that you have believed in your death, believed in it totally, believed in it, not with your mind, but with your body, feeling that one day the fingers that are holding this very page will be yellow, icy ... ?

No: of course, you don't believe in it—and that is why, up to now, you haven't jumped from the tenth floor into the street, that is why up to now you have been eating, turning pages, shaving, smiling, writing ...

That's just what—yes, that is just exactly what I am going through today. I know that the small, black arrow down there on my timepiece is crawling toward midnight and that it will rise upwards again to cross some final line and then that improbable day will begin. I know this, but I still somehow don't believe it—or, maybe it's just that these twenty-four hours are passing like twenty-four years. And that is why I can still do things, rush to things, answer questions, and climb up the gangway to the Integral. I can still feel it rock slightly on the water, and I can understand that you have to hold on to the handrail (the glass is cold under your hand). I see the transparent, living cranes bending their swanlike necks, stretching out their beaks, thoughtfully and tenderly feeding the Integral with scary explosive food for its engine. And I can see clearly the blue, wind-swollen water veins and knots in the river below. But meanwhile: all this was very separate from me—it was foreign and flat, like a diagram on a leaf of paper. And strangely, the flat diagram of the face of the Second Builder suddenly speaks to me: "So tell me: how much fuel will the engine need? If you count three . . . well, three and a half hours . . ."

In front of me—in projection on the diagram—is the number fifteen on the logarithmic dial of the calculator in my hand.

"Fifteen tons. But we'd better take . . . yes, let's take a hundred . . ."

This was because I knew, you see, that tomorrow . . .

And I can see in the corner of my eye that my hand holding the dial is just noticeably shaking.

"A hundred? Why such a large mass? That's, what, enough for a week? Why—much more than a week!"

"Well, what if . . . who knows . . ."

I know . . .

The wind whistles through air that is tightly packed to its very top with something invisible. It is hard for me to breathe, hard to walk, and it's hard for the arrow on the clock of the Accumulator Tower over there, at the end of the avenue, which is slowly crawling along without stopping for even a second. The Tower's dull blue spire is in the clouds, howling obliviously as it sucks in electricity. The pipes of the Music Factory are howling.

As usual, we are in rows, in fours. But the rows are somehow flimsy—maybe it's the wind that is making them waver and bend more and more. Then on the corner we bumped into something and flooded back into a solid, stiffened, packed, quickly breathing wad—and everyone immediately grew long goosenecks.

"Look! No, look—over there, quick!"

"Them! It's them!"

". . . But I—never—no way! No way—I'd rather put my head in the Machine . . ."

"Quiet! You crazy . . ."

On the corner, the door of an auditorium was wide open and a slow, bulky column of about fifty people was coming through it. But "people" is not quite right: there were no feet to them but some kind of heavy forged wheel being turned by an invisible axle. They weren't people but sort of person-looking tractors. Above their heads, flapping in the wind was a white flag, with a golden sun sewn onto it, and in its rays was the inscription: "We are the first! We have been Operated! Everyone follow us!"

Slowly, irrepressibly, they plowed through the crowd—and it was clear that if there had been a wall, a tree, or a building in their path they wouldn't have stopped and would have plowed through the wall, the tree, the building. Now they had reached the middle of the avenue. Screwed together at the arm, they stretched out in a chain, their faces toward us. And we, a tense wad, bristling with heads, are waiting. Goosenecks stretched out. Clouds. The wind is whistling.

Suddenly the wings of the chain, from the right and from the left, quickly bend inward and come at us—faster and faster, like a heavy machine going downhill—and squeeze around us in a ring . . . toward the gaping doors, through the doors, inside . . .

Someone's piercing cry: "They're driving us in! Run!"

And everyone darts. Just by the wall there is still a narrow gap in the living ring and everyone heads toward it, heads pointed forward, heads momentarily as sharp as wedges, with sharp elbows, ribs, shoulders, sides. Like a spurt of water forced out of a fire hose, they spray out in a fan of scattered stamping feet, swinging arms, and unifs. Out of nowhere, for an instant, a vision: a twice-bent, S-like body with transparent wing-ears. And then he is gone, has vanished through the earth, and I am alone among ticking second hands and legs on the run . . .

I was pausing for breath in some entranceway with my back firmly to the doors and just then, toward me, like the wind, came a tiny human sliver.

"I was . . . I was behind you the whole time . . . I don't want—you understand—I don't want to . . . I agree to . . ."

Tiny round hands and round blue eyes were at my sleeve: it was her, it was O. And then she somehow slipped down the wall and settled onto the ground. She huddled in a little ball down there on the cold steps, and I stood above her, stroking her head, her face (my hands became wet). I felt: I was very big and she was completely small—a small part of me myself. It was totally different from what I feel toward I-330 and I now imagine that it must be a similar feeling to that of the Ancients toward their private children.

Below, through hands covering her face, a barely audible: "Every night, I . . . I can't—if they cure me . . . Every night I—alone in the dark, I think about the baby—what it'll be like, what I'll be like with it . . . I will have nothing to live for—you understand? And you must—you must . . ."

A ridiculous feeling but I was sure of it: yes, I must help. Ridiculous, because it was a duty and yet another crime. Ridiculous, because a white duty cannot, at the same time, be a black duty and a crime—they can't coincide. Life is either blackless or whiteless and its color only depends on a basic, logical premise. And if the premise is that I gave her a child illegally . . .

"Well, good—don't cry, don't cry . . ." I say. "You understand: I must lead you to I-330—like I suggested before—so that she can . . ."

"Yes." (Quietly, not taking her hands away from her face.)

I helped her to stand up. And, saying nothing, each thinking about our own things or, maybe, about the exact same thing, we went along the darkening street, among mute, leaden buildings, through the taut, whipping branches of the wind . . .

At some transparent, tense point, through the whistle of the wind, I heard familiar puddle-squelching footsteps behind me. At the crossroads, I looked around: among the over-turned, rushing clouds reflected in the dim glass of the street, I saw an S. At that moment my arms became extraneous and were swinging out of time, and I am loudly telling O that tomorrow . . . yes, tomorrow is the first flight of the Integral and it will be completely unprecedented, miraculous, and awe-inspiring.

O is dumbfounded and looks at me roundly, bluely, looks at my loudly, senselessly swinging arms. But I don't let her say a word—I talk and talk. But inside, separately—only audible to myself—there were thoughts, feverishly buzzing and clashing: "I must not . . . I somehow have to . . . I must not lead him with us to I-330 . . ."

Instead of turning left, I turned right. The bridge offered up its obedient, slavishly bowed-over spine to the three of us: me, O, and S behind us. The lights from the illuminated buildings on the other bank poured out onto the water, smashing into thousands of feverishly jumping sparks, spattered with rabid foam. The wind was droning—as though there is a tight bass string somewhere in the middle-sky. And through the bass, behind us, still . . .

My building. At the doors O stopped, and started on something: "No, but you promised . . ."

But I didn't let her finish; I hurriedly pushed open the door and we were inside, in the vestibule. Above the monitor desk: the familiar, anxiously quivering, drooping cheeks. A dense bunch of ciphers all around—there was some kind of disagreement—and heads were hanging over the railings on the second floor, and then running down the stairs one by one. But I'll come to that later, later . . . Just then I quickly carried O over to the opposite corner, sat with my back to the wall (there, behind the wall, I saw a dark, big-headed shadow crawling along the sidewalk, back and forth), and pulled out my notebook.

O slowly settled down into her chair as if, under her unif, her body was evaporating, melting, and there was only an empty dress and empty eyes that sucked you into a blue void. She was tired: "Why did you bring me here? You lied to me."

"No . . . Quiet! Look over there: do you see—behind the wall?"

"Yes. A shadow."

"He is behind me all the time . . . I cannot. You understand—I must not . . . I will now write two words—you will take them and go alone. I know he will stay here."

A ripe body started to rustle again under her unif, her stomach rounded out slightly, and on her cheeks, barely noticeable: a dawn, a sunrise.

I slipped the note into her cold fingers, squeezed her hand tightly, and my eyes sipped from her blue eyes for the last time.

"Farewell! Maybe one day . . ."

She pulled back her hand. Stooping over, she slowly went off. Two steps and she quickly turned—she was next to me again. Her lips were stirring. From her eyes, from her lips, from all of her: some kind of word, over and over and over again to me. What an unbearable smile, what pain . . .

And then this stooping human sliver was at the doorway, then it was a tiny shadow behind the wall, not looking back, going quickly and then quicker still . . .

I walked up to U's little desk. With anxiously, indignantly blown-out gills, she said to me: "Do you see? It's like everyone has gone out of their minds! That one there swears that he saw some kind of person, naked and covered with fur, near the Ancient House."

From the dense group of bristling heads, a voice: "Yes! And I'll repeat it again: I definitely saw it."

"So, how do you like that, eh? What a lot of gibberish."

And she was so convinced and disdainful of this "gibberish" that I asked myself: isn't that just what's been going on in me and around me recently—isn't it all really "gibberish"?

But I glanced at my hairy hand and remembered: "You probably have a few drops of sunny forest blood in you. Maybe that's why I also . . . you . . ."

No, fortunately it is not gibberish. No, unfortunately it is not gibberish.

KEYWORDS:

(*No Keywords. In Haste. The Last.*)

The day had arrived.

Quick: get the *Gazette*, it may be in there . . . I read the *Gazette* with my eyes (exactly that: my eyes are now like a pen, like a meter that you hold, feel, in your hands—they are external, they are an instrument).

There, in large type, on the whole page:

> THE ENEMIES OF HAPPINESS ARE NOT SLUMBERING. HOLD ON TO HAPPINESS WITH BOTH HANDS! TOMORROW WORK WILL BE SUS-PENDED AND ALL CIPHERS WILL APPEAR FOR THE OPERATION. THOSE WHO FAIL TO APPEAR WILL BE SUBJECTED TO THE MACHINE OF THE BENEFACTOR.

Tomorrow! Can there be—can there possibly be any tomorrow?

In the inertia of my daily routine, I reach my hand (the instru-ment) over to the bookshelf and place today's *Gazette* with the oth-ers, in the gold-painted binder. Along the way: "Why am I doing this? Does it matter? I won't ever return to this room . . ."

And the *Gazette* goes from my hand to the floor. And I stand and look around the whole, whole, whole room. I am hurrying to collect things—I'm feverishly cramming everything that it seems a shame to leave behind into an invisible suitcase. The table. Books. The chair. I-330 once sat on that chair while I was below, on the floor . . . The bed.

Then for a minute, two, I wait ridiculously for some kind of miracle: maybe the telephone would ring, maybe she would tell me to . . .

No. No miracle . . .

I walk off—into the unknown. These are my last lines. Farewell to you, unknown, you, dear readers, with whom I have lived for so many pages, to whom, sick with a soul, I showed all of myself, to the last stripped screw, to the last snapped spring . . .

I am walking off . . .

KEYWORDS:

The Released. A Sunny Night. Radio Valkyrie.

Oh, if only I had actually smashed myself and all the others to smithereens; if only I had actually found myself somewhere behind the Wall, together with her, among the beasts baring their yellow fangs; if only I had actually never returned here again. It would have been a thousand, a million times easier. But now what? Go and strangle that woman? As if that would help anything!

No, no, no! Take hold of yourself, D-503. Affix yourself to a firm logical axle. Lean on the lever with all your strength for a time and, like the ancient slave, turn the millstones of syllogisms. Until you've written it down, you won't get your head around what happened . . .

When I boarded the Integral, everyone was already all assembled, everyone was in their places, all the honeycombs of the gigantic glass hive were filled. There were tiny, antlike people below, under the glass of the decks, standing at telegraphs, dynamos, transformers, altimeters, valves, arrows, motors, pumps, pipes. In the wardroom, some were bent over panels and instruments, probably under command of the Bureau of Science. And next to them: the Second Builder with two of his assistants.

All three of them had turtle-like heads drawn into their shoulders, their faces gray, autumnal, rayless...

"Well, what's happening?" I asked.

"Well... it's a bit grim..." One of them smiled grayishly, raylessly. "Who knows where we'll have to land. Anyone's guess, really."

It was unbearable for me to look at them—at those whom I would forever throw from the comforting numbers of the Table of Hours, whom I would tear from the maternal breast of the One State forever, with my very own hands, in one hour's time. They reminded me of the tragic figures of *The Three Released*—a story that every schoolchild knows. It's a story about three ciphers who, for the sake of experiment, were released from work for a month: to do what they wanted to do and go where they wanted to go.* These unlucky types loitered around the place they usually worked and peeped inside with hungry eyes. They stood in plazas for hours at a time; they performed the very movements that were appointed to that hour of the day as needed by their organism: they sawed and planed the air, they rattled invisible hammers, thumping on invisible blocks. And, finally, on the tenth day, they couldn't bear it anymore: linking arms, they walked into the water and to the sound of the March, they plunged deeper and deeper, until the water ended their torment...

I repeat: it was hard for me to look at them. I hurried to leave.

"I'm just checking the engine room," I said, "and then off we go."

I was asked about something—about which voltage to use for liftoff and how much water ballast was needed in the aft cisterns. There was some sort of sound device in me and it responded to all the questions quickly and precisely, without stopping, while I was with other thoughts inside.

And suddenly in the little narrow corridor, something came to me, inside, and from that moment, basically, it all began.

In the narrow little corridor, gray unifs and gray faces flashed

---

*This was long ago, back in the third century after the Table.

past, and among them, for a second, was that one with the hair pulled down low and the eyes under his forehead. I understood: they were here, and there was nowhere for me to go and only minutes remained, a few dozens of minutes . . . There was the smallest, molecular shiver all over my body as if it was generated by a motor (it didn't stop until it was all over), but my body's building was so light and all the walls, partitions, cables, beams, lights—everything was shivering . . .

I still don't know if she is here or not. But now there is no time left—they've sent for me, they want me upstairs in the command room as quick as possible: it's time to be on our way . . . but where to?

Gray faces, rayless. Tense, blue veins below, on the water. Grave, cast-iron layers of sky. And I raise my similarly cast-iron hand and take hold of the receiver of the command telephone. "Upward—forty-five degrees!"

A muffled explosion—a jolt—a violent, white-green mountain of water at the stern. The deck, soft and rubbery underfoot, is departing and everything below, the whole of life, forever . . . A second later everything below is tightening up and falling deeper and deeper into some sort of funnel: the protuberant, icy-blue sketch of the city, the round little bubbles of the cupolas, the lonely lead finger of the Accumulator Tower. Then: a fleeting wadded curtain of clouds. We break through and then: sun, blue sky. Seconds, minutes, miles and the blueness quickly hardens, filling with darkness, and stars come through like drops of cold, silver sweat . . .

And here was an awesome, unbearably bright, black, starry, sunny night. As if you suddenly turned deaf: you can still see that the pipes are roaring but you are only seeing it—the pipes are mute, it is silent. And so was the sun—mute.

This was all natural—it was what we must have expected. We had left the Earth's atmosphere. But it was all so quick, so arresting, that everyone all around blanched and quieted. But I—I felt things ease under this fantastical, mute sun. It was as if, having had my last contraction, I had already crossed an unavoidable threshold and my body was left behind somewhere there, below, while I was flying off to the new world where everything would be unusual, upside-down . . .

"Hold steady," I cried to the engine room—or perhaps it wasn't me but that sound device inside me—and the machine, with a mechanical hinged arm, thrust the command receiver over to the Second Builder. I was dressed in fine, molecular shivers, audible only to myself—I ran downstairs, to look for . . .

The door to the wardroom: in an hour it would clatter sternly and lock . . . An unfamiliar, shortish cipher stood by the door. He had a face like the hundreds and thousands that get lost in a crowd, but his arms were unusually long, down to his knees (it was as if they had been hastily taken from a different human gene pool by mistake).

A long arm extended and barred the way: "Where are you going?"

It was clear to me: he doesn't know that I know everything. Fine: maybe that's how it should be. And, looking down, purposefully, sharply: "I am the Builder of the Integral. And I—am in charge of this test flight. Understood?"

The arm was gone.

The wardroom. Over the instruments and the maps: heads, circumnavigated with bristling gray, and other heads, yellow, bald, ripe. Quickly, I scooped up everyone—in one glance—and went backward, along the corridor, along the gangway, downstairs to the engine room. There: the heat and the din from the scorching, blasting pipes; the reckless, drunken, never-pausing squats of the glittering cranks; and the dials trembling just slightly . . .

And then—finally—at the tachometer, it was him, his face bent low over a notebook . . .

"Listen . . ." (the din: you had to scream into each other's ears). "Is she here? Where?"

In the shadows, a smile came from under his forehead: "Her? There. In the radio room . . ."

And I was off. There were three of them in there. All of them in winged earphone helmets. And she was like an ancient Valkyrie—a head higher than usual, winged, glittering, flying—and it was as if there were enormous blue sparks on her radio antennae, which were coming from her, along with a faint smell of ozone and lightning.

"Could anyone . . . well, you there . . ." I said to her, panting (from running). "I need to convey a message below, to Earth, to the hangar . . . Come with me, I'll dictate . . ."

Next to the instrument room was a tiny little box of a cabin. We: at the desk, side by side. I found and squeezed her hand tightly: "Well, what now? What happens now?"

"I don't know. Do you understand how wonderful that is: not knowing and flying wherever . . . And soon it will be twelve—and who knows what will happen? And then night . . . where will you and I be tonight? Maybe on the grass, on dried leaves . . ."

Blue sparks and the smell of lightning come from her and the tremble in me is getting faster.

"Write this down," I say loudly, still panting in the meantime (from running). "Time: eleven-thirty. Speed: sixty-eight hundred . . ."

She, from under her winged helmet, not tearing her eyes away from her piece of paper, quietly: ". . . Yesterday evening she came to me with your note . . . I know—I know everything: be quiet. But, then, is the baby—yours? I sent her off—she is already there, behind the Wall. She will live . . ."

I am back in the command room. Again: the crazy night with its black starry sky and blinding sun; slowly, the hand of the clock on the wall is limping from one minute to the next; and everything is dressed in a fine cloud of barely noticeable (except to me) trembles.

And for some reason it seemed that it would be better if all this were to happen not here, but somewhere lower, nearer to the Earth.

"Stop!" I yelled into the engine room.

We were still going forward—by inertia—but slower, slower. And then the Integral caught itself on some hairspring of a second and hung immobile for a blink, until the little hairspring sprang and the Integral dropped like a rock—faster and faster. It continued like this, through silence, through minutes, dozens of minutes (my pulse was audible), as the hand approached 12:00 before my eyes. And I saw it clearly: the rock is me and the Earth is I-330—I was a rock flung by someone, and this rock absolutely had to fall and smash on the ground into smithereens . . . And what if I just let it . . . The hard, blue smoke of the rain clouds below us was already appearing . . . What if . . .

But instead, the sound device inside me, articulate and accurate, seized the receiver and gave the "slow ahead" command—and the rock stopped falling. And then only the four lower extensions began snorting—two fore and two aft auxiliaries—just enough to paralyze the Integral, and the Integral stood in the air, shuddering, as though firmly anchored at a kilometer or so from the Earth.

Everyone poured out onto the deck (almost 12:00, time for the lunch bell) and rushed to lean over the glass railing, without pausing for breath, swallowing the unknown over-the-wall world there, below. Amber, green, blue: an autumn forest, meadows, a lake. On the edge of the blue saucer: some yellow, bony ruins, a yellow, desiccated, threatening finger (it must be the spire of an ancient church that escaped destruction by some miracle).

"Look! Look! Over there—starboard!"

A quick dot was flying along with a brown shadow through the green desert. I had binoculars in my hands and I mechanically brought them up to my eyes: a herd of horses was galloping through chest-high grasses, their tails raised, and on their backs, those chestnut, white, jet-black . . .

Behind me: "And I'm telling you that I saw it—a face."

"Go away! Tell it to someone else!"

"Well, take them, then, take the binoculars!"

But they had disappeared. The infinite green desert . . .

The tremble of the bell penetrated into that desert, filling it, me, and everyone: lunch, in a minute, at 12:00.

The world was strewn into momentary, disconnected fragments. Someone's ringing gold badge lay on the steps but it didn't matter to me: I crunched it under my heel. A voice: "I am telling you— it was a face!" A dark square: the open door of the wardroom. Clenched, white, sharply smiling teeth . . .

When the clock started to strike infinitely slowly, not pausing for breath from one strike to the next, and the front rows had started to move in—at that moment, the square of the door was crossed out with two familiar and unnaturally long arms: "Stop there!"

Fingers dug into my palms (it was I-330, she was next to me): "Who is this? You know him?"

"Surely he is . . . isn't he . . . ?"

He climbed up on someone's shoulders. A face (like hundreds of thousands and yet uniquely his own) up above hundreds of faces: "In the name of the Benefactor . . . You—you know who you are— you will listen to me, every one of you will listen to me. I am telling you: we know. We don't yet know your digits—but we know you. The Integral won't be yours! The test flight will be led to its conclusion, and you—you won't even dare to move—you will complete the mission, with your own hands. And then . . . well, that's all . . ."

Silence. The glass slabs underfoot were soft, wadded, and my legs turned soft and wadded. From her: a totally white smile of mad, blue sparks. Through her teeth, into my ear: "Is this you? Did you 'fulfill' your 'duty'? What have you . . ."

Her hand: torn away from my hands. Her furious-winged Valkyrie helmet was now somewhere far ahead. I was alone, I froze and, saying nothing, I walked into the wardroom like everyone.

But it wasn't me, I'm telling you, it wasn't me! I haven't mentioned this to anyone, no one except those white mute pages . . .

Inside me—inaudibly, recklessly, loudly—I screamed this to her. She sat across the table, opposite me, and she didn't once brush past me with her eyes. Next to her: someone's ripe-yellow baldness. I could hear (this was I-330): " 'Nobility'? But, dearest professor, even a simple philosophical analysis of this word shows that this is a prejudice, a relic of the Ancients, of the feudal epoch. But we . . ."

I felt: my face was paling and now everyone would see it. But the machine in me went through the fifty mandatory masticatory motions to each bite; I bolted myself in, like I was in an ancient nontransparent house, piling up rocks against the door, covering the windows . . .

Later, the command receiver was in my hands. Our flight, in its icy final anguish—through the clouds—into the icy, starry-sunny night. Minutes, hours. And, evidently, there was a logical motor working feverishly inside me the whole time (though it wasn't audible to me myself) because suddenly, at some point in blue space, I saw: my writing desk, the gillish cheeks of U bent over it, a forgotten page of my notes. And it was clear to me: it couldn't have been anyone but her. It's all clear to me . . .

Ah, if only—if only I could get to the radio . . .

Winged helmets, the smell of blue lightning . . . I remember I said something loudly to her and I remember her, looking through me, as if I was glass, and from a distance: "I am busy: I am receiving from below. Dictate it to someone else, to her . . ."

In the tiny little box of a cabin, having thought for a minute, I firmly dictated: "Time: fourteen-forty. Descending! Stop the engines. The end of everything."

The command room. The mechanical heart of the Integral has stopped, we are falling but my heart . . . hasn't managed to fall with us, it has detached and is rising in my throat. Clouds, and then a green dot in the distance, getting greener and more distinct, rushing toward us in a whirlwind: the end is in sight . . .

The deranged porcelain-white face of the Second Builder. It was probably him who shoved me aside with one stroke. I hit my head on something, and there was a darkening, a falling and, cloudily, I heard: "Reverse—full speed!"

A sharp jump upward . . . I don't remember anything else.

KEYWORDS:
Banded. A Carrot. A Killing.

I didn't sleep all night. All night, thinking about one thing . . .

My head, after yesterday, was tightly bound up in bandages. Now, these weren't bandages but a band: a merciless band of glassy steel, riveted onto my head, and I find myself in the same sort of forged circle: I will kill U. I will kill U and then go to I-330 and say: "Now do you believe me?" The most awful part of all this is that the idea of killing—dirtily, anciently, smashing a head with something—is giving me the strange sensation of having something disgustingly sweet in my mouth, and I can't swallow my spit, and I have to spit it into my handkerchief all the time, and my mouth is dry.

In my closet lay a heavy piston rod that had snapped after casting (I was supposed to look at the structure of the fracture under the microscope). I rolled my records up into a cylinder (let her read them all, up to every last letter), shoved them into the fragment of the rod, and went downstairs. The stairway—of endless stairs—was kind of nasty, slippery and oily, and I was wiping my mouth with the handkerchief the whole time . . .

Downstairs. My heart thumped. I stopped, took out the rod, went to the monitor's desk . . .

But U wasn't there: just an empty, icy surface. I remembered: all labor had been canceled today. Everyone was supposed to go for the Operation and it made sense: there was no reason for her to be there, there would be no one to monitor here . . .

On the street. Wind. A sky of rushing, cast-iron slabs. And it could have been a moment from yesterday: the whole world shattered into separate, sharp, independent pieces, and each of them started dropping vertically, then they stopped for a second, hanging in front of me in the air, and then vanished into thin air without a trace.

It was as if all the black, precise letters on this page suddenly shifted, scattered about in fright and there wasn't one word, just nonsense: scatt-abou-infrig. On the street, there was a crowd, similarly dispersed, without rows: going forward, backward, diagonally, crosswise.

And then there was no one. And, in the space of a second, an image shot past and froze: up on the second floor, in a glass cage, hanging in the air, a man and a woman, in a kiss, standing, her body bent backward to breaking point. It was the last time, forever . . .

At another corner, a prickly bunch of heads was stirring. Above the heads—unattached, in the air—a flag with the words "Down with the machines! Down with the Operation!" And detaching (from myself), I thought for a second: it can't be that everyone has such a pain, the kind that can be wrested from one's insides only if it is taken together with the heart, and that every one of us needs to do something, before . . . And for a second there was nothing in the whole world except (my) bestial hand with its cast-iron-heavy bundle . . .

Then: a little boy, facing straight ahead, a shadow under his lower lip. His lower lip was turned outward, like the cuff of a rolled-up sleeve—his whole face was turned outward—and he was shrieking, running from someone, as fast as his legs could carry him, there was stamping coming after him . . .

The little boy prompted a thought in me . . . Yes, U should be at school now, I must get there quickly. I ran to the nearest entrance to the subterranean rail.

At the entrance, someone speeding past: "Not running. The train isn't running today! There . . ."

I went down. It was total chaos. The reflection of faceted crystal suns. A platform, densely packed with heads. An empty, frozen train.

In the silence: a voice. It's hers—she's not visible but I know, I know this stubborn, supple, whiplike, lashing voice—and somewhere here were those sharp triangle eyebrows, jerked up to the temples . . . I yelled: "Let me! Let me through! I have to . . ."

But someone's pincers had me—by the arms, the shoulders—hard as nails. And in the silence, a voice: ". . . No! Run upstairs! There you will be healed, there you will be fed full of sumptuous happiness, and once you're satiated, you will slumber evenly and snore to an organized beat—can you not hear this great symphony of snores? You funny ciphers: they want to liberate you of the torturously gnawing question marks that wriggle like worms . . . But you're standing here and listening to me instead. Go quickly—upstairs—to the Great Operation! What does it matter to you that I stay here alone? What does it matter to you if I don't want them to want things for me—if I want to want things for myself—if I want the impossible . . . ?"

A different voice—slow, heavy: "Aha. The impossible? That means chasing after your idiotic fantasies and letting them swing their tails in front of your nose? No: we're going to grab that tail and stamp on it, and then . . ."

"And then—you'll gobble it up and you'll start snoring—and then you'll need a new tail in front of your nose. They say that the Ancients had an animal: a donkey. In order to make it go forward, and continue forward—they attached a carrot to a stick in front of its snout, just far enough away that it couldn't get at it. But if it did get it, it gobbled it right up . . ."

Suddenly the pincers let me go; I threw myself into the middle, where she was talking—and at that moment everything began to fall apart, contracted itself. Then a cry from behind: "They're coming, they're coming this way!" The lights jumped and went out (someone had cut through the wire) and then: an avalanche, screams, a wheeze, heads, fingers . . .

I don't know how long we rolled like that underground. Finally: little steps, twilight, it got lighter, and we were on the street again, fanning out into different directions . . .

Now: I'm alone again. The wind and twilight were gray, low, and right over your head. Deep in the wet glass of the sidewalk: upside-down lights and walls, and figures, moving around, feet up. The unbelievably heavy bundle in my hand was pulling me into the depths, toward the bottom.

Downstairs, U was still not behind the little desk and her room was empty and dark.

I climbed up to my room and turned on the light. My temples, tautly squeezed by the band, were thumping and I walked around, chained to one and the same circle: the table, the white bundle on the table, the bed, the door, the table, the white bundle . . . The blinds were lowered in the room on the left. On the right, above an open book: knobbly baldness with an enormous yellow parabola for a forehead. Wrinkles on the forehead: a row of yellow illegible lines. Occasionally our eyes met and then I felt: these yellow lines are about me.

. . . It happened at exactly 21:00. U herself walked in. One thing distinctly remains in my memory: I was breathing so loudly, and when I heard how I was breathing, I wanted so much to quiet it somehow—but couldn't.

She sat down, smoothed her unif over her knees. The pink-brown gills quivered.

"Ah, my dear, then it is true—you are injured? I only just found out—just now . . ."

The rod was on the table in front of me. I jumped up, breathing even louder. She heard it, stopped in mid-word, and also stood up for some reason. I could already see the place on her head, my mouth had a disgusting-sweet . . . the handkerchief, where was the handkerchief—I spit on the floor.

The cipher on the other side of the wall, to the right (with his yellow, purposeful wrinkles dedicated to me) . . . It was necessary that he didn't see it, it would be even more unpleasant to do it if he was to watch it . . . I pushed the button—without permission—but so what, does it matter anymore? And the blinds fell.

She, obviously, felt it, understood it, and rushed to the door. But I intercepted her and, breathing loudly, not looking down from that place on her head for even a second . . .

"You . . . you have gone out of your mind! Don't you dare . . ." She backed away and sat down, or more like fell, on the bed, trembling and sticking her hands, palms together, between her knees. All wound up, still holding her firmly with the leash of my eyes, I slowly put out my hand toward the table—moved only one hand—and grabbed the rod.

"I beg of you! A day—just one day! Tomorrow—really tomorrow, I will go and make everything . . ."

What is she talking about? I raised it threateningly . . .

And, to my mind: I killed her. Yes, you, my unknown readers, you have the right to call me a murderer. I know that I would have brought that rod down on her head if she hadn't screamed: "For the sake of . . . the sake of . . . I'll do it—I . . . now."

With shaking hands, she ripped off her unif and an expansive, yellow, pendulous body toppled back onto the bed . . . And only then did I realize: she thought that I had lowered the blinds so that . . . in order to . . . that I wanted to . . .

It was so unexpected, so stupid, that I burst into laughter. And just then, the tightly wound spring inside me sprang, my hand went weak, the rod rumbled on the floor. Here I saw, with my own eyes, that laughter was the most terrible weapon: you can kill anything with laughter—even murder itself.

I sat at my desk and laughed—a reckless, final laugh—and couldn't see any way out of this ridiculous situation. I didn't know how this would have turned out if it had followed its natural course—but then, suddenly, there was a new, external, complicating factor: the telephone rang.

I threw myself at the receiver and grasped it: maybe it's her? But in the receiver, someone's unfamiliar voice: "Please hold."

An agonizing infinite buzzing. From far off: heavy footsteps, getting closer, more booming, more cast-iron, and then ...

"D-503? Uh-huh ... This is the Benefactor. Report to me at once!"

Ding—the receiver hung up—ding.

U was still lying on the bed, eyes closed, gills widely spread into a smile. I raked her dress up from the floor, threw it at her and, through my teeth: "Well, quick! Quick!"

She drew her waxy body half up onto her elbows; her breasts splashed down her sides and her eyes were round.

"What?"

"Nothing. Come on—get dressed!"

She was all knotted up, tightly clutching her dress, her voice flattened.

"Turn around."

I turned around, leaning my forehead on the glass. Lights, figures, sparks trembled on the black, wet mirror. No: it is me, the trembling is inside me ... Why does He want me? Can it be that He already knows about her, about me, about everything?

U, already dressed, was at the door. Two steps toward her and I squeezed her hand so hard that it was as though I had extracted what I most needed in drops from her hand: "Listen ... Her name— you know, to whom did you name her? No? Just tell the truth— I need it ... I don't care whether—just tell the truth ..."

"No."

"No? Well, why ...? You went there to tell them ... and?"

Her lower lip was suddenly inside out, like the little boy's, and from her cheeks, down her cheeks there were droplets ...

"Because I ... I was afraid, that if she was ... that they would have ... you would have ... you would stop lov ... Oh, I can't— I couldn't have!"

I understood: this was the truth. A ridiculous, funny, human truth! I opened the door.

KEYWORDS:

Empty Pages. The Christian God. About My Mother.

It's strange, my head is like an empty white page: I don't remember how I got there, how I waited (I know that I waited)—not one sound, not one face, not one gesture. It is as if all the wires between me and the world had been cut.

When I regained consciousness, I was already standing before Him and I was too scared to raise my eyes: I could only see His enormous cast-iron hands on His knees. These hands weighed heavily upon Him, upon His knees. He slowly stirred His fingers. His face was somewhere in the clouds, up above, and since His voice was reaching me from such a height, it didn't roar like thunder, it didn't deafen me, but it sounded like a regular human voice.

"So then . . . You, too? You—the Builder of the Integral? You, to whom it was given to become the greatest conquistador? You—whose name should have begun a new, brilliant chapter of the One State . . . you?"

Blood had splashed into my head and cheeks. Again a white page: nothing but a pulse in my temples, a resonant voice above— not one word. Only when He had stopped talking did I regain consciousness again and I saw: the hand moved ahundredton-ly, slowly crawling, a finger was fixing toward me.

"Well? Why do you stay silent? Is it so or not? Is 'executioner' the word?"

"It is," I obediently answered. And then I clearly heard each of His words.

"What? You think I am afraid of that word?! Have you ever tried tearing off its shell and looking inside? I will now show you. Remember: a blue hill, a cross, a crowd. Some are up above, spattered with blood, nailing a body to the cross; others are below, spattered with tears, watching. Doesn't it seem to you that the role of those above is the hardest, the most important? Yes, and were it not for them, would this whole grandiose tragedy have been put on? They were hissed off the stage by the crowd: but then the author of this tragedy—God—should reward them even more heartily. The most merciful Christian, God himself, slowly burning all the recalcitrants in the fires of Hell—is he not an executioner? And were there really fewer burned at the stake by the Christians than Christians who were burned themselves? And yet, understand this, and yet, they glorified this God as a God of Love. Absurd? No, the opposite: it is testimony, written in blood, to the ineradicable good sense of a human. Even then—wild, shaggy as they were—they understood: true algebraic love toward humankind is inhuman—and the sure sign of truth is its cruelty. Like fire—the sure sign of fire is that it burns. Can you show me a nonburning fire? Well—argue the case, dispute me!"

How could I argue? How could I argue when these were my (former) thoughts exactly—only I haven't ever been able to dress them in such forged, shining armor. I said nothing . . .

"If this means that you are in agreement with me—then let's talk like grownups, when the children have gone to bed: about everything right through to the end. I ask you: what have people—from the very cradle—prayed for, dreamed about, and agonized over? They have wanted someone, anyone, to tell them once and for all what happiness is—and then to attach them to this happiness with a chain . . . What are we now doing, if it isn't this? The ancient dream about paradise . . . Remember: in paradise, they don't know desire, they don't know pity, they don't know love. There, angels, the slaves of God, are blissful, with surgically excised imaginations (which is why they are blissful) . . . And here, just when we have chased down this dream, when we have grabbed it like this—" His hand squeezed: if there had been a rock in it, sap would have sprayed from it. "When all that remains is to skin the kill and portion it out in pieces—at this very moment you—you . . ."

The cast-iron rumble suddenly cut short. I was all red, like iron on an anvil under a thumping hammer. The hammer, saying nothing, hung over me, and the waiting—this was even . . . scari . . .

Suddenly: "How old are you?"

"Thirty-two."

"You are exactly twice the age of a sixteen-year-old ignorant! Listen: it can't be that it has actually never entered your head that they—we don't yet know their names but we are sure that we will get them out of you—that they only need you because you are the Builder of the Integral—only so that, in order to, through you . . ."

"Don't! Don't!" I cried.

It was exactly like shielding yourself with your hand and screaming at a bullet: you can hear your funny "don't" while the bullet has already burned a hole in you and you are writhing on the floor.

Yes, yes: The Builder of the Integral . . . yes, yes . . . And then: the memory of U's infuriated face with quivering brick-red gills on that morning, when they both were together in my room . . .

I remember very clearly: I started to laugh and lifted my eyes. Before me sat a bald, Socratic-bald, person, and there were fine droplets of sweat on his baldness.

How simple everything is. Everything is so majestically banal and so simple, it is just funny.

Laughter choked me, shooting out in puffs. I shut my mouth with my palm and violently flung myself out of the room.

Steps, wind, wet, jumping fragments of lights, faces, and while running: "No! Have to see her! Have to see her one more time!"

Then: again an empty white page. I only remember: feet. Not people, but specifically feet: hundreds of feet, a heavy rain of feet stamping arhythmically, falling on the street from somewhere. And a sort of merry, mischievous song, and then a shout (it must have been at me): "Hey, hey! Over here, to us!"

Later: a desert-like square filled all the way to the top with tightly packed wind. In the middle there is a dull, bulky, terrible mass: the Machine of the Benefactor. And an unexpected image arose inside me, echoing up: a bright-white pillow; a head thrown back onto the pillow, with half-closed eyes; a sharp, sweet little stripe of teeth ... And all this was sort of ridiculously, horribly connected to the Machine—I know how but I still don't want to see it or to say it out loud—I don't want to—just don't.

I closed my eyes and sat on the steps that went up toward the Machine. It must have been raining: my face was wet. Muffled cries, somewhere far away. But no one hears it, no one hears me cry: deliver me from all of this—deliver me!

If only I had had a mother like the Ancients: my—yes, exactly— my own mother. She would know me as—not the Builder of the Integral, and not cipher D-503, and not a molecule of the One State—but simply a fragment of humanity, a fragment of herself, trampled, squashed, thrown away ... And whether I am nailing or being nailed—maybe it's all the same—she would hear what no one else heard, her old-woman lips, overgrown with wrinkles ...

KEYWORDS:

Infusoria. Doomsday. Her Room.

Morning at the cafeteria. The cipher on my left seemed spooked and whispered to me: "Well, eat, will you! They're watching you!"

I smiled, using all my strength. And it felt like some kind of crack on my face: I smile and the seam of the crack splits wider and wider, and gets more and more painful to me . . .

The next thing was: I had just managed to pick up a little cube with my fork, when instantly, the fork shuddered in my hand and jangled onto the plate. The tables, walls, dishes, and air shuddered and clattered and rang outside with an enormous, round, sky-high, iron din that vibrated through heads and buildings, and then died off, faraway, like fine, barely perceptible circles on the surface of water.

In that instant, I saw blanched faces drain; and mouths that were going at full steam brought to a standstill; and forks frozen in the air.

Then everything went the wrong way, was derailed from age-old tracks, everyone leapt up from their places (not having sung the Hymn), chewing crazily, off the beat, choking and grabbing at one another: "What? What happened? What?" And the disorganized fragments of what was the fine-tuned, great Machine—everyone rained down on the elevators—down the stairway—stairs—

a stomp—snatches of words—like tatters of a letter, ripped, swept about with the wind . . .

They also rained down from every nearby building, and after a minute the avenue was like a drop of water under a microscope: infusoria, locked in the glassy clear drop, darting around wildly, from side to side, up and down.

"A-ha" (someone's triumphant voice, in front of me). I see: the back of a head and a finger directed at the sky (I very distinctly remember the yellow-pink fingernail and below the fingernail, a white half-moon crawling out of the horizon). It was like a compass: hundreds of eyes, following this finger, were turned up to the sky.

There were clouds fleeing from an invisible pursuit, racing along, crushing one another, jumping over one another; and there were the dark, cloud-tinted aeros of the Guardians with their tubes like hanging black prosces; and, even farther along, there, in the west, there was something that looked like . . .

At first no one understood what it was—even I didn't understand. I, for whom (unfortunately) everything is clearer than to everyone else. It looked something like an enormous swarm of black aeros: barely perceptible fast-moving dots, somewhere unbelievably high in the sky. They approached with hoarse, guttural drops of sound from above, and finally: there were birds above our heads. Sharp, black, piercing, falling triangles filled the sky, a storm was beating them down and they settled on the cupolas, on the roofs, on the columns, on the balconies.

"A-ha." The triumphant head turned around and I saw that it was the overhanging-forehead cipher. But the only remnant of his former self is in those words previously used to describe him. He had somehow crawled out from under that permanently overhanging forehead of his, and on his face—around his eyes, around his lips—bunches of rays were growing like hair. He was smiling.

"You understand?" through the whistle of the wind, wings, cawing, he yelled to me. "You understand? The Wall—they blew up the Wall! Un-der-stand?!"

There were twinkling figures going by, somewhere in the background, with their heads extended out, running inside quickly, into the buildings. In the middle of the street: an avalanche of new, surgically altered ciphers marching over to the west, rapidly and yet somehow slowly (from the burden) . . .

Hairy bunches of rays around his lips and eyes. I grabbed him by the hand: "Listen: where is she—where is I-330? There, behind the Wall? Or . . . I need to—are you listening? Right now, I can't stand it . . ."

"Here," he yelled to me drunkenly with happy, strong, yellow teeth. "She is here, in the city, activated. Oh yes—we are activated!"

Who is "we"? Who am I?

There were hundreds just like him surrounding us, having crawled out from under their dark overhanging foreheads, loud, merry, strong-toothed. Swallowing the storm with open mouths, waving these openly visible, peaceful, and benign-looking electrocutors (where did they get hold of them?)—they were moving to the west, behind the new, surgically altered ciphers, but bypassing them on the parallel, on the forty-eighth avenue . . .

I stumbled against taut ropes of twisting wind and ran to her. Why? I don't know. I stumbled: empty streets; a foreign, wild city; the incessant celebrating of the avian uproar; doomsday. In several buildings, through the glass of the walls I saw (it cut into me): female and male ciphers shamelessly copulating, without even lowering the blinds, without any tickets, in broad daylight . . .

A building, her building. The bewildered doorway, all the way open. Downstairs, behind the monitor desk: empty. The elevator was stuck in the middle of the shaft. Panting, I ran upstairs along the endless stairway. A corridor. Quickly—like spokes of a wheel—numbers on the door: 320, 326 . . . 330, yes!

And through the glass door I see: the whole room was strewn about, messed up, crumpled. A chair had been toppled over in someone's hurry—facing downward, all four legs up—like a dead dog. The bed: somehow absurdly moved away from the wall at a slant. On the floor: the fallen, trampled petals of pink tickets.

I bent over, picked up one, two, a third: the letter "D" and the digits "503" were on all of them, I was on all of them, melted drops of me, spilled over an edge. And this is all that was left . . .

For some reason, it seemed that they shouldn't be like this, on the floor where people could walk over them. I grabbed another handful, put it on the table, smoothed them carefully, looked at them, and burst out laughing.

Before I didn't know this, but now I know, and you'll know it, too: laughter comes in different colors. It is only the distant echo of an explosion occurring inside you: it might be festive rockets of red, blue, gold, or it might be shreds of human bodies flying upward . . .

A name flashed on the tickets that was totally unfamiliar to me. I don't remember the digits, just the letter: "F." I brushed all the tickets off the table onto the floor and stepped on them—on myself, with my heel—"Take that—and that!" And I left . . .

I sat in the corridor, on the windowsill opposite her door, still waiting for something, stupidly, for a long time. Footsteps started to shuffle from the left. An old man: a face, like a punctured, empty bubble, collapsed into creases—and the puncture was sapping something transparent, slowly flowing downward. Slowly, vaguely, I realized: tears. And it was only when the old man was already far off that it occurred to me, and I called out to him: "Listen, listen, do you know where cipher I-330 . . ."

The old man turned around, recklessly waved a hand and hobbled on.

In the twilight, I returned to my building. In the west, the sky squeezed itself into blanched blue spasms every second and emitted a dull, muffled drone. Roofs were strewn with black, extinguished smolderings: birds. I lay on the bed and I was immediately set upon by wild beasts, a dream smothered me . . .

KEYWORDS:

(*I Don't Know. Maybe the Keywords Are Simply: A Thrown-Away Cigarette.*)

I regained consciousness in bright light—opening my eyes was painful. I squinted. In my head: an acrid, blue puff of smoke, everything was in a cloud. And through the cloud I heard myself: "But I didn't turn on the light—how is it that . . ."

I leapt up. Behind the desk, having propped up her chin with her hand, I-330 was looking at me with a smirk . . .

I am writing at that very desk right now. Those ten, fifteen minutes are already past, cruelly twisted into the most tightly wound band. It's as though the door has only just closed behind her, and that it may still be possible to catch up to her, grab her hand, and then maybe she would start to laugh and say . . .

I-330 was sitting behind the desk. I flung myself at her.

"You, you! I was—I saw your room—I thought you had—" But halfway through I struck upon the sharp, immobile javelins of her eyelashes and stopped. It came to me: this is exactly how she looked at me then, in the Integral. And now I must immediately, within the space of a second, be able to explain everything to her—in a way that she will believe it, otherwise she never will . . .

"Listen, I-330, I have to, I have to tell you everything . . . No, no, I, right now—I just need a sip of water . . ."

The inside of my mouth was dry, as though coated with blotting paper. I tried pouring the water but I couldn't. I put the glass down on the table and tightly seized the jug with both hands.

Now I saw: a blue puff of smoke—it was from a cigarette. She brought it up to her lips, pulled on it, and greedily swallowed the smoke as I drank the water—and she said: "Don't bother. Shut up. It doesn't matter—you can see: I came anyway. There, downstairs—they're waiting for me. And you want these last minutes together to be spent . . ."

She tossed the cigarette to the floor and leaned all the way backward over the armrest of the chair (there was a button on the wall and she had a hard time reaching it). I remember how the chair lurched and two of its little legs came up from the floor. Then the blinds fell.

She walked up and hugged me tight. Her knees through her dress—a slow, gentle, warm poison covering me . . .

And suddenly . . . This happens sometimes: you're deeply plunged into a sweet and warm dream and suddenly something punctures it, you shudder, and your eyes are wide open again . . . And so it was now: the trampled pink tickets on the floor, in her room—and on one of them, the letter "F" and some digits . . . They were lumped into one ball inside me and I can't even say now what feeling it incited in me, but I squeezed her so hard that she cried out in pain . . .

Another minute of those ten or fifteen on the bright white pillow: a head thrown back with half-closed eyes; a sharp, sweet stripe of teeth. And the whole time I was being reminded of something nagging, ridiculous, torturous, something that I shouldn't be thinking . . . that I musn't think about even now . . . And I squeezed her, more and more tenderly, more and more cruelly, and the blue spots under my fingers became brighter and brighter . . .

She said (not opening her eyes, I noticed this): "They say that you were with the Benefactor yesterday. Is this true?"

"Yes, it's true."

And then the eyes flew open—and I watched with pleasure how quickly her face paled, faded, and disappeared: she was all eyes.

I told her everything. Except (I don't know why ... no, that's not true, I do know why), except one thing: what he said at the very end, about the fact that they had only needed me because ...

Gradually, like photographic paper in the developing tray, her face emerged: cheeks, a white stripe of teeth, lips. She got up and walked over to the mirrored door of the closet.

Again, it was dry in my mouth. I poured myself some water but drinking it was unpleasant. I put the glass down on the table and asked: "Is that why you came—because you needed to know about that?"

From the mirror to me: a sharp, mocking triangle of eyebrows, lifted slightly, to her temples. She turned around to say something to me but said nothing.

She didn't need to. I know.

Say good-bye to each other? I moved my extraneous legs and they grazed the chair—it fell facedown, dead, like the one in her room. Her lips were cold—at one time the floor had been just as cold, here, in my room, by the bed.

When she left, I sat on the floor, bent over the cigarette she'd thrown away—I can't take it anymore—I don't want to anymore!

KEYWORDS:
The End.

All this was like the last grain of salt thrown into a saturated solution: quickly, prickling with needles, crystals began to crawl, harden, freeze. And it was clear to me: everything had been decided and tomorrow morning I would do it. It was just like deciding to kill yourself—perhaps it's only then that I will rise again. Because only that which killed can rise again.

In the west, the sky shook in blue spasms every second. My head was burning and banging. That is how I sat through the whole night and fell asleep at about seven in the morning, when darkness was already sagging, beginning to turn green, and the roofs, studded with birds, were becoming visible . . .

I woke up: it was already ten (obviously there hadn't been a bell this morning). On the table stood the glass of water—still from yesterday. I greedily swallowed all the water and ran off: I needed to do all this quickly, as quickly as possible.

The sky: desert-like, pale blue, completely eaten away by the storms. The thorny angles of shadows, everything is chiseled in the blue autumn air—thin—frightening to touch in case it snaps, shatters, and flies apart as glass dust. And the same inside me: I shouldn't think, mustn't think, mustn't think, otherwise—

And I didn't think, perhaps I wasn't actually seeing either, but was recording everything. Here on the street: branches from somewhere with green, amber, crimson leaves on them. Up above: aeros and birds intersecting and rushing about. Nearby: heads, open mouths, arms waving like branches. They must have been the source of this howling, cawing, buzzing . . .

Then: empty streets, as though they'd been swept by some sort of plague. I remember: I stumbled over something unbearably soft, yielding, and yet immobile. I bent over: a corpse. He lay on his back, his bent legs spread apart like a woman's. His face . . .

I recognized the thick African lips and it was as if his teeth were spraying with laughter even now. His eyes tightly screwed up, he laughed right at me, in the face. A second later, I stepped over him and ran off because I couldn't stand it; I needed to do everything quickly, otherwise I felt I would break, I would cave in, like overloaded train tracks . . .

Happily, it took only twenty steps until the sign appeared with its gold letters: BUREAU OF GUARDIANS. I stopped on the threshold, drank down some air—as much as I could—and went in.

Inside, in the corridor, ciphers were standing in a line, in an endless chain, with pieces of paper, with fat notebooks in their hands. Slowly they moved a step, another step, and stopped again.

I started to rush along the length of the chain; my head was fragmenting, I was grasping at sleeves, I was begging them, like a sick person begs to be given something that, with a second of the sharpest agony, would end it all immediately.

Some woman, with a tautly drawn belt over her unif and two sciatic hemispheres distinctly sticking out, which she moved from side to side the whole time as if they were, in fact, her eyes. She snorted at me: "His stomach hurts! Take him to the bathroom—there, the second door on the right . . ."

And, directed at me: laughter. And from this laughter, something came up to my throat, and I would now scream or . . . or . . .

Suddenly someone grabbed my elbow from behind. I turned around: it was transparent, wing-ears. They weren't pink, as usual, but crimson. The Adam's apple on his neck fidgeted—it was about to rip through his thin neck skin.

"Why are you here?" he asked, quickly drilling into me.

I seized hold of him, too: "Quickly, into your office . . . I have to tell you everything—right now! It's good that it is you in particular . . . It, maybe it is horrible that it's you but it's good, it's good . . ."

He also knew her, which tormented me even more, but maybe he would shudder, too, when he heard it all, and then we would be killing her together and I wouldn't be alone in my final second . . .

The door slammed. I remember: some sort of piece of paper was stuck down under the door and it scraped along the floor when the door was closing. Then we were covered with some kind of special, airless silence, like a cap. If he had said just one word— didn't matter which, the most nonsensical word—I would have disgorged everything immediately. But he said nothing.

I was so tense all over that there was a buzzing in my ear. I said (not looking): "It seems to me that I always hated her, from the very beginning. I struggled . . . But, however—no, no, don't believe me: I could have saved myself but didn't want to, I wanted to die, this was more valuable to me than anything . . . that is, not to die, but that she . . . And even now—even now that I already know everything . . . You know, do you know, that the Benefactor summoned me?"

"Yes, I know."

"But what He told me . . . You see—this all doesn't really matter, it's like having the rug pulled out from under you—and you, along with everything that is here on the table—the paper, the ink . . . The ink spills and everything is smudged . . ."

"Go on, go on! And hurry up. Others are waiting."

And I—choking, getting mixed up—recounted everything that had happened, everything that I've written here. About my real self, about my shaggy self, and what she said then about my hands—yes, that was exactly how everything started—and how I didn't want to fulfill my duty then, and how I lied to myself, and how she got counterfeit certificates of illness, and how I was rusting from one day to the next, and about the corridors down below, and how there, behind the Wall . . .

All this: in senseless lumps, balls. I was choking, I didn't have enough words. He nudged me the words I needed with crooked twice-bent lips and a smirk. I gratefully nodded: yes, yes . . .

And then (what was going on?) he had started speaking for me, and I was only listening . . . "Yes, and then . . . That's exactly how it was, yes, yes!"

I feel: it started to get colder under my collar as if from ether alcohol, and I asked with difficulty: "But how do you . . . ? But there is no way you could have . . ."

He had a smirk on his face, he was saying nothing, curving more and more and then: "But you know—you've been attempting to conceal something from me, and here, while you've enumerated everything you noticed behind the Wall, you're forgetting one thing. You were saying . . . no? But don't you remember, what you saw there in passing, for a second—you saw . . . me? Yes, yes: me."

A pause.

And suddenly, like a lightning strike to the head, it was shamelessly clear: he is also *them* . . . And my whole self, all my agonies, all that I, exhausted, with my last strength, brought here, like a victory—all this was simply funny, like the ancient anecdote about Abraham and Isaac. Abraham, in a cold sweat, was already waving the knife over his son—over his own self—and then suddenly there was a voice from above: "Don't bother! I was just joking . . ."

Not moving my eyes from his ever-curving smirk, I propped myself up against the edge of the table with my hands and slowly, slowly, slid back with the armchair. Then I grasped all of myself in an armful and ran headlong past the screams, the steps, the mouths.

I don't remember how I came to find myself downstairs in one of the public latrines by the station of the subterranean rail. Up at ground level, everything was perishing, the greatest and most intelligent civilization in all history was collapsing, but down here, by some irony, everything had stayed like it was: splendid. And to think: all this is condemned, all this will grow over with grasses, and there will only be "myths" about all this . . .

I started to groan loudly. And at that very moment I felt someone tenderly stroking me on the shoulder.

It was my neighbor, from the room to the left of mine who was always busy at his desk. His forehead was an enormous bald parabola, and on his forehead were the yellow, illegible lines of wrinkles. And these lines were about me.

"I understand you, totally understand you," he said. "But still, be calm: it isn't necessary. Everything will return, inevitably return. The only important thing is that everyone finds out about my discovery. I am telling you this first: I have calculated that there is no infinity!"

I looked at him wildly.

"Yes, yes I am telling you: there is no infinity. If the world is infinite—then the average density of matter in it must be exactly zero. And since it is not zero—this we know—then, consequently, the universe is finite, it is of a spherical form and the average density = the inverse of the universal radius squared, multiplied by . . . Wait, I just have to calculate the numerical coefficient, and then . . . You understand: everything is finite, everything is simple, everything is calculable. Then we will conquer, in the philosophical sense—do you understand? But you, with all due respect, are hindering me from finishing this calculation, you—are screaming . . ."

I don't know what I was more amazed by: his disclosure or his firmness in this apocalyptic hour. In his hands (I saw this only now) was a notebook and a logarithmic dial. And I understood: even if everything perishes, it is my duty (before you, my unknowns, my beloveds) to leave my records in finished form.

I asked him for some paper and, on it, I wrote these final lines . . .

I just wanted to mark a period, like the Ancients put crosses over the holes where they sank their dead, but suddenly my pencil shook and fell from my fingers . . .

"Listen." I tugged at my neighbor. "Yes, listen now, I'm talking to you! You must—you must answer me: and so, where does your finite universe end? What is there—and what is next?"

He didn't manage an answer: from above, down the stairs, there was stomping—

KEYWORDS:

Facts. The Bell Jar. I Am Certain.

Day. Clear. Barometer: 760. Is it possible that I, D-503, wrote these 200 pages? Is it possible that I, at one time, felt—or imagined that I felt—any of this?

The handwriting is mine. And this now is the exact same handwriting, but, happily, it is only the handwriting that is similar. None of the ravings, none of the ridiculous metaphors, none of the feelings: only the facts. Because I am healthy, I am completely, absolutely healthy. I smile—I can't not smile: some kind of splinter has been dragged from my head and my head is light, empty. More precisely: not empty, but there isn't anything extraneous that hinders smiling (the smile is the normal condition of the normal person).

The facts are these. On that evening, my neighbor, having discovered the finiteness of the universe, and I, and everyone who was with us, were taken, since we did not have Operation certificates, and carried off to the nearest auditorium (the number of the auditorium is familiar for some reason: 112). There, we were bound to tables and subjected to the Great Operation.

The next day, I, D-503, appeared to the Benefactor and told Him everything that I knew about the enemies of happiness. How could this have seemed so hard to do before? Incomprehensible. The only explanation: my former sickness (a soul).

In the evening of that day I sat at one table with Him, with the Benefactor (for the first time) in the famous Gas Room. They brought in that woman. In my presence she was supposed to give her testimony. This woman stubbornly said nothing and was smiling. I noticed that she had sharp and very white teeth and that this was beautiful.

Then they led her under the Bell Jar. Her face became very white and since her eyes were dark and big, this was very beautiful. When they started to pump air out from under the Bell Jar, she threw back her head, half-closed her eyes, and squeezed her lips—this reminded me of something. She was looking at me, strongly gripping the armrests of the chair and looking, until her eyes closed completely. Then they dragged her out, quickly brought her back to her senses with the help of electrodes, and then put her back under the Bell Jar. They repeated this three times and she still didn't say a word. Others, who had been brought in together with this woman, turned out to be more honorable: many of them started to talk after the first time. Tomorrow they will all mount the steps of the Machine of the Benefactor.

Postponing it would be impossible because there is still chaos, howling, corpses, wild beasts, and—unfortunately—a significant amount of ciphers betraying reason in the western quarters.

But, across the city, on the fortieth avenue, they have managed to construct a temporary wall of high-voltage waves. And I hope we will win. More than that: I know we will win. Because reason should win.

About the Translator

Natasha Randall makes her living as a translator and writer in New York City. She completed her studies in Russian literature and language at the University of Edinburgh, and her work has appeared in *The New York Times, Los Angeles Times, St. Petersburg Times, Strad* magazine, and on National Public Radio.

A NOTE ON THE TYPE

The principal text of this Modern Library edition
was set in a digitized version of Janson, a typeface that
dates from about 1690 and was cut by Nicholas Kis,
a Hungarian working in Amsterdam. The original matrices have
survived and are held by the Stempel foundry in Germany.
Hermann Zapf redesigned some of the weights and sizes for
Stempel, basing his revisions on the original design.

Modern Library is online at
www.modernlibrary.com

MODERN LIBRARY ONLINE IS YOUR GUIDE TO CLASSIC LITERATURE ON THE WEB

THE MODERN LIBRARY E-NEWSLETTER

Our free e-mail newsletter is sent to subscribers, and features sample chapters, interviews with and essays by our authors, upcoming books, special promotions, announcements, and news. To subscribe to the Modern Library e-newsletter, visit **www.modernlibrary.com**

THE MODERN LIBRARY WEBSITE

Check out the Modern Library website at **www.modernlibrary.com** for:

- The Modern Library e-newsletter
- A list of our current and upcoming titles and series
- Reading Group Guides and exclusive author spotlights
- Special features with information on the classics and other paperback series
- Excerpts from new releases and other titles
- A list of our e-books and information on where to buy them
- The Modern Library Editorial Board's 100 Best Novels and 100 Best Nonfiction Books of the Twentieth Century written in the English language
- News and announcements

Questions? E-mail us at **modernlibrary@randomhouse.com**. For questions about examination or desk copies, please visit the Random House Academic Resources site at **www.randomhouse.com/academic**.